Cathy's Golden Dream

. . . For somewhere in the nearing future, her physical handicap would be no more; she was on the threshold of freedom from those "limitations." She wouldn't have to prove she could master speech therapy in spite of being blind. She could master it or fail or simply quit on the same footing as any other student. If she wanted to switch to another field, if she wanted to leave school and get a job, if she wanted to withdraw her savings from the bank and travel for a year, it would be as easy for her as walking through an open door. . . .

GIFT OF GOLD

BEVERLY BUTLER

A word fitly spoken is like apples of gold in pictures of silver.
PROVERBS 25:11

AN ARCHWAY PAPERBACK
POCKET BOOKS • NEW YORK

POCKET BOOKS, a Simon & Schuster division of
GULF & WESTERN CORPORATION
1230 Avenue of the Americas, New York, N.Y. 10020

Published by arrangement with Dodd, Mead and Company
Library of Congress Catalog Card Number: 73-3151

ISBN: 0-671-41327-9

First Pocket Books printing August, 1973

10 9 8 7 6 5

Printed in the U.S.A.

Dedicated to

SISTER MARY HUBERTA VERMEULEN

with love and deepest appreciation

Acknowledgments

WITH each new novel I write, I am impressed again with the limitations of my personal fund of knowledge and with the generosity of those to whom I go for expert information and advice. Among those generous people who went out of their way to help me with this book, I would especially like to thank Mrs. Geri Knowler Nold, who, as a blind speech therapist herself, had many valuable suggestions to offer; Mrs. Ellen Brandt, who shared with me not only her knowledge and enthusiasms but also a day in her speech therapy classroom; Mrs. Barbara Bogk Rogalski and Miss Susan Wise, who, as student speech therapists, made vivid for me the joys and trials of college work in that field; and Miss Angela Bourne, who, as a resource teacher for blind children in California, must surely have bestowed the golden gift of individuality on many of her students during her too-short life.

—BEVERLY BUTLER

GIFT OF GOLD

1

ROBINS WERE chirping among the campus oaks as if it were still midsummer, but it wasn't the September sun pouring in through the third-floor therapy room window that was raising the film of moisture on Cathy Wheeler's upper lip. She touched a finger to the dial of her Braille watch under cover of picking up the notebook that had just fallen—or been pushed—off the table. Only twenty minutes into the period. A whole thirty more to go. She had known an entire college semester to move by faster than this period this morning.

"Boys," she said to the pair of gigglers on the other side of the table, "please don't do that." She wasn't quite sure what "that" was, but it seemed safe to assume that anything involving that much chair scraping and producing that much mirth ought to be stopped.

They did stop, but the notebook slid to the floor again as soon as she moved her hand away from it, and there was a fresh burst of giggles.

"All right, if that's where it wants to stay, let's leave it there," she said to hide the fact that she didn't know which child was guilty, although she strongly suspected the five-year-old, Craig.

She began to wind the little music box in front of her and set it going on the table. "Now watch me, Roddy," she told the four-year-old. "Watch my tongue." She began to sing to the tune of "Twinkle, Twinkle, Little Star," tinkling from the box, her mouth wide open to display the acrobatics of her tongue. "La-la, la-la, la-la-la . . ."

There was a snicker from Craig, but Cathy pretended not to notice him. She was a college student, after all, the trained adult here who knew what she was doing—or anyhow, was supposed to be doing. Any minute now, Dr. Paulus, the new chairman of the school's department of speech therapy, would be popping her head in at the door to check that all was going well in this, Cathy's first clinic session with real patients. From what little Cathy had seen of Dr. Paulus so far, things had better be going well—or else. It wouldn't do to be caught looking as if a pair of bratty little boys were succeeding in making her feel inadequate and silly.

"La-la, la-la, la-la-la," she continued doggedly through a second chorus of the song. "There now, Roddy, let me hear you do it."

The music box was running down. She picked it up and rewound it.

"I wad dad," whined Craig, who, for no organic reason that could be discovered, chose to speak as if he suffered from a perpetual cold in the head. Although it was barely half an hour ago since Cathy had walked into the clinic's waiting room and met him for the first time, she was beginning to recognize that there were a good many other things as well that Craig chose to do for no discoverable reason.

"No, you leave it alone," she said, pushing the box farther to the right and away from the fingers that grabbed at her hand to snatch the prize. "You had your turn and you'll have another, but now it's Roddy's turn. Come on, Roddy. Let's hear you. La-la, la-la . . ."

Roddy, whose problem was a cleft palate, breathed a reluctant, "Hya-hya, hya-hya."

"Your tongue, Roddy," Cathy corrected. "Remember the end of your tongue. What's it doing? Get it up there against your front teeth and push. Push."

Something grazed her ankle. There was a whimper of protest from her guide dog, Trudy, who had been lying quietly under the table up to now. Cathy reached down to soothe her and encountered a small oxford swinging in toward Trudy's middle. The shoe escaped her fingers, but from the direction in which it retreated, she had no doubts as to its owner.

"Craig," she said sharply. "Are you trying to kick my dog? Don't you dare!" This was one area in which she would tolerate no fooling around.

Craig tee-heed and slid off his chair with a plop that brought an appreciative chortle from Roddy. Trudy emerged from beside Cathy's chair, giving herself a shake and uttering a sneeze of German shepherd disgust. Roddy was now on the floor beneath the table, too.

Cathy stood up, trying to remember that she was supposed to gain the children's liking and respect as early as possible. Losing her temper and shouting wasn't the approved method.

"Boys, get back in your seats. Please. Later, if you're good, you can pet the dog."

Trudy circled behind her to evade a slap-thud imitation of dog steps that was being done on hands and knees. Cathy rounded the table and ducked below it, both hands spread and grabbing. She closed on a passing leg, then on the arm that, hopefully, went with it. She dragged her captive out onto his feet.

"You sit," she said, lifting him above the nearest chair and plunking him down on it hard. "You hear me? You sit still and behave."

She dove under for the second child. Her fingers grazed his belt and slipped off as he scuttled out of range. Overhead, the music box emitted a flurry of telltale plinks, departing for the rear of the room. Trudy's toenails at once clicked toward the front of the room. Cathy made a reckless lunge and seized what dissolved at once into an outraged wail.

Of course, it was at this moment that the door opened to admit the cool voice of Dr. Paulus. "Anything wrong, Miss Wheeler?"

"Trudy, stay," Cathy ordered. That would be the ultimate straw: having her dog go racing off along the clinic corridor.

She struggled to her feet, still clutching the wailer. She would gladly have thrown him at Dr. Paulus or at anyone else who would elect a scene like this to crash. Her hair was straggling into her eyes, she could feel a run oozing the length of her left leg, and she was aware that the little music box—she had shopped a month to find one that played the tune she wanted—was being tapped experimentally against the windowsill, or something equally solid, behind her.

"Hello, Dr. Paulus. No, I believe everything is about under control. We've had a slight misunderstanding about what is good behavior and what's bad in a classroom, that's all." She smiled, knowing she was fooling no one into imagining she was calm and collected. With a shade more conviction, she added, "I think I'm winning."

"I see," said Dr. Paulus. Her voice continued to be cool and unamused. "All right, then, boys, let's go back to our seats. I want you to show me the work you've been doing this morning."

Her voice was lovely to listen to. Every syllable was as clean and pure as a perfect crystal, yet liquid and musical. Her tone, however, left no question as to who was in authority here.

Cathy's prisoner stopped dangling like a dead weight from her arm and stood up straight. "Can you show Dr. Paulus a picture of something that starts with your sound?" she prompted, releasing him.

"I wadda show by pidjer," came from the windowsill tapper in accents that were unmistakably Craig's.

The realization prickled over Cathy that, in the skirmish, she had temporarily lost track of which child was who. Thank goodness, Dr. Paulus' first thought hadn't been to be introduced to them.

Cathy stretched her hand to Craig as he plinked by. "Give me the music box, please."

He side-stepped and went on to his place at the table, leaving her extended hand empty except for an inquiring lick from Trudy.

"Craig," she said on a note that was meant to be ominous but that sounded merely frustrated.

"Give the music box to Miss Wheeler, please," Dr. Paulus directed with the serenity of one not in the habit of being disobeyed. "Children who come to our clinic must do what their therapist tells them or she won't be able to help them learn."

Cathy's lightweight sweater was suddenly too heavy and too hot. It dried none of the dampness breaking out on her forehead to have Craig rise from his chair and deliver the box to her like a sweet little lamb. Dr. Paulus' speech, she knew, was not designed only for Craig's benefit. A student therapist who couldn't achieve cooperation from her patients had lost the battle before it was begun.

She felt like a reprimanded child herself as she resumed her seat, beckoned Trudy to lie down again, and retrieved the notebook of pictures from its resting place on the floor. But you're not being fair, she thought. How am I going to prove to them that I'm the boss if you barge in at the crucial moment and take over? Go away, Dr. Paulus. Let me handle this. I'll straighten things out.

But Dr. Paulus didn't go away. She seated herself at the end of the table and remained there, exuding an atmosphere of authority that was almost solid enough to touch. The children were as conscious of it as Cathy was. She couldn't have asked for two more docile patients as she flipped through the pages of carefully selected pictures, each of them bearing a transparent Braille label to help her guide the discussion. Roddy actually produced a good, strong "l" when he identified the lion she pointed to for him. This wasn't terribly astonishing in itself, for Roddy had been a patient at the speech clinic for two semesters already and his report stated he was capable of making most of the sounds he had been drilled in if he would just put forth the effort. This was simply the first time he had seen fit to exert himself today.

Both boys turned their faces to Dr. Paulus for approval each time they answered. It didn't matter who was holding the book for them or asking the questions.

They knew who was in command now, and it wasn't Cathy.

When Dr. Paulus finally left, a scant five minutes before the bell rang, Cathy wasn't sure whether she wanted to burst into tears or to erupt fire like a Hawaiian volcano. Sister Bernard would never have interfered like this with a student's first day in clinic. Never in a million years. It was Sister Bernard's theory that a girl learned more by being on her own through that initial session with her first patients that any supervisor could teach her in an entire semester of sitting by and clasping her hand. But Sister Bernard had been transferred to a college in Oregon during the summer—or so the student grapevine had it—to spend the next five years organizing a speech therapy department there, and Dr. Paulus, an unknown quantity, had been imported to St. Chrysostom College, here in the Midwest, from an eastern university to take her place at the head of the speech therapy department. Only not quite so unknown a quantity as she was two hours ago, Cathy thought bitterly as the bell ended the period.

Well, there was nothing to do about it but gather up her teaching materials and hope that things would go better when Roddy and Craig returned to her on Friday.

"Okay, boys, we're done for today," she said, forcing a smile.

She reached for Trudy's harness and walked the two boys down the hall to the waiting room, where she could deliver them into their mothers' keeping. It was necessary to explain Friday's assignment to the mothers, going into detail about the notebook each child was to work on by pasting pictures into it that bore a relation to his particular sound problems, and suggesting ways to encourage him to use these sounds outside the clinic. Her smile began to stiffen into her jaw as she talked, but she managed to maintain it to the end.

"And will you be Craig's therapist on Friday?" Craig's mother asked.

"Why, yes. Certainly. I'll be his therapist right up through December, the whole semester," Cathy answered. No one, not even Craig's mother, could expect her to add that she was overjoyed at the prospect.

She wondered at the purpose of the question, anyway. Although she and the mothers hadn't met until today, she would have thought that, when the children had been brought for diagnosis or to enroll, someone somewhere along the line would have briefed the parents on the college's clinic procedure.

"You're a regular speech therapist, then? I mean you do everything the others do? Like—well—one of the mothers was telling me how sometimes they use a tongue depressor in a child's mouth, and—" The woman's voice trailed off uneasily.

Cathy saw what Craig's mother was getting at, but she was in no mood to rescue her graciously. If the woman lacked the nerve to ask a question straight out, her curiosity would have to go unsatisfied. Cathy's business here was to correct speech problems, not to volunteer intimate details of what it is like to be blind.

"I am not a regular therapist yet," she said, shaking her head and smiling some more. "I'm a student, the same as everyone else here. We're most of us juniors this year."

"But you will be taking Craig for the whole semester?" his mother repeated. "Alone? On your own? Like the others? I mean, it's certainly wonderful that you can, and—and— That's a beautiful dog you have there.

It's perfectly incredible, isn't it, how they can train those animals to be practically human? Craig, honey, don't kick the doggie. He might bite you."

"Trudy doesn't bite people, ever," Cathy said, thinking more's the pity. She stepped back, pulling the big dog closer to her, beyond reach of Craig honey's toe. Plainly, her teaching was going to have to cover more than decent speech patterns this semester.

"Well, I won't keep you any longer, Miss Wheeler. There is Dr. Paulus, and I want to speak to her before we leave. It's been so inspirational talking to you."

"Thank you," Cathy murmured to the footsteps already bustling away. If the woman was looking for information as well as inspiration, she might as well speak to Dr. Paulus. The chairman should know as much about Craig's classroom experience today as the therapist who was supposed to have been in charge.

In the hall, Cathy dropped her smile like a false mustache. She headed for the lavatory on the second floor to comb her hair, tidy her twisted skirt and rumpled sweater. There was nothing to do about the run in her stocking but live with it to the end of the day.

Her next destination was the library, there to write up her notes on her patients while the "happy" memory was fresh in her mind.

"Here comes Cathy," Amy Reinhardt chirped from the back of the room when Cathy and Trudy eased in through the heavy library doors. "Over here, friend. Join the post mortem."

The post mortem sounded more like a protest meeting. Karen Bergen interrupted herself only long enough to say "Hi," as Cathy took the chair Amy pushed out for her, then resumed indignantly, "Twice. Twice, mind you. The first time, okay. I was expecting that. But ten minutes later she popped in again, like she thought she'd better sneak back and catch me at something."

"She did the same to me, the very same," broke in Laura Riley, another student therapist. "The second time I didn't even hear her. I just happened to glance over my shoulder and there she stood, like she'd been there half an hour. After that, I couldn't do a thing for watching the door and wondering when she was going to fade in again."

"That's nothing. I cracked down so hard on my kids to get them behaving like angels, in case she checked a third time, that I guess I scared them. Anyhow, when I looked down, there was this huge puddle under little Jimmy's chair." Monica Vohl's snort of a chuckle held no contrition.

"I don't know if I belong in this discussion," Cathy said. "She walked me and my patients to my therapy room, but she dropped in for a visit only once. Of course, she stayed for nearly half the period. Dr. Paulus, I mean. I assume that's who it is we're talking about."

"You're darn right it is. Old fish-eye herself," Monica said. "I should have had her mop up the floor in my room or else I should have left the wet mop in her office. It was really her mess."

Cathy entered wholeheartedly into the laughter this picture provoked. Somehow, laughter reduced Dr. Paulus to a manageable size. She began to seem slightly ridiculous, and you can't be afraid of someone ridiculous.

Afraid? Cathy tucked her feet under the chair to give Trudy more room beneath the table. No, afraid was putting it a measure too strongly. Yet, now that she knew she wasn't the sole object of Dr. Paulus' special attentions, a fist inside her unclenched from a knot that had been as much defensive as resentful.

"The least she could have done was warn us she'd be looking in more than once," Karen said. "Sister Bernard never spied on her students. She didn't let anybody get away with anything, but she didn't spy."

"Sister Bernard!" In Amy's mouth the name was a prayerful ejaculation. "I could have done so great this morning if Sister Bernard had just been here to glance in once. I know I could. My two little girls are darlings. We fell in love at first sight. But then, after Dr. Paulus surprised me by her second visit, I got so nervous my teeth were almost chattering. I have this terrible feeling that she's lurking around corners, trying to catch me at something."

"She did catch me," Cathy said. "I was dragging a child out from under the table, bodily. I'm afraid there wasn't too much love being lost in my room." All at once, she saw the scene as Dr. Paulus must have seen it. "I don't wonder she had to come in and sit down. Imagine being met at the door by a huge German shepherd, there's no therapist to be seen and only one little boy, who's standing by himself at an open third-story window, as if he might be about to jump out."

The more she described it, the more hilarious the incident grew. Mutters of "quiet" and "sh-h-h" from neighboring tables began to override the giggles, reminding them that people around them were trying to study.

Karen and Laura hushed immediately. They opened their books and started to rustle through the pages, but Amy declared, "I'm too wound up to concentrate right now. What I want is a big, cold drink of something. Come on, Cathy. Let's go down to the grill."

Cathy hesitated. If she didn't get her notes written up during this period, she would have to stay after her last class this afternoon to do it or else wait until tonight. Neither alternative was considered ideal procedure. On the other hand, starting in on her notes now would mean disregarding the small but ominous beginnings of a pain behind her left eye. A glass of lemonade and an aspirin at this stage might be all she needed to dissolve it, or at least to insure it remained small.

Before she was decided, one of the library doors whished quietly open. A draft from the hall breathed across her neck. There was a stifled, "Oh-oh," from Karen, and a sheet of paper fluttered to the floor.

"Good morning, Dr. Paulus," someone said brightly from the other end of the room.

"Good morning," Dr. Paulus replied in her beautiful voice. If her footsteps hadn't been noiseless on the smooth tile floor, they would have been masked anyway by Karen's scrabbling pursuit of her paper, but Cathy had a pricking of the thumbs that this table was to be the target of the new chairman of the speech therapy department.

"Good morning, Dr. Paulus," Amy said, injecting the dazzle of her smile into the sound.

"Good morning, Miss—Reinhardt. Miss Vohl. Miss Bergen. Miss Riley." It might have been the effort to recall names she had known only since last week that held Dr. Paulus' tone to a cool neutral. "Miss Wheeler?"

"Yes?" Cathy said, responding to the rising inflection placed on her name. Then she wondered if she had mistaken the cue and should have said, "Good morning," instead. The thought flickered through her mind that it wasn't easy to like someone who persistently threw you off balance.

"Do you have some free time this afternoon or tomorrow when you could stop by my office?" Dr. Paulus asked.

Cathy's dismay was as sharp as it was unreasonable. "I'm in class until three-thirty today," she said—too quickly.

Dr. Paulus' reply was no less prompt. "Three-thirty will be fine." In the same fluid, neutral voice she added, "You know where to find my office, of course."

"Of course."

"Very well, I'll expect you this afternoon at three-thirty."

Woolly silence wrapped the table after her retreating footsteps, a whisper more audible than when she had entered the library, were erased by the shush of the door's opening and closing once more. Not a paper rustled. Not a chair creaked. Not a breath was expelled loudly enough to be detected.

Cathy at last reached down for her briefcase propped against the table leg, and hoisted it onto her lap. A mute "Twinkle, twinkle" broke from the music box inside, and a guarded laugh from Laura dispelled the wool.

"What do you suppose she's got up her sleeve now?" Karen asked, leaning forward as if to confine the question to the center of the table.

"You don't think she heard us laughing and guessed what it was about?" Cathy said. She knew there wasn't a chance in the world it could be that, but she wanted reassuring.

"Impossible," Amy declared with heartening conviction. "No one was laughing or talking by the time she came in. Anyway, you usually can tell when somebody's been listening. My mother always has this funny kind of smirky look around the eyes."

These offhand barbs Amy occasionally directed at her mother never failed to make Cathy wince. Her own family life with her parents and younger brother was such that she counted it a plus that St. Chrysostom was situated right here in her home town, so that she could live at home while attending college. She had accumulated all the boarding school experience she ever wanted in the six months she had spent at the state school for the blind after she had lost her sight through glaucoma when she was fourteen. Without her parents' faith in her and help, she might never have been able to fight her way back to a normal life among sighted classmates and friends, where she belonged. It gave her a disquieting sense of being rich in the presence of poverty whenever Amy dropped a reminder that "home" and "mother" had meanings quite different for her.

Monica, however, took no notice. "This Paulus doll is nobody's mother. She's nobody's sweetheart, either, and she's not about to be."

"From the way she marched through that door and zeroed right in on you, Cathy, I'd say she must have come down here on purpose to look for you," Laura said. "Maybe she's developing a fondness for your company."

Cathy made a wry mouth. "Don't be smug. She's probably so impressed by my classroom performance this morning that she wants to groom me as her assistant. In which case, I'll see that you people are invited in for private conferences next."

Whatever lay behind the unexpected summons, it was all to the good, she told herself, that Dr. Paulus should have found her here in the studious atmosphere of the library, instead of downstairs in the grill, loafing over a glass of lemonade. It would be wiser to get those notes written up during what was left of this period, she decided, delving into her briefcase for paper, a braille slate, and a stylus. That cold drink and the aspirin would have to wait.

By three-thirty that afternoon, however, Cathy was throbbingly aware that she had chosen wrongly. The nugget of pain behind her eye had expanded bit by bit to claim the whole upper quarter of her face in a slow, pulsing ache. An aspirin at lunch and another swallowed two hours later at the start of Sister Janice's Measurements in Education class had done nothing but stir up the acids in her stomach to a disquieting pitch.

She halted Trudy a few steps short of Dr. Paulus' office and drew two deep, steadying breaths of air in her lungs. These headaches of hers were the effects of nervous tension, she reminded herself, so if she could just relax—After all, what was there really to be nervous about? Deliberately, she loosened the taut grip of her fingers on Trudy's harness.

"Okay, Trudy," she directed, "right and in."

Trudy's tail fanned the back of Cathy's legs as they entered the office. For her, this room was Sister Bernard's, and Sister Bernard seldom failed to have a piece of cookie or cracker or some other agreeable token of friendship tucked away in her desk. The fact that it was no longer Sister Bernard presiding at the desk didn't mean to her that there might be a change of policy as well.

"Miss Wheeler, yes. You're right on time," Dr. Paulus said, and a file drawer rolled shut. "I'll be with you in a second. There's a chair right ahead of you."

Cathy located it with a cautious poke of her briefcase. It was the old wicker rocker that used to stand invitingly beside the window. Sister Bernard had liked it there because she said it reminded her of a corner of her grandmother's old-fashioned kitchen, and it was a refuge where she could sit and collect herself when the urgencies of too many meetings in too many places, too many problems to be solved in too little time, and too many decisions to make on the basis of too limited knowledge gathered themselves into a pressure wave that threatened to run her over. Now the chair was far from the window, standing at the front corner of the desk like any other impersonal piece of office furniture.

Cathy lowered herself into it warily, half-prepared to find its rounded contours had been squared and straightened. This wasn't quite fair, she admitted, for if Dr. Paulus were more formal than Sister Bernard, it didn't have to follow that she had no desire to be friendly. The trouble lay in that nobody was quite sure yet what she was or what she intended to be.

"I am at a serious disadvantage this semester." The beautiful voice cut in on Cathy's thoughts as if Dr. Paulus were tuned to the same wave length. "I know none of you people personally as Sister Bernard did. All I have to guide me for the present is what your file says about each of you, and I'm discovering that records of that sort leave out the details that are sometimes most important—important from my point of view, anyway." She closed the office door and returned to her desk. "I hope eventually to find time for a private interview like this with each of the upperclassmen."

"I suppose it is hard, taking charge of a complete department in a strange school," Cathy said politely. "I hadn't thought of it like that."

But why was the honor of the first private interview

being awarded to her? Why not to one of the seniors, since there was less time left for getting acquainted with them than with the juniors? Or if it must be a junior, why start with Wheeler? Why not start with Martha Adams and the A's, or else with Lynn Ziebenaur, at the other end of the alphabet, and work back? Sister Bernard wasn't always fully organized, but that was surely how she would have done it.

"I'm afraid that, for some people, the greatest difficulty will be to accept the fact that I am not Sister Bernard," Dr. Paulus said, tuning in on her again. "I don't believe in substituting a carbon copy for an original, and certainly no one could be more totally an original than Sister Bernard. My concern is to maintain the high standards she has established here, and to encourage the growth of the speech therapy department and the college to the best of my ability. Which means, of course, I must act according to what seems to me to be in the best interests of all involved."

"I'm sure you will do a fine job," Cathy murmured. At any rate, she thought, we're agreed on one point: we both admire Sister Bernard. But she was utterly without a clue as to where all of this was leading. Nothing in Dr. Paulus' smooth tone hinted that she might be fishing either for sympathy or praise. Was she trying to justify her sit-in of this morning? Or perhaps issuing a subtle notice by way of Cathy that the juniors had better resign themselves to more of the same?

Dr. Paulus released a light breath that might have been a sigh. "Very frankly, Miss Wheeler, I'm curious about how you happen to be studying speech therapy. I should think it presents a number of aspects that would be particularly difficult to master for a person with your handicap. Knowing Sister Bernard and her high standards as I do, I'm interested in what conditions you had to meet for her to consent to training a blind student."

"Conditions? There weren't any conditions aside from the ones everybody had to meet—grade points, high school credits, and the like. Sister Bernard said I probably knew more about what a blind person could do than she did, so if I were willing to stand or fall on the same ground as a sighted student, she felt I had as much right in the program as any other qualified applicant." Cathy's smile was for Sister Bernard, who not only taught that physical handicaps could be overcome but practiced what she preached. "So far, the work hasn't been more than I can manage."

"I must admit that is the impression your academic record gives," Dr. Paulus said, and Cathy wondered if that lovely, cool voice ever warmed in the least degree. "But tell me, why did you choose speech therapy to study?"

What there was in the question to put her on her guard, Cathy hardly knew, but it alerted her like the dinging of a railroad crossing signal. This wasn't the moment to confess that she had stumbled onto speech therapy by accident in her senior year of high school. Her earliest, dearest dream had been to become an artist. In high school, that had changed to becoming a journalist, painting pictures with words instead of the colors she could no longer see. It was through sheer ignorance—an idea that speech therapy had something to do with ghostwriting speeches for public figures—that she had signed up to hear a career-day talk on the subject. The possibilities in it of a field for herself, however, began to beckon her as soon as she discovered her mistake.

"It seemed a ready-made profession for a person like me who has to be aware of voices and speech variations as a part of everyday living. Also, speech therapy deals in language, and I've always enjoyed studies of that sort." She groped in a back pocket of her memory for the carefully selected and polished reasons she had written in her college application that senior year at high school. "A speech therapist makes a positive contribution to society. She restores the power of communication to people who would otherwise be cut off from society. These are things I would like to be able to do, and to do them on a professional level."

"There are other professional areas in which valuable service is rendered to people in need of trained assistance, areas in which you would be almost ideally qualified to work. Have you ever thought of directing your studies toward work with the blind?"

"No," Cathy said, startled into curtness. Then, with scarcely less finality, she added, "That is, I've thought about it enough to know that I am definitely not interested."

She had been braced for practically anything but a train on this old track. What she resented was the implication the question always carried that, because she was blind herself, both necessity and natural inclination should restrict her activities to the world of the blind. Her high school counselor had taken the stand that college was too competitive a situation for anyone without sight, but that, if she were determined to learn that the hard way, her best chance would be in rehabilitation or special education for the blind. Under pressure, he had grudgingly allowed that she might have an outside chance in journalism, but he refused even to discuss speech therapy, declaring it would demand a degree of professionalism too high to be practical in her case. It was then that she had known she intended to study speech therapy.

"I should think you would be an invaluable asset to people suffering the same handicap as yours," Dr. Paulus pursued, seemingly unaware that the subject was closed. "From my own observations and from what I've heard from your classmates and teachers, I would say you have an enormous amount to give in the line of adaptability, creativeness, and inspiration."

"Thank you," Cathy said, but the flush warming her face was not modesty's response to a compliment. Her hands were locked together in her lap, containing anger that, like this morning's tension, was the more volatile for being mixed with nebulous flecks of fear. She not only disliked this turn of the conversation, she didn't trust it. When people referred to her as an inspiration, often as not it was by way of oiling the hinges of a trap door about to be dropped away from under her feet.

"But if I do have those qualities, they'll surely serve me just as well in speech therapy, don't you think?" Her smile hoped to reduce all this to the idle speculation it was. "I'm into my junior year. It would be the same as throwing away two years of study if I changed my mind now."

Dr. Paulus' voice was serene, untarnished silver. "Wouldn't it be better to throw away two years now than to find you had wasted four years later?"

"Wasted?" The heat raced from Cathy's face in a dizzy flight, leaving ripples of distortion around the word and what it might mean. "I don't understand. How could they be wasted?"

Trudy stretched herself on the carpet and moaned in

comfort, as if to emphasize that the idea was preposterous.

Dr. Paulus shifted in her chair. "I'm sorry to put it so bluntly, Miss Wheeler, but I believe it is a possibility that neither you nor I can afford to ignore. Your academic record is, of course, above reproach. So is your ingenuity in modifying methods and materials for your own use that normally require sight. I noticed, for example, the inconspicuous Braille labels beneath the pictures you were showing the children this morning. Nevertheless, textbooks, hearing tests, and classroom materials form only a minor portion of what's involved in being an effective speech therapist."

"But what—why—" Cathy fumbled, and repeated, "I don't understand."

Her mind was stunned to a standstill. Even anger had deserted her. All she could feel was the heavy beat of the ache in her head.

"A speech therapist's greatest asset is her ability to work successfully with people. No matter how skilled she is technically, if for some reason she isn't able to communicate her skill to a patient, the time and energy and expense that went into educating her have been wasted."

"Are you talking about the little boys this morning? Do you mean because when you came in they were misbehaving?" Involuntarily, Cathy crossed her legs to hide the run in her hose. Her temperature began to rise again, now that she had a glimmer of what was wrong. "Things will be different Friday. I'll have them under control, I promise you."

"I doubt it will be that simple. With young children, it's important to be able to tell in advance where trouble is going to happen and to be at that place to prevent it before it does. Those children this morning were taking flagrant advantage of the fact that you couldn't see what they were doing."

"I wasn't firm enough at the start, I know," Cathy said. "I won't make the same mistake Friday." She wanted to add, "I'd have had them under control eventually today if you hadn't come in and taken over. You were as much of the problem as anyone." But one thing she wasn't about to do was to whimper excuses.

"Unfortunately, the difficulty extends beyond the children. The attitude of the patient's family toward his therapist can influence his progress as much as that of the patient himself, especially when the patient is a child." Dr. Paulus paused. "To put it briefly, Mrs. Fenger was very disturbed today when she learned that her son was in the hands of a blind student. Neither your records nor any argument I could provide on your behalf could persuade her that he would receive as competent treatment from you as from a sighted student."

Mrs. Fenger. Craig's mother. The woman who had said, "It's certainly wonderful that you can," and thinking all the while, "You can't." She, too, had called Cathy an inspiration.

Cathy shook her head slowly, cautious of the ache that swung above her eye like the bubble in a carpenter's level. "She doesn't have to worry. I wouldn't be in speech therapy if I weren't fairly sure I could do it. As for Craig, her boy, I already have my lesson plan partly worked out for Friday with some ideas I want to try on him. She'll have to be persuaded when his speech begins to improve."

"Craig won't be in your class Friday. Mrs. Fenger insisted that he be assigned to another therapist immediately, and, since there was an opening in the schedule of one of the seniors, I felt that it would be the best course for all concerned. If the parents are prejudiced against the therapist, so will the child be, and there is very little the best of therapists could accomplish in the face of such a barrier."

It's not only the parents who are prejudiced against me, Cathy thought bitterly. It's you. You're not going to give me the ghost of a chance if you can help it. But she sat silent, her throat too dry for a word to get by.

"The point I'm making is this," Dr. Paulus said into the void. "For every student St. Chrysostom accepts, one equally qualified or nearly so must be turned away. The college isn't large enough to accommodate all who apply. Its reputation has long since outstripped its facilities. It isn't fair to that reputation or to the girls denied admittance if the school should expend four years of training on a student who may be severely limited in both ability and opportunity to put it to use."

The point she was making was only too clear. Cathy could feel herself being remorselessly impaled on it. "You want me to quit? To drop out of speech therapy?"

"I'd like you to give it serious thought. We're just a week into the fall semester. It would be relatively easy for you to switch to a different program, if you decide to act within the next few days."

Relatively easy! Easy for her to rethink the lines of her future in just a few days? Easy to leap into a set of new courses for which she had no background or preparation? Easy to collect the textbooks for those courses and have them tape-recorded in their entirety so she could study from them in time to catch up with and keep up with assignments being handed out already?

Easy to scrap two years of hard college work as if it were nothing? Easy to eat humble pie in the presence of everyone who had said from the start that she would never make it? Easy!

The rocker tilted Cathy forward as if it were struck from behind. "What about my other patient? Roddy, the cleft palate? I take it his mother hasn't asked to have him reassigned, so I still have a patient to work with. Mrs. Fenger is just one person, after all."

"Mrs. Fenger, I'm afraid, is representative of a large proportion of the population. I can practically guarantee that you would run into this same attitude on the part of prospective employers when you tried to find a job."

Cathy refused to be shaken by the probable truth of this. "There are blind speech therapists working professionally," she said. "I know. I've read about them. I know it can be done."

She was thinking, you can't throw me out just like that. Not if I won't go. You have to have a reason, a real reason like bad grades or broken rules or something. You have no power to weed me out if I won't go. She knew that perhaps that wasn't so, but she had nothing to lose by fighting.

The office was still except for the electric hum of a small clock on the desk. Then Dr. Paulus asked, "Are you willing to abide by the consequences if your semester's work in the clinic is judged inferior? In that event, you would no longer be in the position of choosing to drop the program. The department would require you to do it."

"But if my work is satisfactory?" Cathy bargained. The headache was throbbing like a drumbeat between her and the sound of her voice.

"That would be grounds for reopening this discussion," Dr. Paulus said, giving nothing. "Don't decide now. Sleep on it and come in—this is Tuesday—come in Thursday to tell me what you'll do. In the meantime, try some honest probing into how badly you want to become a speech therapist and why."

"Thank you. I will." Cathy stood up, in hopes that the interview was over. To her surprise, her knees were trembling.

"Just one more thing." Dr. Paulus tapped a set of papers together and stood up, too. "Should you choose to stay in speech therapy this semester, there will be a replacement for the Fenger boy, so you will continue to have two patients to work with in the clinic. Here is the diagnostic report on the child it will probably be. He is a five-year-old, mentally retarded, who doesn't speak. You will want time to study this before you decide on any course of action."

A bright blade of triumph thinned Cathy's headache for an instant. Dr. Paulus was quite aware that she couldn't force a determined student to drop out. She had been prepared all along to yield if Cathy called her bluff.

Just how cleverly prepared didn't begin to sink in until Cathy reached her locker on the ground floor. There, the reverberations of that parting shot caught up to her: "study this before you decide on any course of action."

She was to consider from the report not so much how she would treat this new patient, but if. Would she bow out gracefully now, her own record intact, or be drummed out in disgrace at the end of the semester when she had failed to convert a speechless moron into a prattling prodigy? Whatever she did, the deck was stacked so that Dr. Paulus could not lose.

Cathy slid her notes of the morning's clinic into her briefcase, then closed her locker and leaned her head against the cool metal of the door. How badly do I want to become a speech therapist? And why? The answers should have been ready on the tip of her tongue, but they eluded her somehow in the mist of ache and confusion. She wanted only one thing right now—to go home.

But even that, it turned out, was not to be accomplished without its price. When she pushed open the heavy outer door for herself and Trudy, they stepped into the spatter of water hitting the paved walk and the fizz of raindrops slanting among the leaves. At some time today, while her attention had been elsewhere, this morning's sunshine had dissolved into a sodden rain.

2

CATHY STOOD a minute under the stone arch of the doorway, coming to terms with her dismay. The bus stop was at the far edge of the campus, more than a city block distant, and there was a dreary, settled-in beat to the rain that suggested small likelihood of its letting up in the next few minutes.

Not even a plastic rain scarf with me, she thought ruefully. Good-by, hairdo.

She pulled her sweater sleeves down to her wrists for what minor protection they could give, and took a firmer hold of her briefcase in her right hand, Trudy's harness in her left. "Trudy, forward."

Trudy descended the three steps to the walk at the funereal pace that was her response always to wet weather. Cathy gave the harness a half-hearted jiggle to urge her along a little faster, but she knew that neither that nor an outright command would achieve anything like Trudy's normal brisk pace. She never refused to work in rain, but she made it quite plain that she considered the necessity an imposition.

Cathy hunched her shoulders and ducked her head as the full sweep of the rain struck her. It wasn't a cold downpour, anyway. She could be thankful for that. Besides, they might as well plod around the puddles on the walk as to splash through them at a run because, the way things were going today, the bus she wanted had probably left five minutes ago.

Gradually, the cars swishing by on the wet street ahead grew a little closer. Cathy listened to them to keep herself from thinking about anything else—about anything at all. The sharp beep-dee-beep-beep of a car horn startled her into raising her head, but the face-on onslaught of the rain persuaded her to lower it again at once.

Then she heard the shouts, too thin and high-pitched to make out until a deeper, masculine voice joined in. "Cathy! Ca—thee-ee!"

She lifted her briefcase in an uncertain wave, not quite believing she could be the particular Cathy being paged. The world was crammed with Cathys, and a sizable number of them attended St. Chrysostom College.

"Hurry up! Come—" Some of the words lost themselves in passage as the lighter voice soloed again. "—ride . . . Larry's car."

It was Amy Reinhardt. Cathy suddenly recognized the voice. Amy, apparently offering her a ride via Larry Tobin, the young shoe salesman who was her current favorite.

Cathy swung the briefcase in a higher arc and gave Trudy's harness a genuine shake this time. Trudy stopped and shook herself, sending a spray of raindrops over Cathy's already soaked legs.

"Come on, Trudy, forward," Cathy urged. "Don't you want to go for a ride?"

Trudy's ears lifted, and her dragging steps picked up a fraction more speed. It wasn't much speed, but it got them down the remainder of the walk and to the waiting car at last.

"Hurry up. Hop in. The back door's open," Amy called from inside. "Larry will drop you off at your house."

"I don't know if we should." Cathy's headache lurched against the front of her skull like a shifting sandbag as she bent to speak through the open door. Rain landed on her neck, setting off a rash of goose pimples beneath her sweater. She couldn't be more miserable than she was. "We may ruin your car, we're so wet. We can just as well wait for the bus."

"Water can't hurt this car," Larry called. "Get in. No bus is going to deliver you right to your door."

Trudy was halfway in as it was, and tugging at the leash to get the rest of herself aboard.

"Well, okay, if you're sure," Cathy capitulated. She lowered herself in and onto the seat. "Thanks, Larry. Thanks a lot."

She checked for the safety of Trudy's feet and tail and slammed the door. It was only then that she realized they didn't have the back seat to themselves. A bulky shoulder and a knee loomed to her left as she straightened to hunt for the seat belt.

"All set?" Amy asked, leaning over the back of the seat. "Oh, you know Greg Breck, don't you?"

"Sure she does," Greg said, as if the possibility of his ever being forgotten by anyone who had ever met him were unimaginable. "We met a week ago in your student lounge or whatever you call that place with all the tables and no food. Larry and I were scouting in different directions for Amy because she wasn't where she said she'd be—as usual. You were the gal who sent me down to the locker room, where she wasn't either. I never forget a redhead."

Cathy was annoyed at herself for putting a hand up to smooth her hair. It needed no smoothing, anyway, not these limp, wet locks hanging where there had been soft waves half an hour ago. She did remember him. It had been on registration day, and the lounge was full of girls writing out their class cards. No one could direct him to Amy, and a few hadn't even known who Amy was, but that didn't phase him a bit. He had gone from table to table, not missing a one, tossing off lavish compliments, asking names, and cracking stale jokes, like the manager at a supermarket grand opening handing out samples of bologna. Larry and he were roommates, she recalled—or worked at the same store or something. The facts were hazy in her memory, and it didn't really matter.

"Isn't this great?" Amy demanded in her little-girl chirp that lent everything she said the quality of a small adventure. "This is Larry's day off, so when I saw it was raining, I called him to come pick me up. Then, just by luck, we glimpsed you on the walk as we turned the corner. I thought your last class was done at three-thirty and you'd be long gone by now."

Cathy didn't remind her of the private conference Dr. Paulus had called. That would lead to questions she didn't want to answer, especially not in the presence of outsiders like Larry and Greg. She didn't know if she could bring herself to answer them for Amy, either, at least not until she had a few more answers for herself.

"It's great to be rescued," she said, making a show of enthusiasm. "Thanks again, Larry. But I'm wondering if

Amy warned you how far I live from the college before she volunteered your services."

"Who cares how far it is?" Greg replied. "Haven't you heard that getting there is half the fun? Or can be?" he added with heavy significance.

"The tank is full of gas, the windshield wipers work, the roof doesn't leak, and there's nowhere anybody has to be at any special time," Larry said as he or Amy switched on the radio. "Don't worry about a thing. Except maybe Greg back there."

Cathy wasn't worried about Greg. She wasn't that interested in him. Besides, Trudy, her broad head resting on Cathy's knee, her curved ears alert, ought to be enough of a third party to keep him from becoming overly friendly. What did trouble her was Larry's hint that this might be an aimless cruise, rather than a direct ride home—a cruise shot through with the frenzy of electric guitars and crashing drums.

"What's the matter? Got a headache?" Greg asked.

Cathy realized her hand was pressing her forehead. "A little." She turned the gesture into another upward push at her drooping hair, irritated by this hint that she was under observation.

"Too bad it's not an aching tooth," Greg said. "I've got a dentist friend who could take care of that for you in a jiffy. No pain. No charge. He'd do it for the pleasure of seeing if you could smile." He crooked a finger under her chin. "Maybe I ought to have a look, just in case."

Amy giggled. "Greg has friends everywhere. He's taking night courses in public relations at the university. I guess what he's learning there really works."

Cathy refused to gratify him with the shove he was inviting. She merely lifted her chin away. "Like a charm," she said in a tone that should have withered him.

"Sweet young things from the local convent school are our next assignment," Greg said blandly. "I've been reading ahead."

Amy twisted around in her seat. "Don't get funny about St. Chrysostom, Gregory Breck, or that's one lesson you're going to flunk. It's an accredited women's college, with a national reputation, which means if you think a college run by nuns is just a convent school, you're sadly mistaken. Cathy and I had our first day of clinic today, and we're here to testify that they don't let you get by with a thing."

"That's right. Today was kiddie day for you, wasn't it?" Larry tapped the horn. The car veered slightly and hummed on without changing speed. "How were they? Pretty rough on you?"

"Not the children. The two little girls I've got—Sally and Beth—are darlings. We had such fun getting acquainted. I know I'm going to love them and love teaching them. Their doting mommies have let them get into such an advanced stage of baby talk that I'm going to be the one who teaches them every word they'll speak."

Amy's eagerness fairly twinkled. There was obviously no question in her mind about becoming a speech therapist. And none in her future, either. Cathy turned her face to the window to conquer a pang that wasn't as vicious as envy but a good deal sharper than wistfulness.

"Well, when you get tired of the little darlings, I can tell you what to do," Greg said. "Ship them over to my friend the dentist. He'll straighten their crooked little teeth and change the shape of their crooked little mouths and send them home talking like Winston Churchill."

"If they did have crooked teeth and crooked mouths, which they don't, they'd talk exactly the same when they left the dentist as they did before," Amy informed him. "Speech is something that's learned. It's a habit pattern, set up in the brain, and to change it you have to practice and practice until you've worn a new pattern into the brain. It's the same principle as learning to use your left hand gracefully for things when your right one is in a cast. Only, learning proper speech is a lot harder. Right, Cathy?"

"Right," Cathy said, although she wasn't really listening. She wished they would either cut the volume of the radio or else leave her out of the conversation—or both. Her energies were centered on simply enduring until she finally reached home.

"Sure, sure." Greg patted her wet sleeve. "If that's the propaganda you want handed out while you have a good time playing peek-a-boo with the cute little kiddies, it's okay with me. I suppose you've got to tell the mamas something so they'll get hot and bothered about junior's saying 'wed thocks,' instead of 'red socks," and pay you gals to take him on."

Cathy knew he was trying to provoke a retort from her, but she didn't answer. She didn't have to. Amy flamed up like a rocket leaving for the moon.

"In the first place, we don't get paid while we're students; the clinic does. In the second place, you'd get hot and bothered, too, if you were junior being laughed at because it always comes out 'wed thocks' no matter how hard he tries to say it right. And in the third place, plenty of people have speech problems a lot more serious than that. What chance does a person have, do you think, of making a decent living or having friends or doing anything else if he stutters so badly people stop listening before he gets the message out, or if people can't stand to listen to the ugly sounds he produces when he talks, or if he can't talk at all because of a stroke or accident or something? You're lost if you have no way to communicate, and speech is the type of communication that sets human beings apart from the animals."

Cathy detected echoes of Sister Bernard in the words, but the passion was purely Amy's. Perhaps if I could have blazed like that for Dr. Paulus, Cathy thought, things would have been different this afternoon. But had she ever felt such a blaze in herself when the subject was speech therapy? Her cheek touched the cold glass of the window, and a shiver ran through her.

"Hey, there." Greg surprised her by taking hold of her hand. She was appalled to have him lean forward and say, "Tobin, this girl is cold back here."

Larry chuckled. "Must be you've got a communications problem of your own. You better hire Amy."

"No, I mean she's shivering. She's cold. And this coach's heater is still on the casualty list, isn't it?"

"Who was figuring to need a heater this early in September?" Larry asked, with more justice than gallantry. "My jacket's back there somewhere. Put that on, Cathy."

Cathy pulled her hand from Greg's, which seemed to be prepared to stay linked indefinitely. "No, no, I'm fine. I'm perfectly okay." But another shiver cut her short by setting her teeth to chattering.

"I tell you what," Greg said. "Swing left at the next light, Tobin. We'll go down to the Bavarian Hut. They serve hot chocolate that's hot enough to melt the cups. So is their coffee."

"No, please, not on my account," Cathy protested. What she meant was, please, just leave me alone. Don't fuss about me. Just let me go home.

But no one paid any attention. Greg had an arm around her, supposedly to aid him in draping Larry's jacket across her shoulders. Amy was applauding the idea of a detour like a happy cricket. Trudy rose up in the crowded space between the seats to poke an anxious nose into Cathy's face. Larry called on everyone to acknowledge that a car without a heater, such as his, was much to be preferred over a car not yet delivered, such as Greg's.

Cathy tried once more to make herself heard in the commotion, but it was like trying to flag down a tornado. She gave up the effort and settled into the welcome warmth of Larry's jacket. Maybe if Greg were allowed to blow unopposed for a while, he would eventually blow himself out.

"Turn right on Twenty-ninth," he directed. "There's an alley in the middle of the block. Take that, and we can pull up about ten steps from the side door of the place. Rudy, the manager, is a friend of mine. He'll let us in there, and you girls won't even have to get your feet wet."

If Cathy could have mustered the energy, she would have asked him how he proposed to dry those ten steps between the car and the door. She was glad she didn't, for the steps proved to be protected by an awning of some sort. They did all troop from the car to the side door without wetting their feet, and Greg did know Rudy, the manager, who greeted him like an old friend.

Greg also knew which table they should choose and

distributed them around it, himself at Cathy's left, Larry to her right, and Amy opposite her. Greg called the waitress by her first name while informing her they wouldn't need a menu, and ordered hot chocolate for Cathy without troubling to ask if she would like it. Greg recommended the same for Larry and Amy and ordered coffee for himself.

"Have to watch my figure, you know," he said.

Amy snorted. "Thanks a lot. What about our figures?"

"I'm keeping an eye on those, too. It's my favorite kind of scenery," he said. "Besides, teeny-tinies like you never have to count calories, and our melancholy redhead here lacks the basic ingredients for ever becoming a jolly fat girl."

Cathy retreated behind a sip from the glass of ice water the waitress set in front of her. She thought longingly of the little box of aspirins in her purse, but she wouldn't dare risk swallowing one while Greg Breck was on the scene. In two seconds flat, he would be spearheading a rescue operation by way of roaring ambulances and wailing sirens, and she would end up strapped into a hospital bed, untold miles farther from her home.

Neither was there much to hearten her in the fragrance steaming from the cups when they arrived. Hot chocolate had always been too thick and too sweet a concoction for her taste, and this promised to be the sweetest and thickest ever. It was the hottest as well. She retracted her fingers from the curve of the cup before she actually touched it, and still she could feel the heat in her fingertips.

"Use a spoon," Larry advised. "If the handle doesn't

evaporate, it's probably safe for the fillings in your teeth."

"Mmmm, delicious," Amy murmured. "Dip in through the whipped cream. That cools it."

Cathy slipped her spoon in cautiously, and more cautiously raised it to her lips. The first swallow rolled down her throat in a smooth trickle of warmth. So did the second, and her stomach winced in pleasure. She woke to the discovery that she was hungry. Could that be what lay at the root of her headache?

"This place is darling," Amy told her. "Checkered tablecloths and candles full of drippings at every table. Big, dark beams up above. Mugs and steins and little carvings on the walls. Don't they have zither music here at night and folk dancing?"

"Saturday nights," Larry answered. "I've dropped in here once or twice to watch. It's old-time country dancing—polkas, waltzes, schottisches—that kind of stuff. The food's good, too, if you can read German enough to know what to order."

"Greg can," Cathy said before she could stop herself.

Greg accepted the tribute as if that were what it had been meant to be. "I don't have too much of a problem. My policy is when in doubt, look at the price and point out the dish you can afford." His cup clinked on his saucer. "Listen, I've got a great idea. Why don't the four of us come here Saturday night for sauerbraten and fun?"

"Sure. Why not? That is, if the girls are willing," Larry said.

Cathy's spoon halted its slow revolutions in her cup. A full-scale evening with glorious Greg? She did a frantic tally of the people at the table. Surely, if she counted urgently enough, she would find a fifth person here, someone who could be numbered instead of her in Greg's "four of us."

"This Saturday? I can't," Amy said, proving herself the friend Cathy had always known her to be. "I have to be in New Concord this weekend. Sunday is my mother's birthday."

"Where is New Concord?" Greg asked. "Not much more than an hour from here, is it? We could drive you there after the sauerbraten and polkas and still get you up home in time for the birthday."

"You don't know my mother." Amy's laugh wasn't altogether mirthful. "I have to take the first bus after I get out of class Friday, and I don't come back until the last one Sunday night. All I'd have to do would be to phone her there's a change of plans, and she'd be down here the next morning to see for herself what's so important, and that would be the end of that."

The desire to bless Mrs. Reinhardt had never come upon Cathy before, but she did it ungrudgingly now, secure in the knowledge that Amy wasn't exaggerating. Mrs. Reinhardt had a way of dropping in on events in Amy's social life, if she knew them in advance, offering to drive Amy and her date to and from the movie so the three of them could become better acquainted, or rearranging an evening date into a cozy luncheon for three at the Women's Club in the interests of Amy's getting the good night's sleep she needed, or simply "being there" in Amy's rented room, to see her off to the party and to welcome her in on her return. "Amy and I are bound together by closer ties than most parents and children," she had confided to Cathy on their first meeting, which was at the freshman get-acquainted picnic two years ago. "Since her daddy died when she was eight, we've grown to be a complete little world in ourselves." Frequent long weekends at home and a lengthy casualty list of boy friends was part of the price Amy kept paying to enlarge that world just a bit for herself.

"Can't you tell her there's an exam late Friday or something?" Greg suggested, like Dr. Paulus, unable to recognize no when he heard it.

Cathy ventured a sip from her cooling cup, and wondered why she had been in such a rush to get away from Craig Fenger's mother. If she had been a shade more courteous, a shade less curt, there might have been no interview with Dr. Paulus this afternoon. What was it Mrs. Fenger had asked, anyway? Hadn't she merely been wanting Cathy to assure her that no harm could possibly come to Craig in her hands? An understanding attitude from Cathy, a generous explanation of how she adapted the routine methods and materials for herself . . .

"Well, Cathy," Greg boomed in her ear, "I guess that leaves it up to the two of us. What do you say? How's your schottische?"

"My what?" Like a delayed broadcast, his words registered in her mind, and she set her cup down hard. "Oh, no! I couldn't. Thanks, but Saturdays are pretty well booked up for me."

"Booked up how?" Greg leaned toward her so that his shoulder nudged hers. He picked up her left hand and laid it palm down beside her cup. "No ring. And I don't see any frat pin. He can't be that steady and not have a 'No Trespassing' sign on you anywhere."

Cathy withdrew her hand to her lap. Among Greg's several qualities that didn't appeal to her was his free and easy handling of her as if she were goods on a display counter.

"Weekends are when I do my heavy studying," she said, because the truth, lame though it sounded, was the first thing that entered her mind. "I'm booked up with books."

Amy instantly turned traitor. "Oh, Cathy, why don't you go? By this Saturday you'll have earned a night off. It'll be fun."

Except that this may be the one weekend of study that is most vital of all, Cathy thought. The least slip now and Dr. Paulus would snap her up like a toad catching a fly. She started to shake her head but stopped and concentrated on not raising her hand to press against the ache there instead.

"Cathy! Cathy Wheeler!" a new voice hailed her. "What are you doing here?"

Only it wasn't new. It was as old as grade school and the halls of Wilson High.

"Joan Norton!" Cathy nearly stepped on Trudy's foot in her eagerness to move her chair away from the table by way of encouraging the interruption. "What are you doing here, is the question. How long has it been? More than a year."

"Ages," Joan agreed, the clack of her heels bringing her to the table. "Mummy and I were shopping next door, and we saw you in here on our way to the car. Mummy went on to the car, but I couldn't pass up this chance to talk to you. It's too perfect."

Cathy introduced her former schoolmate to the others, explaining, "Joan used to read for me in high school."

"And walk her home, and steer her through the halls at school, and do practically everything—until she began bringing the dog. We know all each other's secrets, don't we?" Joan said—and probably believed it was true.

Greg—who else but Greg?—pulled up a chair for her from another table. "I shouldn't sit," Joan protested, sitting, "because Mummy's waiting. I only ran in for a second, and I have to run right out."

She was making wide gestures as she spoke. Cathy could trace them by the scent Joan was wearing—something reminiscent of geraniums—which swooped in the wake of each movement like the vapor trail of a jet.

"Now here's a gal with the sign in plain sight," Greg said. "Shiny diamond, third finger, left hand. No doubts about where she stands."

"You bet it's in plain sight," Joan said. "This diamond cost two hundred dollars plus tax."

"You're engaged?" Cathy struggled not to sound astonished, but all through high school the boys had scattered ahead of Joan like deer pursued by a hound. Who would have dreamed that Joan would gain her heart's desire, a man of her own, only a couple of years after graduation?

"You better believe it. The date is set, the church is reserved, and I bought my wedding dress this afternoon."

"Congratulations," Cathy said before she remembered the proper wish to a bride was "felicitations." Congratulations, she had read somewhere, implied victory in a contest, the winning of a coveted prize, and brides, in theory, should be considered as the lovely prize won, not the doughty winner.

Joan, however, was oblivious to such fine distinctions. "Can you believe it? I'm going to be a bride. Finally! I've got a list a yard long of people I'd like to invite so I could laugh in their faces, but of course, we can't afford that big a wedding."

Amy laughed, then apparently realized what Cathy knew already: that Joan was quite serious. Joan generally was.

Amy mended her mistake by jumping up and coming around the table. "May I see your ring? Let Larry have a good look, too. When's the wedding?"

"November first. That sounds like forever, but it's really less than two months off. And there's everything still to do." Joan brought her hands together in a punctuating clap that lifted Trudy's muzzle from Cathy's foot. "That's why I'm so glad I saw you in here, Cathy."

Cathy tried not to inhale too deeply of the geranium scent that was billowing her way. "Why?"

"I need a third bridesmaid. I'm going to have my two cousins, Olive and Nadine, and I'd like you to be the third. Will you? It would solve everything."

"Me?" Cathy found herself oddly flattered at the same time that her knowledge of Joan Norton was warning her there was probably no reason to be so. Weren't bridal attendants usually chosen from relatives and dearest friends? Certainly, she qualified on neither score. "I don't know. I'm not sure—"

Greg uttered a groan. "Don't tell me you're going to give her that line about being booked up with books."

Joan's laugh penetrated to the remotest corners of the restaurant. "That's Cathy Wheeler for you. You haven't changed a bit, I gather. Honestly, I worry about this girl. It seems like the only diamonds she's ever going to be interested in are the ones she knits into argyle socks."

"Aha!" Greg said. "Now we're getting somewhere.

Girls don't knit argyle socks unless there's some guy to wear them. Who gets the socks?"

Cathy shrugged from under the hand he dropped to her shoulder and said distinctly, "Why don't you call me some evening, Joan? Fill me in on the details of the wedding and all?"

Anyone but Joan would have understood the hint. Joan continued gaily at undiminished volume. "If there's a guy in Cathy's life, it's one I've never heard of—except maybe one named Steve, who walked out yea these many years ago. No, she started doing argyles because a girl in school was foolish enough to say it was too tricky to do unless you could see the colors and patterns and everything. Don't ever tell Cathy Wheeler something's impossible unless you want her to try it. The last I saw, she had three beautiful pairs done without a mistake, and without a soul to give them to."

"Mark wears them ice skating," Cathy said. If Greg were unaware that Mark was her younger brother, that was his problem. She doubted that anyone was listening to her, anyway. Joan still had the floor.

"You have to admit, Cathy, you can't resist a challenge, even if it's to do something you wouldn't care two cents about otherwise. My theory is it's your way of compensating for being blind. I suppose that's only natural, though, considering the dumb things most people do or say when they see a blind person."

Cathy reached for her glass of water to conquer a horrible premonition that her chocolate was about to rise up and give Greg an excuse for calling the emergency squad, after all. Her head and her stomach had taken about as much discussion of her blindness as they could manage for this day.

"Would you believe," Joan went on, bending toward Greg, "that when I used to ride the bus with her—"

"Excuse me," Larry broke in, "but could that be your mummy up there? That lady who just came in?"

"Where?" Joan leaped from her chair. "Oh! . . . No, thank goodness. But I do have to run. She'll be having fits."

"Thanks," Cathy directed a wan smile at Larry.

"Any time," he murmured, and she knew why Amy thought him worth hanging on to.

"No need of thanks," Joan said. "You'll be doing me a favor. I had my heart set on three attendants, but I couldn't think of who else to ask until I had this brainstorm, seeing you in here. Mummy said why not ask you, because I've certainly done you enough favors for you to return one. And I know Pete will be so surprised. It's perfect."

"Pete?" A premonition of a different sort lanced Cathy as she realized that Joan hadn't yet identified the groom. "Pete who?"

"Pete Sheridan, of course." The shrillness of Joan's giggle betrayed that she recognized it was far from an "of course" announcement. "But you must have heard we've been dating. It started during his first leave after he went into the army."

Cathy shook her head slowly. "I haven't heard much of any of the Sheridans since they sold their house and moved across town to an apartment. I knew Pete went into service right after graduation, but that's about it."

Yet as children, she and Pete had lived more like Siamese twins than neighbors, riding their bikes together, building snow forts, working jigsaw puzzles, going swimming, pooling their pocket money for a how-to paperback on Indian crafts or a bargain sale on chewing gum. It was an intimacy that couldn't survive the new pressures and excitements of entering their teens. She and Pete were traveling divergent roads well before the Sheridans finally moved away. But for Pete, her old playmate, to be getting married. It was like a door closing on a part of her life, an abrupt snap of scissors through the cord between childhood and now.

And for Pete to be marrying Joan Norton, the girl whose very name used to gag him when they were in school together! That was a jolt. Although, come to think of it, hadn't it crossed her mind once or twice in the past that the gentleman did occasionally protest too much?

"It's a long story. I'll have to call you." Joan was drifting step by reluctant step toward the exit. "But anyhow, you can tell any of the old gang you meet that I've got him, just like I always said I would. And here's a tip for you two girls, in case you need one: it sure helps keep a lonesome soldier interested and grateful if you let him call collect from anywhere he happens to be. It did terrible things to my bank account and to my father, but it was worth it."

Repeating her thanks to Cathy and her promise to phone soon with further details, she faded into the near distance and was gone.

Amy released a throat-clearing sort of giggle. "Is she always—? Does she always—? I mean, I'm not knocking your friend or anything, but does she—?"

"She does. And she is. Always." Cathy did what she could to round her mouth to a smile. "Like she said, there are no secrets where she is."

"Well, she's a gal who knows what she wants and how to get it," Greg said. "You've got to give her credit. There's about two good swallows in your cup and the same in mine. What do you say we drink to the power of positive thinking?"

He clinked his cup against Cathy's, and she choked down what remained of her chocolate, trusting that empty cups would set the wheels in motion again to bring her home at last. That was as positive as she could think for the present. A gal who knows what she wants . . . How badly do you want . . . Why . . . Cathy pressed the paper napkin to her lips and breathed a silent prayer that no one would suggest a second round of drinks.

"You aren't going to act as bridesmaid for her, are you?" Amy asked. "She sounded as if she thinks you've agreed already, but you won't, will you?"

"I don't know. I don't suppose so," Cathy answered, but without conviction. "Pete Sheridan is an old friend. We grew up together."

And now we are grown up, she thought. The things we do aren't games any more. For richer, for poorer, for better, for worse—they're for real. The thought blew a shiver of loneliness through her, but it carried a breath of new strength as well.

"Old friends aren't to be trusted. My advice is to acquire new ones at every opportunity," Greg said. "Which brings us back to the question of whether you and I have a date together Saturday night."

"I'm afraid not. Thanks just the same, but I honestly do have some heavy studying to do this weekend." If her smile was small, it was genuine this time. "I have a new patient being assigned to me, and I've got to be ready for him."

And for Dr. Paulus. Why? Perhaps Joan was right; it was like the argyles. Or like climbing a mountain because it was there. If the end product were a pair of socks she didn't need or a snowball that melted or permission to continue a program of studies she wasn't even certain she cared that much about, this was beside the point. Not to be defeated, that was reason enough for putting up an all-out fight. At any rate, it would have to do for a reason until a better one came along.

Larry rattled the ice in his water glass. "Drink up, Breck. Here's a girl who knows what she doesn't want and she's not about to take it. You've got to give that kind credit, too." Coins jingled in his pocket. "Let's see if your luck's any greater in getting your friend the waitress over here to give us our bill."

3

LEONARD PERKINS. That was his name. Leonard Perkins: age five years, seven months; vision, hearing, vocal organs normal; I.Q. 75; no intelligible speech except for the single word "mama." That was what in essence the diagnostic report boiled down to. Cathy could recite the report almost in its entirety, Roman numerals, sub-headings and all, by the time she presented herself at Dr. Paulus' office the next afternoon.

"You have studied the report on the patient who will replace the Fenger boy in your class?" Dr. Paulus asked.

"I have," Cathy said. She had studied scarcely anything else last night, after copying the report into Braille at her mother's dictation. Her heels were planted hard against the office carpet to brace herself for any further attempts from Dr. Paulus to jerk it out from under her. "I knew a number of retarded children when I was at the state school for the blind. I think I can handle him."

"Then you have chosen to remain in the speech

therapy program this semester?" Dr. Paulus paused, but not as if she actually expected an answer. "Very well, I will notify his parents at once that the clinic will accept him. Unless they have made other arrangements for him since filing their application, which is unlikely, you can plan on his becoming your patient the beginning of next week. Have you any questions?"

Cathy could think of none it would be prudent to ask. And that was the end of the interview. No arguments. No objections. No veiled threats designed to pressure her into changing her mind. No hint of the determined opposition she had been grimly prepared to resist. She left the office mentally staggering, as though she had given a mighty thrust to a door already open.

Could it be that Dr. Paulus had recognized that it would be a waste of time to try to dissuade her, once Cathy's decision was made? Or was it that Dr. Paulus knew more about Leonard Perkins than was revealed in the report, and was counting on that hidden trap to work Cathy's downfall? Did he perhaps have a violent temper? Did he throw wild tantrums or grow hysterically frightened at a moment's notice? Could that single word of his, "mama," mean he was so dependent on his mother that she would have to stay with him during the therapy sessions, protecting him from Cathy's every attempt to encourage him to work?

Cathy was half-ashamed to harbor such cloak-and-dagger suspicions, but the questions continued to haunt her through the week.

"All I know is you better keep Trudy out of his way," Mark advised her from the wisdom of his fourteen years. "Remember Lenny in *Of Mice and Men?* It probably goes with the name." His voice thickened into slurred stupidity. "It was such a nice, soft doggie. I jus' kept huggin' it and pattin' it and squeezin' it, and then, all of a sudden, it didn't wiggle no more."

"Thanks a heap," Cathy said. "Maybe I'd better take a whip instead of a tape recorder. Only I knew several retarded kids at the school for the blind when I was there, and none of them sounded like that. They didn't act like that, either. Come to think of it," she went on for the benefit of her own misgivings, "the retarded kids were a pretty well-behaved group on the whole."

She had returned home to finish her education in the public schools after just one semester at Burton, the state school for the blind, so her contact with those retarded pupils had been limited by time as well as by inclination. Not that I actually disliked any of them, she hastened to reassure herself. It was simply that they were such plodders. But they did learn. Slowly, of course, but they learned. That was what she wanted to bear in mind as she searched through her last year's texts for the chapter on teaching the nontalker—that thought, and not the nagging question of why this particular retarded child, Leonard Perkins, had been selected by Dr. Paulus from the clinic's waiting list.

None of the monsters Mark had conjured up for her, however, and nothing she had imagined for herself prepared her for the child Dr. Paulus introduced to her in the waiting room the following Tuesday.

"I think if you take his hand," said the tired-voiced woman who was Mrs. Perkins, "he'll go with you without any fuss. Leonard loves everybody."

Cathy extended her hand toward the scuffing, shuffling sounds she assumed to be Leonard—a Leonard apparently pawing the ground to be off. "Hi, Leonard. My name is Cathy. Would you like to come with me for a while?"

Her hand went shut on a cluster of fingers as wispy and dry as stems in a winter bouquet. They lacked only fur to convince her she had been given a monkey's paw. As it was, a half-forgotten tale of a shriveled monkey paw and the grisly wishes it bestowed flashed into her head like a breath on the back of her neck. She couldn't be positive that her handclasp loosened at once solely to avoid crushing those tiny, brittle fingers.

"Good," she said, because Dr. Paulus was right there, looking on. "We're all set. You come around on the other side, Roddy, and hold Trudy's harness, if you want to, and we'll go."

Dr. Paulus did not escort them to the therapy room. Cathy was thankful for that, although the journey involved as little fuss as Mrs. Perkins had predicted. Roddy, as Cathy had hoped, was too impressed by the importance of holding Trudy's harness to invent capers in the hall, and Leonard trotted along beside her like a docile balloon bobbing at the end of a string.

Or rather, he fluttered like a tissue paper kite, she decided, when the business of settling him in a chair next to her at the work table required her to touch more of him than his hands. He was hardly taller than a two-year-old, and she could circle his two wrists in her thumb and forefinger nearly twice without straining. It was like grasping a pair of drumsticks by their tapered ends. Everything else about him—his head, his shoulders, the foot he swung rather than kicked against her leg—was proportionately small.

So much for Mark's hulking Lenny, she thought. At least he's not going to be a discipline problem. I can pin him down with one finger. That meant she could concentrate on keeping Roddy under control, which, last Friday, when he was her lone patient, had proved to be a full-time job.

"Roddy," she said, "this is Leonard. He's your new partner. Why don't you tell him hello?"

"Hayo," Roddy said, indifferent both to Leonard and to enunciation.

"Hel-lo," Cathy corrected. "Where's the tip of your tongue? Let me hear it say that l." She repeated "Hel-lo," to cover a vague shudder as Leonard's hand brushed her arm and flitted away.

A good therapist never permitted personal emotions to enter into her relationship with a patient, she reminded herself. It was a rule she had always interpreted to be a warning against growing too fond of a patient, but she could understand how it might have a broader application. This weird, fidgety, silent gnome of a child was giving her the creeps.

"Hay-lo," Roddy said, only half-trying. He ruffled the pages of his assignment scrapbook, then demanded, " 'Ell him a-hay hayo."

Cathy interpreted this to be, "Tell him to say hello."

"He can't," she said. "Leonard doesn't know how to talk yet. That's why he's here, so he can learn."

She allowed herself a wry smile at this bit of wishful thinking. But if Leonard couldn't talk, it was becoming obvious that there were plenty of other things he could do. In just the space of this brief conversation, he had scratched his head loudly, clapped his hands softly, bumped his heels against the chair legs, touched her arm, bent to scratch his ankle, and twisted around to pat the back of his chair. Now, at the sound of his name, he emitted a thin, high burble of laughter and jumped from the chair to twine his arms around her waist in a hug. It was like being attacked by a pair of wiry vines.

She shrank from him, in spite of herself, which, perhaps, was the reaction Dr. Paulus was counting on. There was more than Leonard's faulty learning faculties that could foredoom Cathy's therapy attempts to failure.

Cathy made herself hug the matchstick shoulders. He did smell clean. There was that much in his favor. His shirt had the freshness of a garment recently laundered, and the fragrance of shampoo clung to his hair.

"You're going to learn to talk, Leonard," she said grimly. "We'll work at it until you do, won't we?"

"Yes," Roddy said, taking it for granted that he was to be part of "we." "We'll learn you how."

He produced the l sounds carefully.

Leonard uttered his shrill laugh again and ducked from under Cathy's arm to run across the room. Roddy was out of his chair and after him in the same instant. Cathy sprang up, too, propelled by a choking certainty that Dr. Paulus was about to come through the door and the whole fiasco of last Tuesday's clinic would be replayed.

The doors of the cupboard rattled. "Hubbar'," Roddy said. " 'At's a hubbar'."

"Roddy!" But Cathy checked the sharp command on her tongue. It dawned on her what he was saying. "Roddy, if you're going to teach Leonard the names of things, you have to say them clearly and right. That's the cupboard. Say it slowly and clearly so he can understand you."

"Cupboar'," Roddy echoed. He spaced the syllables painstakingly. "That's . . . the . . . cup-board. No, a mirror!"

For Leonard had already moved on to pat his hands up and down the big mirror hanging at child level to help in practicing tongue and lip exercises. Cathy joined him to touch the glass, its wooden frame, the wall beside it, encouraging Roddy to name each object as she did. It didn't matter that Leonard wandered over to the window while she and Roddy were still conquering the final l in wall, or that he was absorbed in removing his shoes before Roddy finished with "windowsill" and "window glass," or that his laugh sliced through the midst of an earnest explanation of the radiator and steam.

Drop in on us now, Dr. Paulus, why don't you? Cathy challenged. Listen to Roddy making a serious effort to use what he's learned.

But Dr. Paulus chose not to drop in until the boys were seated at the table once more. By then Roddy was tired of the role of teacher and was growing silly, hearing more lines to be giggled at than l and t sounds to identify in the nursery rhymes Cathy was reading to him. Her foot was lodged behind the leg of Leonard's chair, keeping the chair and Leonard pressed tight to the table to insure that he stayed in one place at least for a little while. Leonard was pounding his head rhythmically against his fists, perhaps in protest or perhaps merely because he liked to do it.

"I'm just looking in on people to be sure everything is going smoothly," Dr. Paulus said from the doorway. "And that everybody is where he belongs."

Leonard flung himself suddenly backward. Cathy grabbed for the teetering chair. "We're all here," she said above the clatter of bringing its legs four-square to the floor again. "Everything's fine." Her fingers dug the assertion into the wood slats of the chair back.

"Very well." If there was the faintest skepticism in the words, the door closed on it, and Cathy was left to founder or tread water as best she could alone. Plainly, no aid would be forthcoming this morning unless she asked for it, thereby admitting she had blundered out beyond her depth.

Cathy set Leonard straight in the chair, a job easily done with one hand. With the other hand she smoothed the creases in Miss Muffet's page. She wasn't about to founder—not this morning nor this semester.

As for just treading water and no more . . . She had to face the potential truth in that charge when she restored the boys to their mothers and sat down to tally up the morning's experiences. Within a fifty-minute period she had learned that Leonard's eyes went to anything that moved or gleamed or cast a shadow, and that wherever his eyes went, Leonard must go, too; that pictures on a card or in a book appeared to bear no relation for him to anything identifiable; that it was next to impossible for him to sit quietly anywhere for any reason; that his span of attention was nonexistent. Her textbook advised her to stimulate the child's interest by imitating his early attempts at speech and make him feel speech was a worthwhile achievement by prompt praise for his every attempt. Nothing that she had said to Leonard today, however, had received the least response that would suggest he even heard her, let alone that he was capable of listening, and the only sound that had come from him during the whole period was that unnerving laugh. There wasn't much to build on.

"He understands everything we tell him," Mrs. Perkins said. "Well, a great deal of what we tell him. He'll bring his ball or his pillow, whichever we ask for, and he'll turn on TV for us or turn it off, and he goes straight to the closet for his coat when his daddy asks if he wants to take a ride. My husband and I are amazed at him sometimes, he understands so many things."

But Cathy's ears caught the questioning inflection in the woman's voice, as if she would like Cathy to confirm for her that this evidence was truly significant. Besides, Trudy could distinguish between her ball and her dish when told to fetch one or the other, and she would run for the closet where her harness hung if someone mentioned going for a walk. Furthermore, she could be trusted to turn right or left correctly, select the up stairway or the down, and find her way out of a complicated building, if told to do so, as well as daily displaying intelligence and judgment to which Cathy could feel safe in entrusting her life. The chances for Trudy's learning to talk looked better than Leonard's by far—a fact of which Dr. Paulus, Cathy had no doubt, was smugly aware.

"But there has to be some way to get through to him," she said when she described Leonard to the girls at lunch. "If his I.Q. is 75, that's supposed to mean he is educable, so he ought to be able to learn, if I can figure out a way to teach him. They wouldn't let a patient into the clinic that's impossible." She heard an echo in her voice of Mrs. Perkins' pleading "tell-me-that-I'm-right" tone.

"His mother must be the lady who was talking to my Sally's mother when I got to the waiting room," Amy said. "I got there late, so I didn't see which child belonged to her, but I knew I hadn't noticed her in there last week. She was saying they'd been trying for two years to get their youngster into the clinic, and that it was like a miracle that, at last, he'd been accepted. Imagine!"

Karen Bergen crumpled a sandwich wrapper. "Imagine what? That she'd wait two years, or that she thinks getting near us is a miracle? I'll bet the clinic has a waiting list as long as your arm of speech problems that don't fit the needs of us student therapists one year or another. We're supposed to be learning as much from the patients as they are from us."

Cathy bit into the satiny cheek of a plum without tasting it. She could see that list unrolling like a scroll, yards and yards of it, and at the very bottom, so close to the edge he was practically a reject, Leonard Perkins. But not quite a reject. Oh, no, Dr. Paulus was too clever for that. No one could accuse her of replacing Craig with a patient that had been diagnosed impossible. If his position on the list suggested he was an improbable, that was altogether different; scheduling him could be defended as providing a valid learning experience for a student therapist.

To be sure, Cathy had guessed a week ago that this was to be the maneuver, but guessing wasn't the same as hearing the proof of it in Mrs. Perkins' own words. There was no doubt now about how Dr. Paulus bargained or that she was out for blood.

"If you were late this morning and didn't get hung up by the thumbs for it, that's the real miracle," Monica told Amy. "Paulus took me apart because I'd been changing a typewriter ribbon and I didn't get all the smudge scrubbed off my hands. She marched me off to the washroom to scrub again, and then she was peeved because that made me five minutes late in getting my patients into the therapy room. She's a real neurotic aboat soap and clocks."

"There was no miracle," Amy said. "She caught me." Wistfully, she added, "Sister Bernard was never that picky about little things."

"She used to be." Laura Riley set her milk carton on the table with an affirmative tap. "My cousin Maureen —she graduated the year we were freshmen—told me Sister Bernard never let them get away with a thing in the beginning. There was a time when she knew everything about the girls from whom they were dating to how late they stayed out on school nights to when was the last time they had washed their hair—day students and residents. It's just in the past few years that all the other things she had to do got to be so much that she kind of eased up on the students."

Cathy frowned, thinking back over the last two years. "It seems to me Sister Bernard kept a pretty sharp eye on us, busy as she was. She tried to, anyhow. I remember she once told me the trouble about being a chairman of a department was that you had to be everywhere at once to do things nobody else could do."

"I wish she had thought of that when they decided to haul in Paulus to do her job for her," Monica muttered.

"Dr. Paulus is rated tops in the field," Karen said, a false note of virtue creeping into her voice. "We should be congratulating ourselves that we have her. That's what Sister Janice told me. And she also told me Dr. Paulus was one of Sister Bernard's first and favorite students. What do you think of that?"

"Horseradish!" Amy exploded, injecting actual violence into the unoffending noun. "How could Sister Bernard have a favorite like that? They're not a bit alike. Sister is so kind and warm and ready to understand, and she's loved by everybody who knows her, while Dr. Paulus . . ."

"Yes? Go on," Monica prompted, and led them all in a burst of laughter at Dr. Paulus' expense.

"Well, I don't really know Dr. Paulus well enough to say what she's like," Amy retreated. "I guess what's making me maddest is that my mother thinks it's such a glorious blessing that we have a new chairman—any kind of chairman that's not Sister Bernard. She was always afraid I was being influenced too much by Sister Bernard." Her lunch bag rattled in sudden defiance. "But I don't care. I think Sister Bernard is the most beautiful human being I ever met, as well as the greatest speech therapist around, and if I can be even a tiny bit like her, I'm going to try."

"You'll get no argument on that here," Monica said. "I'm for bringing Sister Bernard back and dumping Paulus any day."

"Oh, I don't know. Maybe we ought to give her a chance. Maybe we're not being quite fair to her." Laura's laugh was half-apologetic. "She must be working hard to do the best she can. Otherwise, why would she switch patients around like she did for Cathy?"

"That wasn't Cathy's idea. That was the little darling's mama," Monica supplied before Cathy could answer. "A junior wasn't good enough for her precious. She had to have him taught by a senior, and Paulus, instead of telling her take it or leave it, let her switch."

Cathy didn't correct her. None of the girls knew the whole story behind the rescheduling of her patients, and she preferred to keep it that way. Not that it wouldn't be gratifying to whip their indignation against Dr. Paulus to a blistering lather and to bask in the protective blaze of their loyalty for herself.

But that kind of loyalty carried too high a risk of degenerating into sympathy for her. Sympathy at first for the raw deal she was being handed because she was blind, then sympathy for her because she was blind. If once they began to feel sorry for her on that score, it would be a long time, if ever, before they would accept her again as simply another student, an equal, one of the group. Dr. Paulus would have won a subtle victory, more lasting, perhaps, than the goal she contemplated.

Cathy rolled her plum pit inside her sandwich bag, pretending to listen but not actually hearing as Monica continued to hold forth on the tribulations Monica herself had encountered in the clinic today. Not only could Cathy not confide in her classmates, neither could she go to Sister Regina, the college president, to demand fair treatment. Dr. Paulus would claim necessity as her sole motive, cite Mrs. Fenger's objections, the need to fill in the vacancy in Cathy's schedule on short notice, the fact that a 75 I.Q. indicated Leonard was teachable, and it would sound as if Cathy were whining for special concessions or crying "foul" to hide her own incompetence.

The outcome would be no different if she allowed her father to bring his heavy artillery to bear on the college. "I'll pay a visit to your college president and we'll soon have this monkey business straightened out," he had threatened last week when Cathy reported her interview with Dr. Paulus. "In my book, this Paulus woman is way off base. If that's going to be her policy—toadying to hysterical mothers, instead of backing up her students as reliable products of her department—she might better turn in her badge and quit. That attitude wouldn't get her far in my business, and I'll tell her so, among other things."

And he would, too. Cathy knew it. Nor would he retire from the scene until he had wrestled the opposition into settling matters to his satisfaction—or else had an ironclad explanation as to why it couldn't be done. Yet the winning card would still belong to Dr. Paulus. She might conceivably be forced to yield to pressure and to substitute a less difficult patient for Leonard Perkins, but she would see the action as justifying her belief that Cathy wasn't equipped to cope with patients who didn't conform exactly to the textbook patterns. That would be the implication written into Cathy's record, the damning inference any prospective employer would draw: the patient presenting a challenge in temperament or treatment was beyond her abilities.

And what if that implication is right? whispered a traitorous voice at the edge of Cathy's mind. What if Leonard is teachable, and Dr. Paulus is counting on appearances to discourage you from putting a concentrated effort into finding out?

Cathy's lunch bag skittered from a twitch of her fingers and dropped to the floor. Between her sidelong swoop to pick it up and her return to sitting upright, the answer had crystalized. No effort would be more concentrated than hers. The first thing she would do when she reached home today would be to call the city library for the blind and ask for any and all materials that were recorded or in Braille that dealt with the mentally retarded.

The idea generated prickles of electricity through her for the rest of the afternoon. She coaxed Trudy into running the last of the three blocks from the bus stop to her home, and they arrived on the front stoop panting and excited. The fact that the door was locked didn't penetrate to her until she had pressed the latch twice. Then she remembered that this was the day her mother would be late in getting home from her church guild activities.

Ordinarily, Cathy had a sense of letdown when she entered a house empty of the people who belonged in it, but as she let herself in and bent to undo Trudy's harness, she couldn't be sorry not to have to discuss Leonard just yet. She could recount the harrowing details better when she was able to add that she had already taken a positive step toward dealing with them. She detoured through the kitchen to release Trudy into the freedom of the back yard, then, from force of habit, ran upstairs to use the phone outside her bedroom in the upper hall.

The phone began to ring before she lifted the receiver. "This is Dr. Kruger's office," said a feminine voice in response to her rather startled hello. "Is this Catherine Wheeler?"

When Cathy acknowledged that it was, the voice went on to explain that Dr. Kruger was being called out of town for the remainder of this week because of a death in his family. A Dr. Rosenthal would be caring for his patients while he was away, but appointments could be rescheduled for a later date for anyone who preferred to see Dr. Kruger personally.

"And, of course, we have you down for this Saturday, the twentieth," the voice finished.

Cathy had forgotten there was such an appointment pending. It was for a routine eye examination, which, like dental checkups, came around every six or eight months. In her opinion, there was more nuisance value to it than anything else, but the word "reschedule" flicked her on an exposed nerve.

"No, that's fine. Saturday's fine," she said. She'd had all the rescheduling she could bear for a while. "I'm sorry about Dr. Kruger. The death, I mean."

"Thank you," the voice said. "We'll be expecting you at ten o'clock, then, Saturday."

Which means I can scratch Saturday morning as a time for extra cramming, Cathy thought as she replaced the receiver. There were those headaches, though. They had been bothering her for a year now, but never so frequently or so badly as they had become in the past few months. Maybe it was as well to make sure they weren't a symptom of more eye trouble, which was what her mother feared. Or if they were, it would help to learn if something could be done about them.

The back door burst open downstairs. Trudy's toenails clattered across the linoleum, accompanied by a clumping tread that had to be Mark.

"Mom! Mom! Hey, Mom?" His bellow filled the kitchen.

"She's not home," Cathy called. She went to the head of the stairs where she might have a better chance of being heard amid the shouts he continued to roar out as if the house were on fire. "She's not home yet. She's chauffeuring the Golden Age ladies to the fall flower show at the arena. What's wrong?"

"Nothing's wrong. I just wanted to tell her something." His bellow deflated to a notch above a mumble. "Well, I guess I'll get started on my route."

"Okay." But she hesitated, her hand on the stair rail. It wasn't her brother's normal style to turn off his exuberance that fast. "Do you want me to tell her something for you when she gets home?"

"No, I'll tell her." He tramped past the foot of the stairs, paused, and came back. "But listen. Guess what? Remember I told you about this guy on my route that I found out he's a veterinarian?" He swung himself up two or three steps. "He drove by the bus stop this morning and gave me a lift to school, and I can have a job with him weekends and after school if I want." Each fresh detail carried him up a few steps more, his hand squeaking along the railing at arm's length ahead of him.

"Hey, great!" she said. Mark had been talking veterinary medicine since he was ten. "A real job, with pay and everything? Doing what?"

"Oh, cleaning cages, giving baths, running errands, walking some of the dogs, wiping up messes—stuff like that." He was being nonchalant now, tapping a foot on the triangular step at the bend of the stairs, the step that always groaned rather than creaked. "I'll get just about as much as I make peddling papers, probably, but heck! I'd do it for free."

"Yick!" Cathy said, her nose wrinkling. "You're welcome to it. I'd have to be pretty hard up for money before I'd trade a nice, clean paper route for that."

"That's because you don't want to be a veterinarian."

He descended to the bottom of the stairs in a trio of window-quaking bounds. She was on the verge of picking up the phone again when he called from the living room.

"Cathy, did you know you have a letter here? A tape from Israel."

It was proof of the expansive mood he was in that he was halfway up the stairs to hand it to her by the time she was halfway down to receive it. Trudy galloped up to join them, confident this commotion must be leading to a grand chase through the house.

"Atta girl, Trudy," Mark cheered. "Looks like you escaped getting squashed by Big Lennie. Did he try it?"

"Big Lennie is about three feet tall and weighs about thirty pounds," Cathy said. "He couldn't squash a grape if he jumped on it."

"Honest?" He sobered, but only for an instant. "Maybe that's his problem: no space for a brain. What'll you bet he turns out to be a genius in disguise as soon as you teach him to talk? Then your fortune will be made, because people all over the world will bring their dum-dum Lennies to you to be treated."

"Yick!" Cathy said, no less feelingly than before. It didn't strike her as curious until afterward that she had used the same term of distaste in reference to her chosen career as she had to his.

The tape, she knew, was from Ruth Meyer, a high school friend who was in Israel now, working on a kibbutz.

Cathy cocked an ear as the living room clock chimed four. She ought not to play the tape right away. There was so much else she ought to get done first—notes to study, chapters to read, her clinic report to type up for inspection . . . so much else to get done that she was heartily sick of doing.

The realization sent her to the phone, where she dialed the library number, at once, a number she knew by heart.

"That line is busy," said the girl at the library switchboard. "Will you wait?"

"Thanks, no," Cathy decided. The wait could be anywhere from two minutes to a quarter of an hour, and she had other things to do. "I'll try again in ten minutes."

A seven-inch reel of tape lay on the recorder on her desk, ready to be threaded into the take-up reel, so it could unwind for her the mysteries of Chapter Five of her human development text. She lifted it off and set Ruth's little three-inch correspondence tape in its place. Ten minutes was such a short period when you came right down to it that, actually, all it was good for was sampling what Ruth had to say. After the library call was out of the way, she could settle into half an hour or so of real studying before she stopped to help with supper.

She silenced a murmur from her conscience by snapping on the switch, and Ruth's voice sang into the room. "Hi, Cathy. *Shalom!*"

Sheep were bleating in the background. They were some of the flocks belonging to the kibbutz, Ruth explained. "It's impossible to get lost in this area. If you can't hear these darn sheep, you can smell them a mile away."

She talked of gritty dust and simmering heat, and of the boulders and perpendicular rocks that passed for trails where she was. "What I dream of is a whole day under a real shower where nobody is counting the water by the drop."

Another thing she yearned for was something chocolate to eat. "Don't spread this around too much, but Israeli chocolate tastes like tinfoil. I'll give you my entire sweater collection at home for a dozen giant Hershey bars, if you can get them here intact. That means not whitey stale, not melted into soup, not full of bugs, and not hijacked by some other chocolate fiend along the route."

Cathy leaned her elbows on the desk, her chin propped on her fists, and listened to the catalog of discomforts and complaints that poured forth with a happy lilt that reminded her of the remembered sparkle of mica flecks in a sunbathed rock. The ten minutes stretched to twenty, but when the tape reached the end of the first track, she flipped the reel over and set track two going without a thought of calling a halt.

"I want to stay here at least another year, if I can," Ruth said. "My folks aren't too enthused about it, the way the Middle East is bubbling and boiling. They want me home, where it's safe. But I don't know. I've never felt so right anywhere in my life.

"That doesn't mean I'm not interested in what's happening at home, though, so tape me everything about everything as soon as you get the chance. I'm dying for news. Until then, since this tape's running out, *shalom.*"

The end of the tape flicked from the reel and the recorder's automatic cutoff brought abrupt silence to the room. Cathy sat on, motionless, pinned by a swell of reverberations too loud and too clear. You and Mark, she thought, and was surprised by the envy that barbed it. You and Mark—and Joan.

Yes, Joan. There was a piece of news that would divert Ruth's mind from the sheep for a moment or two. Joan Norton's wedding. And Cathy, her resistance worn through by an hour-and-a-half phone debate the evening after their encounter at the Bavarian Hut, Cathy was to be a bridesmaid.

"I knew you'd do it," Joan had trilled when Cathy gave in. "Nobody can say no to a bride. And don't think I'm asking you so that the wedding will be different enough for them to maybe write it up in the paper. That's my cousin Olive's idea. Although, of course, how many brides are there around who'll be having a blind bridesmaid? I'm asking you because I want a friend in my wedding party, not just relatives. This is going to be the biggest day of my whole life, the thing I've been working at for nineteen years, and it's got to be perfect, now that it's coming true."

Cathy pursed her lips and stood up to replace Ruth's tape in its mailing carton. But the thought she had been trying to side-step would not be ignored: Ruth accepting hardship and danger for the sake of feeling "right"; Mark willing to do the lowest and dirtiest chores of animal care for free to be near a real veterinarian; even Joan, slogging on single-mindedly through the years of ridicule and slights to attain at last the man and the wedding band her heart was set on. None of them appeared to have the faintest doubt that the prize was worth every measure of blood, sweat, or tears they had to pay for it. When had she ever cared like that about speech therapy?

What does it matter? she asked herself. Plenty of people are doing plenty of jobs and doing them well, not because the job is the passion of their life but because that's how the cards happened to fall. If it weren't for Dr. Paulus, the question might never have entered my head, and I'd have become a speech therapist, just the same. That wasn't the question Dr. Paulus had actually asked her, anyway. Dr. Paulus' real question was: why do you want to be a *blind* speech therapist?

Cathy shut Ruth's tape away in a drawer and swung on her heel to march to the telephone. There was one thing she did care about. That was beating Dr. Paulus.

This time, the line to the library for the blind was open. "Work with the mentally handicapped? We surely have something on that," Mrs. Ellis, the librarian, said confidently. "Hold on while I check."

Her voice was less confident when she returned. "There seems to be everything here but mentally retarded. There's mental illness—psychiatry, rehabilitation, how to stay mentally healthy—but none of that is it. Here's one on educating the blind, a book of poems for a deaf child, the story of a World War II amputee . . . Fiction wouldn't help, would it? Faulkner's *Sound and the Fury?* That has an idiot in it."

"No," Cathy said. "That won't help. Besides, I've read it."

"Mentally handicapped, mentally handicapped," Mrs. Ellis mused as if she could wish the material into being. "No, nothing in Braille or talking books or tape . . . Wait! There is a tape-recorded book here on brain-injured children. It was read by one of our library volunteers for a student several years ago. I've forgotten who. Would that help?"

"I don't know." Cathy had never heard the term "brain-injured" before. "It sounds like it might be on the right track. Would you send it out?"

"I'll put it in tomorrow's mail." Mrs. Ellis' tone was as pleased as though she had found a gold nugget. "And don't forget we'll have volunteers record any book for you that you send in. September is a pretty full month for us. Our time is so limited and we're doing texts for young people all over the state, but we can always squeeze in another title if it's urgent."

"Thank you," Cathy said. "I may do that."

The time lag between the selection of a print book and its transcription into a recorded version she could use would be months, though. Weeks, at the very best.

The semester would be half over before she could hope to begin to study.

As she lowered the receiver into its cradle, she had a vision of the library shelves lined to capacity with print books containing the information she needed. Information that she could have for the flicker of an eye, the lift of a hand, if she weren't blind. Information that she wouldn't have to have if she weren't blind, because there would be no Leonard, no questions, no obstacles, no problems for her, if she weren't blind.

Her fists clenched themselves in a spasm of frustration, and she shouted at the blank wall beside the phone, "I'm sick to death of being blind."

At the sound, Trudy came racing up the stairs to see what was the matter. Cathy knelt to rub her cheek against the dog's silky head. Trudy licked her face and whined softly, willing to understand if she could. Cathy stood up, feeling somewhat consoled and more than a little ashamed, and went downstairs to the kitchen to fix Trudy's supper.

4

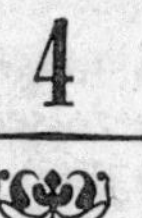

A WAITING ROOM is a waiting room is a waiting room, Cathy thought as she sat in Dr. Kruger's outer office Saturday morning, waiting. She crossed her legs for the tenth time, and for the tenth time uncrossed them again, trying for a more comfortable position in the overstuffed armchair that was too deep and too soft and too sleekly upholstered in a plastic imitation of leather.

It didn't matter what kind of office was attached to a waiting room—dentist, doctor, college president, high school principal. The basic ingredients were always the same: people speaking in hushed tones, if at all; furniture that didn't fit you; a spatter of typewriter keys now and then; an occasional ring of the telephone, quickly answered; boredom dragging the minute hand of your watch inexorably past the time of your appointment—ten minutes, fifteen, twenty-five. And always a compulsive flutter in your stomach, even when the examination ahead was to be a routine repetition of dozens that had gone before.

Cathy yawned to settle her nervousness, checked her

watch once more, and leaned across the broad arm of the chair to ask in a voice suitably low, "Dad, what time do you have?"

"What?" The magazine her father was reading rustled a shuffle of pages. "Oh, ten thirty-five. Why?"

Cathy shrugged and squirmed back into the depths of her chair, being careful not to kick Trudy, who lay sprawled at her feet. There seemed no need to answer his question, since they both knew her appointment had been for ten. In all the years they had been coming to this office, it had never failed that there was a gap of at least forty-five minutes between appointment time and the time when she was called into the examining room. Her mother was inclined to take these into account when she was the chauffeur for these visits, but her father believed in being punctual and preferred being actually a few minutes early, whether the rest of the world cooperated or not.

In all the years they had been coming here—how many, many years was it? At four she had been under treatment for cataracts. There had been eyedrops and surgery and heavy glasses that showed her most of the things she wanted to see. At fourteen the problem had become glaucoma, a condition linked somehow, they said, to the earlier trouble. That had meant surgery again, then hemorrhages inside her eyes and scarring, and almost overnight her vision was completely gone. What more could go wrong, she didn't know. It would seem that, once you had descended the scale to zero, there was nowhere else to go. Except in algebra, of course, with its whole fantasy world of numbers on the minus side, but that didn't apply here. Yet Dr. Kruger continued to schedule her for periodic checkups, and she continued to sit periodically in this chair or another just like it, her stomach doing peculiar acrobatics and her watch marking off the wasted minutes.

She picked up the notebook she had brought to study from. "Any factors which interfere with a child's physical, emotional, or social well-being are potentially relevant to—"

Someone in the inner office sneezed, and her mind released its imperfect grasp on the meaning of the sentence. She drew in a breath and started over: "Any factors which interfere with a child's physical, emotional . . ."

What about a therapist's emotional well-being, she wondered. Or physical or social—doesn't anyone care about that?

Yesterday evening, however, had been one instance in which her speech training, especially in dramatic reading, had proved its practical worth. She had been able to achieve exactly the right mingling of apology and regret when Joan called to tell her the wedding party was to go shopping for shoes this morning.

"It's an appointment I can't cancel, Joan. I've had it for months, and I won't be able to get in again for half a year. Maybe if I had known a few days earlier—But I thought we all agreed Wednesday night, when we went dress shopping, that we were all busy this weekend."

"Yes, I know, but Olive saw this shoe sale advertised, and she and Mummie think we can't afford to pass it up," Joan said, repeating the explanation she had already given twice. "Nadine had other plans, too. So did I, as far as that goes, but we're willing to sacrifice a little. You'll be the only bridesmaid who isn't there."

Cathy wasn't swayed a jot by the knowledge that Joan's cousin, Olive, was promoting the disruption.

"I'm sorry, but I honestly can't make it. I don't have any free time at all this Saturday."

She was determined not to suggest Saturday afternoon as an alternative. Too much might hang on her getting that book on brain-injured children read, and if she were to do any other studying besides, Saturday afternoon was the only time she could do it. That was largely thanks to Olive Tyler, too.

"What's that?" Joan had asked. Her voice was suddenly muffled, as if her hand were covering the receiver. Cathy could distinguish Mrs. Norton's voice in the background, but not what she was saying. "Oh, okay." Joan became unmuffled once more. "Mummie says tell me your shoe size, anyway. Then if they find the shoes they're looking for, they can have a pair put aside for you. It won't matter that much if you can't try them on first. You'll only be wearing them that one day, the day of the wedding."

Cathy suspected that Mrs. Norton was just as well pleased not to be hampered by her presence on the shopping trip. A blind bridesmaid was very nice as a conversational item to be submitted to the newspaper, but she was an awkward nuisance to have to pilot from store to store on a shopping tour. Also, Cathy doubted that her opinion would be seriously missed as long as Olive was on hand to determine what Joan ought to want for her bridesmaids and what was best for the bridesmaids themselves.

Olive had met Joan and Cathy and Trudy in the doorway of the dress shop last Wednesday evening, when Mrs. Norton had let them out of the car and driven off to find a parking place. Cathy's initial impression was of a solid object barring the entrance and yielding reluctantly to their efforts to squeeze by.

"Do you realize," the object had demanded in tones that would have done credit to the matron of a reformatory for girls, "that you are ten minutes late? We have been here since seven o'clock."

"I'm the bride." Joan had laughed and nudged Cathy, as if that were the prime joke of the year. "I'm supposed to be all of a flutter and flighty."

"Aunt Lydia said seven, and Nadine and I were here on the dot," the reformatory matron insisted. She was not noticeably amused. "We have other things to do. You can't expect us to keep giving up our precious time for your affairs if you aren't going to show some responsibility in return."

Cathy was inclined to second that idea. Joan had phoned at noon and left the message with Cathy's mother that this was to be the evening the wedding party went looking for their bridesmaids' gowns. What Cathy's homework schedule might be on Wednesday nights or how she might rearrange it at such short warning were concerns outside Joan's scope of interest.

"Did you see that dress I told you about?" Joan asked, still unrepentant. "You could have been using the time to try it on."

"This place has nothing in it you'd want at a wedding," the matron informed her in a voice that must have carried to the ears of every clerk in the shop. "This stuff is either way out of our price range or it's junk, or both. We'll go down the street to Tucker's as soon as Aunt Lydia gets here. They always have a much better selection."

"You've got to look at this one gown I found. I think it's perfect." Joan began moving to the left, down an aisle. "After all, I am the bride."

Cathy murmured to Trudy to follow, but, within half

a dozen steps, Trudy halted. A bulky something was looming dead ahead.

The something gave a leap that quivered the floor boards beneath the carpet, and gasped in a wisp of a voice, "Dogs scare me. He's so big."

"Oh, I guess I forgot to introduce you," Joan said, returning. "Cathy, this is Nadine Sweetland. The other one is Olive Tyler. I don't have to introduce you to them because they already know your whole life story."

Cathy's smile of acknowledgment was shadowed by a doubt as to whether she was about to perform according to their expectations. She had a feeling she would be happier not ever knowing what version of her life story they had heard. Neither cousin bothered to reply to her "Hello."

"Here comes Aunt Lydia," Nadine said in her breathy whisper.

A hand made of steel springs clamped itself on Cathy's elbow. "This way," Olive said, sounding no less like a reformatory matron, now that she had a name. She swung Cathy in a tight half-circle that faced her toward the door. "Aunt Lydia, we're going over to Tucker's. It's hopeless here."

"That's what I told you in the first place, Joan," Mrs. Norton said. "Come on along, then. The stores close at nine. We don't have all night."

Cathy hesitated, not sure whether this was to be the final word on the subject, but the steel hand on her elbow shoved her forward to the door. She pushed it open to save herself and Trudy from being crushed against the glass, and, in a moment, the whole group was out on the street.

"But you didn't even look at the gown I meant," Joan protested as they trooped off in what was assuredly the direction of Tucker's. "It's the newest color: autumn flame. It's beautiful, kind of an orange red, like maple trees, and they have it done up in velvet—"

"You don't want red velvet for a November wedding," Mrs. Norton said, marching herself and Joan past Cathy and Olive to take the lead. "It would look like a Christmas pageant or something for Valentine's Day. If you must have a seasonal tie-in, November first is closer to Thanksgiving."

And closer yet to Halloween, Cathy thought. She was trying to work her arm free of Olive's grip without provoking a wrestling match.

"I'm okay, Olive. Trudy will get me where we're going. You don't have to worry."

"Trudy?" Nadine wheezed behind her. "Is that his name? Don't you feel funny, walking with him? You should see how everybody turns around and stares."

Olive released Cathy's elbow and seized her hand. "You take my arm. That will work better." And Cathy's hand was bent firmly into the crook of Olive's elbow. "I know about blind people. I used to live three blocks from the home for the blind."

Cathy surrendered rather than create a scene. The evening promised to produce enough of those as it was. And Olive was right. It was better holding to her arm and following her movement than being trundled ahead of her like a wheelbarrow.

Tucker's proved to be a dress shop in which two of the salesgirls were acquaintances of Olive. "We're hunting for a bridesmaid's gown with style to it," Olive informed them. "Something that can be shortened afterward and worn somewhere else without looking like a leftover from a wedding."

"Nothing that is cut too low," Mrs. Norton added.

"It should have sleeves and a modest neckline, or possibly a jacket top. Floor length, of course. This is a traditional wedding."

"But not a sheath," Nadine sighed in the fragile voice that, Cathy gathered, must be the only tiny thing about her. "An A-line or something a little full. Nothing too fitted."

"Something to flatter three different figures: fat, scrawny, and in-between," Joan summed up gaily—and perhaps not altogether without malice. "I'm the bride. I've already got my dress, so you haven't any problem with me."

The salesgirls scurried off to see what they could find, and Olive steered Cathy to a small wrought-iron chair placed against the wall. "Why don't you sit down? You'll be out of the way here."

Cathy flushed, her mouth becoming a tight line of vexation, but, once more, Olive was right. She would be out of the way here, and circumstances being what they were this evening, that wasn't the worst place she could be. If the rest of Olive matched the talons she had for hands, the "scrawny" figure must certainly be hers, and there was some solace in reflecting on that.

For a while, Cathy leaned forward to catch the discussion that broke over each of the gowns the salesgirls presented. Color, fabric, and style were not matters beyond her ken or her interest, and she had misgivings of her own about Joan's "autumn flame." There were some hues that didn't go well with her shade of red hair—bright auburn was the kindest term for it—and she wouldn't be surprised if the effect of a flaming orange-red on her would be, in her grandmother's phrase, "like death warmed over." Still, it was Joan's wedding, and her repeated insistence, audible throughout the shop, that the bride's preferences should carry some weight, struck Cathy as reasonable. The controversy kept moving gradually farther back in the store until she lost track of who was winning what points, and she began to concentrate instead on giving the appearance of being too occupied with her own meditations to notice she had been abandoned.

Cathy's performance would have been more convincing if the chair were more comfortable. Its seat was the size of a small pie tin and had an upward curve built into it that grew to resemble the dome of the state capitol more and more, the longer she sat on it. As a final proof that it was designed to be admired rather than sat on, the seat was upholstered in glossy, friction-free patent leather that slid her down the slope as fast as she could restore herself to the top.

Another five minutes of this, she vowed finally, and Trudy, you and I are going to get up and follow them, whether they want us or not.

Before she could act on this, a second chair was dragged across the carpet and thumped down next to her. "You've got the right idea," Joan said. "I'm going to sit it out on the side lines, too, until they get sick of looking here. Then we'll go back to Demoiselle's and try the velvet autumn flame. Olive has to get her two cents in, just because she works in her father's dry cleaning business and thinks she knows all there is about fashion."

"How old is she?" Cathy asked. Her lowest guess would be forty.

"I don't know. Twenty, twenty-one. She graduated from high school before we did, but she skipped some grades or something, too. She's really intelligent. Her grades and mine used to be identical—except that she went to Longfellow High, where the standards are lower scholastically."

Cathy had been treated to descriptions of Joan's intellectual prowess often enough in the days when Joan used to read for her so that she didn't feel the need to pursue the subject further now. As she hoisted herself to the top of the dome again, she realized that no one had yet mentioned the groom tonight. Not in her hearing, anyway. "What's Pete doing this evening?"

"Pete? Sulking, I suppose," Joan said with a proprietary chuckle. "He wanted to go to a movie tonight; but naturally I couldn't. He keeps wanting me to do all sorts of things that interfere with the wedding arrangements. The other night Mummie had to tell him in plain English that the bride is the important one in a wedding, and he'll have to take a back seat for a while."

Pete could hardly be blamed for sulking, Cathy thought, and she could readily imagine that he was doing it. He never did take kindly to being disappointed or delayed or relegated to second place. It was a mystery to her how he had survived two years in the army as an enlisted man, even though, according to Joan, it hadn't taken him long to climb to the rank of sergeant.

"What's he doing these days besides going to movies alone?" she asked. "He's out of the service now, isn't he?"

"He's out, except for being in a reserve unit for the next six years, and Mummie thinks there may be a way of getting around that. I certainly don't want a husband who's going to be gone once a week and on assorted weekends playing soldier, if I can help it." Joan gave a violent wriggle. "What weird chairs! I'd love to see Nadine try to sit on one. She'd split at the seams."

So Nadine was the fat member of the party, quite as Cathy had guessed. "Is she younger than you?" she hazarded.

"Seventeen. Chronologically, that is, but really she and I are about the same age. I'm not so ancient myself, you know. I'm younger than a lot of girls who aren't married yet." Joan's laugh was sudden and incredulous. "Can you believe it? In six weeks I'll be a Mrs., and set for the rest of my life."

Set for life. Cathy tasted the phrase as if it were an almost tangible fragrance of holiday bakery. "It must be a strange feeling," she said, as much to herself as to Joan.

"It is, kind of," Joan admitted. "It's like waiting for Christmas used to be, only a thousand times better. Me, a Mrs." She paused to contemplate the grandeur of it. "And as soon as we get settled, we're going to get busy and find a man for you, Catherine Wheeler. Pete's got to know somebody somewhere who'll think you're the right girl for him."

"And he'll cherish and care for me the rest of my days." Cathy's smile was wry, not only because of Joan's assumption that desperation could work miracles but because she found a part of herself wondering if that would be such a poor solution, provided it could be that simple.

"Joan! For heaven's sake, what are you hiding off here for? If this is all you care about your own wedding, I don't know why the rest of us should bother." It was Mrs. Norton, zeroing in on them at a rate that brought Trudy scrambling up out of a doze. "If you're interested in the dress we've decided on, come and see it. And bring Cathy."

Cathy brought herself, following the jangle of Mrs.

Norton's bracelet, toward the fitting rooms. Nadine was there, holding aside the curtain for them to enter.

"Here she is," she whisper-sang off key, "Miss America."

She and Joan went into a twitter of giggles that ended in a squeak as Trudy stretched to nose Nadine. Cathy let Trudy draw her a step farther into the cramped room and halted so as not to block Joan's view of the gown.

"It's pumpkin satin," Olive said, swishing this way a step and a step that way, to model it. "It's A-line, a lace panel down the front, elbow-length sleeves. This is the only one they have in stock, but they'll order the other two. Do you want to feel it, Cathy?"

Cathy did not want to feel it, not while Olive was still in it. The line between feeling a garment and handling the person inside it was embarrassingly thin. But Olive had her by the wrist, pulling her arm forward, and there was no graceful means of retreat.

Cathy compromised by touching her fingertips to a sleeve and a shoulder and stooping quickly to gather a handful of the satin hem. The material was lighter weight and more grainy in texture than she would have expected of satin, but other than that, the swift, tactile inspection left her no better informed about the dress than if she had been allowed to keep her hands to herself. The sense of touch did not lend itself to glancing, but then, no one was looking for her honest opinion of the dress, much less asking for her approval.

"Pumpkin is a deep orange shade, a little on the brown side," Olive explained. "It's an autumn color."

Cathy straightened up. "Yes, I've seen pumpkins. At Halloween."

She ought to thank Olive for being so precise about

describing things. Neither of the Nortons nor Nadine showed any desire to take such pains. Yet Olive's precision had in it the condescension of a teacher reviewing the obvious for the class dunce. It was hard to scrape up much gratitude for that.

"It is kind of pretty," Joan conceded. "Although, I'd say it was more the color of pumpkin pie than Halloween pumpkins. I suppose it's okay. But the autumn flame velvet—"

"No autumn flame and no velvet," her mother told her. "Come on. I'll show you what they have in hats to go with this."

Nadine trotted after them, a floor board creaking here and there at her passing, and, once more, Cathy discovered herself left behind. And, once more, she admitted that it was the principle that stung her, not the fact. What she wondered at was how Olive could allow the headgear to be considered while she was still here in the fitting room, too.

Cathy couldn't help a sigh. "Poor Joan!"

"Why?" Olive snapped. "Because of that ridiculous red velvet idea? She doesn't have to wear the dresses, we do. She won't know the difference on her wedding day, anyhow. She doesn't have to pay for them, either. Bridesmaids pay for their own dresses, you know."

"Naturally, I know."

The truth was that, never having been a bridesmaid before, Cathy hadn't known until two days ago, when Amy and Karen undertook to fill her in on some of the details it would involve. She was prepared for the dresses to come higher than the price Olive named, and said so.

A zipper growled, and Olive began rustling herself

out of the gown. "When you earn your own living, you soon learn that money doesn't grow on trees."

"Yes, Joan told me you work for your father." Cathy pulled Trudy tighter against her side. Olive might be scrawny, but, judging by the sounds, she occupied all the space available in flouncing from one dress to another.

"I run one of his shops. I've worked every day since I was sixteen and finished high school." Hangers clattered on a rack. "A lot of kids my age thought they'd die if they couldn't go on to college, but I never needed it, I'm proud to say. You're in college, though, aren't you?"

"I'm a junior at St. Chrysostom College," Cathy answered. It was odd that her tone should be apologetic. Perhaps the apology was because there must be stuff in Olive to admire, but she didn't want to have to do it.

"Of course, for you college is something you need. I don't suppose it will be that easy for you to get a job just anywhere, even with a trunkload of diplomas."

In essence, this was Cathy's own philosophy. A college degree and the training it represented would be vital assets to her, if she was to compete successfully in a sighted world. Stated in Olive's patronizing terms, however, those assets sounded like pencils to be sold on the street corner by a blind girl too proud to stand there just holding out a beggar's cup.

Cathy gave her a sweetly wide-eyed smile. "According to Joan, getting married is better than college or managing a shop." She didn't imagine opportunities in that line were bombarding Olive thick and fast.

"College? Who's talking about college?" The rings of the curtain rattled on the rod, yielding to a shove from Nadine. "Here, Olive. Aunt Lydia walked off with your purse along with hers, by mistake. What's this about college?"

"Cathy's a junior at St. Chrysostom College," Olive said.

"That's right. Joan told me," Nadine breathed. "That's what I'd like to do after high school—go to college. But my father's not sure it's worth the money to educate a girl. Why would you go to St. Chrysostom, though? That's a girls' school, isn't it?"

"It's a women's college," Cathy said. Why that should shock Nadine, she didn't know, but she felt compelled to add, "It rates at the top among schools of its size in the country, especially its speech therapy department."

"But no men!" Nadine teetered on a giggle. "Where's the future in that?"

"Men aren't all that scarce around a women's college. You'd be surprised." Cathy heard an echo of Olive's superiority creeping into her voice, but she couldn't seem to stop it. "You'd be surprised, too, at how many girls there are who want something more out of their future than the chance to trap a man."

"I don't suppose that would make much difference to you, anyway," Olive said. Electric crackles marked the trail of the comb she was whipping through her hair. "You don't get much chance to go out socially, do you?"

What do you know? We've both added each other up to a zero, Cathy thought. The joke would have been funnier if Olive weren't speaking again from her knowledge of what it is like to be blind. She wasn't offering pity—merely stating facts, like a clinical observer. The trouble was, Cathy was growing tired of being observed.

"There's this man down at the courthouse you should meet," Nadine suggested in an eager whisper. "He runs the concession stand there. He's done it for years. And he doesn't even have a dog. He uses a white cane."

"And you think we'd have a lot in common?" Cathy asked. She ran Trudy's leash through her fingers to untwist a kink. Surely they would be moving out of here soon. "Don't you think he might be a little old for me?"

At least, he was if he was still the gray-haired concession operator she remembered from the day her class had toured the courthouse when she was in sixth grade.

"You know him?" Nadine was impressed. "Do you people all know each other? I mean people who—ah, who—people who can't see?"

"Of course, they do," Olive said. "They have clubs and things. They don't live in a vacuum, you know."

"They" being the blind, who were actually quite acceptable and inoffensive folk when you got them herded neatly into their own little ghetto where they belonged. Cathy nudged Trudy toward the curtain, having had her fill of this conversation.

"I'm sure they have grand times at those clubs and things, but I'd rather go to a movie. With a fellow who can drive."

"Don't smile, Olive. It could be possible," Nadine admonished. Her bulk was plugging the doorway. There was no way to get by her. No way to silence her, either.

"Don't forget that fellow at Wilson High that Joan said Cathy used to go with," she went on. "You remember she told you everybody thought he was odd, that he never seemed to like the regular, ordinary girls."

Steve Hubert again. Cathy hadn't heard of him or even thought of him for ages. It was true they had been good friends in high school, but Steve had graduated a year ahead of her and immediately afterward moved with his mother back to her home town in Wyoming. The correspondence he and Cathy had promised each other to keep up had died a natural death, as ever more of his attention was claimed by his university studies and hers by the flurry of her senior year. He had long been ancient history in her life, but now, in less than two weeks, his name had been dredged up twice, courtesy of Joan Norton. Why? Joan had been foremost among the "regular, ordinary girls" Steve hadn't found attractive, but surely that old wound couldn't still be rankling. Not in the midst of preparations for Joan's wedding to her real "one and only."

Perhaps it was merely that Joan was thinking pairs these days, and feeling a little nostalgic, too. Probably Steve and Cathy had an automatic association in her mind because they were the combination that figured oftenest among Cathy's admittedly limited variety of choices.

"Doesn't Joan ever talk about anything but me?" She was surprised by the tartness of her voice.

"She and Nadine are always talking about everybody," Olive said, no less tartly, "but I suppose she wanted us to be prepared."

Prepared for what? Cathy elected not to ask that question. Why am I being so sensitive tonight, she demanded of herself. I ought to have grown a thick enough skin by now not to let a few pinpricks like these draw blood. The trouble was there had been too many pinpricks recently. Her skin was raw. The blood was close to the surface.

"Excuse me." It was one of the salesgirls, lifting the curtain and letting new air into the stuffy little cubicle. "I'd like to measure the other two young ladies so we'll know what to order."

The remainder of the shopping ordeal was mercifully short. Olive departed to supervise Joan's selection of headgear, and five minutes later Mrs. Norton appeared to announce that everything was settled, it was time to go home.

The mantel clock had been striking a quarter of nine when Cathy walked in through her front door. She checked her watch twice to be sure there was no mistake about the hour. "I could swear it must be midnight—of some day next week."

For answer, her mother had passed a plate of cookies to her, still warm from the oven. "I thought you might come home in a mood for replenishment."

They were Toll House cookies, Cathy's favorites. She sank onto the living room couch to enjoy them while she exhaled some of the steam that had been building up within her.

"How do you think I'll look in pumpkin satin? Especially after the wedding, when I shorten it and start wearing it around as an afternoon dress to back yard barbecues and things?"

It was then that the phone had rung. Mark sprinted for it from his room, operating as usual on the premise that the Wheeler phone number was known only to his friends. His surprise when he found this time he was wrong was a final massage of salt into Cathy's smarting wounds.

"It's somebody for you, Cath. A guy! He says to tell you it's Greg Breck."

Cathy armed herself with two more cookies and ran to answer on the upstairs phone. That was why her heart had been pounding a little harder, her breath coming a little faster than normal when she said "Hello" into the receiver.

"Hello, yourself." She hadn't remembered that Greg Breck's voice was that warm or that rich. "I was about to give up hope. Would you believe that there are twenty-seven Wheelers listed in this city and the first twenty-three aren't you? I've crippled two fingers and a thumb, dialing the wrong Wheelers. Now you know that I have determination."

Cathy didn't believe he was that determined. It would have been so much simpler for him to get her number from Amy, by way of Larry, which was probably what he had done. Yet if he were handing her a line, it was at any rate one that was intended to please her like a box of candy, and any sweetening was welcome this evening, whatever its source. Besides, he had learned her number from somewhere and he was calling in spite of everything Joan and Nadine and Olive and, yes, she herself—she more than anyone—would have thought probable.

"It's my ego," he explained. "It bruises terribly when I'm turned down. I always have to try again, to make certain whether the rejection was personal."

It had been personal, she recalled later, but not until after she had let him talk her into dinner and dancing to zither music at the Bavarian Hut with him and Amy and Larry for this Saturday evening. She had begun regretting the date the instant she hung up the phone, and her enthusiasm had been waning ever since. Greg Breck was likable enough in his own fashion, provided you happened to like that fashion, she supposed, but she never would have accepted if it hadn't been for Olive.

So now here she sat in this enveloping chair in Dr. Kruger's waiting room, committed to an unpromising evening tonight, thanks to Olive, and wasting this half-hour of potential study time by thinking of Olive, while shoes that wouldn't fit and would be hard to walk in were being chosen for her by Olive. Or anyhow, I'd rather blame her for all this mess than me, she conceded in a moment of frankness, and slapped an impatient hand on her notebook as it started to slide from her lap.

"Any factors which interfere with a child's physical, emotional, or social well-being . . ."

"Cathy," said the nurse at the reception desk. "You can go in now."

Trudy jumped to her feet as if the summons had been directed to her. Cathy gathered in a deep breath to fill the waiting room hollow in her chest and let her lead the way to the inner office.

"Good morning, Miss Wheeler," a raspy but not unpleasant voice greeted her. "I'm Dr. Rosenthal. Dr. Kruger's nurse explained to you, didn't she, that I'll be filling in for while he's out of town this week?"

"Yes," she replied. "How do you do? I was sorry to hear of Dr. Kruger's loss."

"It is a shame. It was his grandfather, you know. Quite an old man, who had been in poor health for several years. It's a blessing when death releases old people who are trapped like that, but it's always a shock to the family, even if they are expecting it."

A hand touched her arm, guiding her to the office chair. Cathy slid onto the seat quickly, glad to escape a faint tremor in his fingers. Often as she had felt that trembling in the many hands that had helped her, it never failed to be a disquieting sensation. Either people were afraid she was too fragile to withstand a firm grip on her arm or they were so tense to perform an immediate rescue, should she stumble, that they were literally quaking. Mostly, though, it was people not used to helping a blind person who got the shakes. How peculiar that an eye doctor, a trained specialist, would be so ill at ease. Olive, whose specialty was far from ophthalmology, had moved her hither and yon with the fortitude of a bulldozer.

"Now then," Dr. Rosenthal said, "I'm going to start by putting these drops in your eyes."

His touch on her eyelids was thoroughly professional. She blinked fast as the drops turned to liquid fire.

Dr. Rosenthal handed her a tissue to mop up the tears. "That's a beautiful dog you have there. She must be a big help to you in getting around."

Cathy agreed that Trudy was, to which he replied, "Mmmmmmm. Now look down at the floor, please."

He made a few more stabs at conversation between tests, and Cathy made polite answers, but there was nothing to indicate that he was listening either to her or to himself. That was just as well, for he was a lot slower than Dr. Kruger, and any real sort of conversation was likely to slow him down that much more.

"Now then, look straight ahead, please. Do you see this light at all?" he asked, coming eventually to the final test. "Where is it?"

This was the test that interested her most. Could she still see some light? Was there a pinpoint of it to the left? The doctor's sleeve rustled, and she knew he was holding his beam of light to her right. She closed her eyes, and the light she thought she saw continued to shine steadily, not dimmed a bit.

"Do you have any perception there at all?" Dr. Rosenthal asked.

Cathy shook her head. "No, not really. I used to, and

the memory is so exactly like the real thing sometimes that it's hard to tell the difference."

She wished at once that she had kept that bit of information to herself. It was the truth, but spoken aloud, it sounded foolish, if not downright unhinged. Her record must show that she'd had no light perception for several years. It was a fact of life, like having red hair instead of rippling gold, and she accepted it as such most of the time, rarely even thinking about it one way or the other. Yet whenever she sat in this elevated clinical chair, a part of her was ready to believe that all of the facts were reversible and that her medical reports were based on a laughable mistake.

"Mmmmhmmm," Dr. Rosenthal said in regard to she didn't know what. "These eyes of yours been causing you any discomfort lately? Any aches or pains or undue tenderness?"

Cathy shifted her feet on the metal footrest. "Do you count headaches? I've been having those off and on since the last time I was in. The worse ones seem to start behind my left eye, but they could be just tension."

"You've been under pressure of some sort lately?" His bland tone offered no clue to what stock he took in her diagnosis.

"Yes, in a way. I'm a junior this year, and we have a heavier work load than we did last year. More responsibility, maybe. And it didn't seem there was much breathing space between the end of summer school this summer and the start of the fall term. It may be I'm just not organized yet."

She dabbed at her nose, yearning to blow it but afraid he would credit it to a gush of self-pity, instead of the leaky aftermath of his eyedrops. Come to think of it, there was a slightly pitiful ring to a number of things she had said to him. Good grief! Was she that far gone in feeling sorry for herself?

She screwed her face into a resolute grin. "But I guess I'll live."

"A junior! In college? How do you manage the studies? You read Braille, I suppose." He walked across the room as he spoke and pulled open a drawer.

"Yes, I read Braille." Acting on the probability that his back was to her, she blew her nose. "Most of my textbooks are recorded on tape, though. There are volunteer groups here and all over the country who do that sort of thing for students. It's a great help."

"But it would be a lot easier if you could see, wouldn't it?" he asked mildly, and tore a sheet of paper from a pad.

Cathy pressed the crumpled tissue to her nose and sat unmoving for a moment, trying to formulate an answer stupid enough to fit such a stupid question. There wasn't any.

She slipped Trudy's leash from her wrist to her hand and stepped down from the chair. "Is there a wastebasket where I can throw this tissue?"

"Right here."

He brought a plastic cylinder of a basket and she dropped the tissue in. Trudy raised a questing muzzle, ears pricked forward, on the chance a wad or two of chewing gum might have been discarded in there, too.

"Of course, if you set your heart on twenty-twenty vision, that would be pretty much like wishing for the moon. Although the moon isn't an impossibility these days, either, is it?" He chuckled softly. "But even a little vision—say, enough to count fingers with—would be welcome, wouldn't it?"

An electric thrill curled the fingers Cathy had rested on Trudy's head to restrain her. For a dizzy second, the floor dipped beneath her feet like the deck of a boat.

"You're not say—There's a chance—I could see again?" She tacked a laugh onto the question to free her throat of a sudden fog in it like laryngitis.

"My motto is, 'Where there's life, there's always hope,' " he answered. "Who knows what's just around the next corner? Once we stop hoping, we might as well be dead."

"Can you? Is there a way? How—What?" She paused to drag in a breath for which there was no room in her lungs. Her mind was operating with a beautiful, calm precision, but somehow the message wasn't getting through to her tongue. "I don't know if I understand."

"You keep on doing the good job you're doing, and leave the understanding to us." Dr. Rosenthal patted her shoulder and, in the same gesture, guided her toward the door. "We're going to do everything that's medically possible for those eyes. You can depend on that."

At the threshold of the waiting room, he pressed a slip of paper into her hand. "I want you back here in a couple of months. Early December at the latest. We want to keep track of what's happening. In the meantime, I've written you a prescription for some drops that ought to give you relief from those headaches."

Cathy had no recollection afterward of whether she thanked him or not. She could recall only that, as she walked to the receptionist's desk to make the appointment for next time, she could feel and hear and see the whole room shimmering.

5

"CATHY! HEY, Cathy Wheeler! Wait!" It was Amy, racing down the hall from the locker room, her child-clear voice defying the Tuesday morning student buzz to drown it out.

Cathy, halfway up the first flight of stairs, turned and waved to show she had heard, then went on up to wait for her on the landing.

Amy arrived, puffing and blowing. "Are you ever the early bird today? What's your hurry? I thought I'd catch you in the locker room, but you took off like the Kentucky Derby."

"I didn't know you were in there," Cathy said. "Why didn't you do something spectacular and attention-getting like saying hello?"

"I did. I even said hi to Trudy. She heard me. She wagged her tail. But you just kind of smiled and floated on out on cloud nine."

Cathy grinned. "Some cloud nine. Dr. Paulus is sitting in on my clinic session to observe this morning. I'm definitely not floating." But perhaps it was nearly as definite that the floor wasn't meeting her shoe soles quite as firmly as usual.

"Ugh! I don't blame you for having your mind elsewhere, then. She sat in on me Friday, and afterward she criticized everything I'd done. Everything!" Amy ticked off the faults with taps on Cathy's arm. "I praised them too lavishly; I treat them more like playmates than patients; I'm not organized; I'm not strict enough; and besides, I was late getting upstairs to the waiting room."

"Well, that's why I'm not wasting time this morning." Cathy gave Trudy's harness handle a jiggle to indicate they should start up the next flight of stairs. "Whatever else she calls me on, she will have to grant that I'm punctual."

"Don't count on it," Amy warned, falling in behind them, for Trudy climbed steps at a rate most people found easier to follow than to match. "She's not the granting type."

"But listen," she said, darting forward to link an arm through Cathy's when they gained the second floor. "What I want to hear about is last night. Larry said Greg's new sports car was delivered and he drove it over to show you right away. Did he?"

"He did." Cathy tried to hide her broadening grin. "It's a beautiful car. Except it's too small to hold Trudy. We had to leave her behind."

Trudy hadn't liked that idea at all. Cathy hadn't been too fond of it, either, at first. She'd also had some misgivings about going joy riding on a school night, especially the night before she was due to be observed in clinic by Dr. Paulus, but what else could she do? Greg had appeared out of nowhere to ring the front doorbell, his new sports car humming at the curb and his every intention to delight her by a surprise whirl around the city in it. He even took Mark along for an initial tour of the blocks in their neighborhood. Cathy couldn't refuse him. More to the point, she didn't want to.

"You're beginning to like him better than you did, aren't you? I could tell Saturday night that you were really having fun. And it's pretty evident that he likes you."

"He's a good dancer," Cathy said cautiously. "And I wasn't dying of a headache Saturday night. That makes a world of difference by itself."

But the worst of headaches couldn't account entirely for the difference between that dreary afternoon of the hot chocolate and the lively sparkle of last Saturday night in the same place with the same people. Certainly, she hadn't gone out that evening expecting sparkle. She was ready to count herself lucky if only Amy and Larry would stick close enough to her to absorb a part of Greg's overwhelming presence.

But Greg's presence wasn't overwhelming Saturday. It was hard to say exactly how, unless he was less pushy in his attentions to her. Or perhaps it was that she was a lot more receptive to being pleased. There was an easiness to their laughter, a savor to the dinner, a lilt to the zither music, an exhilaration to the pounding feet and clapping hands as he swung her through polkas and waltzes—all adding up to an evening of fun, contrary to every anticipation. More than fun. Although none of them knew it but her, it was a celebration.

She hurried on up the third flight of stairs. If she paused on the thought of how it would be to see again, she might well be lost in the dream of it for the rest of the day. It was too heady a draft to sip from while there were other things she must get done. Besides, Dr. Rosenthal had said "hope"; he had made no absolute promise. She had to keep reminding herself of that or she would have no control left whatsoever.

"You like more than Greg's dancing. Something must have clicked. I can tell by looking at you," Amy said, falling in behind again. "How was it last night with just the two of you? Interesting?"

"More like startling," Cathy flung over her shoulder, and was glad for the moment that her face was out of Amy's line of vision. "You never warned me he has a beard."

No one had warned her. Not Amy, not Larry, not Greg himself, not even her parents or Mark. Not a soul had mentioned it. And a beard was an adornment that gave no clues to its presence itself until it was right there in direct contact with you.

"I never thought. Oh, Cathy!" Amy clapped her on the shoulder in a convulsion of mirth. "It's such a handsome beard, too. Not all rag-moppy and scraggly. It's kind of princely. Larry can't grow one because of store rules about employees being clean-shaven, but if he could, I think it would be kind of—well, you know—more exciting."

Exciting? Yes, but not because of Greg's beard. Not after that initial shock of it against her skin as he leaned to give her a peck on the cheek that, all in an instant, had become neither a peck nor on the cheek. Her experience in kissing wasn't vast, but it was sufficient for her to recognize that those who had kissed her before were boys. Greg was a man.

"Are you saying Larry isn't exciting?" Cathy asked as an excuse for the smile she couldn't keep hidden. "You and he must have gone out last night, or how would you know about Greg's car?"

"I thought you'd never ask. We only talked on the

phone last night, but Sunday . . . Cathy, he's the guy for me. I know he is. I've got to tell you about it."

But they were on the third floor now. The elevator rattled open at the far end of the corridor, scattering two or three women's voices, a child's cough, and a clatter of footsteps into the hall. The telling would have to wait.

"Until after clinic," Amy said. "There's my Sally. My Sal-Sal."

A child came toward them, babbling a stream of what was gibberish to Cathy's ears. She couldn't help a quick comparison with Roddy, who was actually beginning to remember his l and t sounds and to put some effort into making them. On the other hand, when had Roddy ever sounded this glad to see her?

"A present for you? What makes you think I have a present for you, Sal-Sal?" Amy dropped to her knees to bestow a hug and a kiss. "That's my present for you."

"Pedda me," Cathy concluded, must be Sally's version of "a present for me."

"No!" Sally cried, demonstrating that there were some words she could speak as clearly as anyone. "No! Pedda me—"

The rest of the protest was lost on Cathy, but Amy understood it.

"What did I tell you about a real present. I said you and Beth could have a present when you made your sounds right for me, didn't I? Did you practice your sounds at home this week?"

Sally launched into another babble of indignation, punctuated by no's—a repeat of her first protest, Cathy guessed, but it was only a guess. She dipped Amy a farewell smile and nod, and moved on toward the waiting room to collect her own patients.

What sort of present was Amy promising in return for good speech sounds, she wondered? If it were anyone but Amy proposing it, the idea would have a disquieting flavor of bribery, like something born of desperation when every other attempt at motivation had failed. Knowing Amy, the presents were more likely just a token of the affection she felt for her little girls; Amy's affections ran strong. Besides, this was the beginning of their third week of clinic—rather early in the game to be desperate enough to resort to bribes. Or was it? If I could find a gift for Leonard that would get him started talking, wouldn't I cut class this afternoon and spend my life savings to buy it? Cathy asked herself.

She paused inside the waiting room door, listening for Roddy's voice or that of his mother among the murmurings of mothers and children. It would be asking too much to hope that she wouldn't hear Leonard or his mother, too, so Dr. Paulus might be deprived of her golden chance to say I-told-you-so at the end of the session today. Last Friday, Leonard's second visit to the clinic, he had spent a good share of the period laughing his weird laugh at the light fixture in the ceiling, had dumped a box of marbles on the floor and clapped his hands while they rolled to the four corners of the room, and had discovered a fondness for patting Trudy. In the three days since then, Cathy had managed to read most of the book on brain-damaged children, but it contained few teaching hints beyond the suggestion that schools should be established and specially equipped to handle such children. The book's primary purpose was to explain that damage to the brain might block or detour but not necessarily destroy a perfectly normal intelligence, while retardation meant that the intelligence was below normal to begin with. Which left her and Leonard right where they were last week.

Or Leonard, anyway. The thought unfurled like a banner in a sudden breeze: I'm a thousand miles from where I was Friday. I'm going to see again!

"Good morning, Miss Wheeler. Here we are."

It was Mrs. Perkins and Leonard. Cathy beamed at them. It wasn't their fault they were problems. They probably wouldn't be if they had a choice.

"Good morning." She smiled down at the general area where Leonard must be and reached for his hand. "Hello, Leonard. How are you today?"

Leonard replied by fastening both hands on the necklace she was wearing. It was a string of artificial walnuts that she had bought on sale for ninety-nine cents last spring, but the nuts had a rough, autumn texture she liked, and she definitely had no desire to have the string broken.

"Are those pretty? Do you like them?" She bent lower to ease the strain on the strand and to cover his hands with hers in an attempt to loosen them.

"That's right, Leonard. Those are walnuts, just like in our back yard," Mrs. Perkins said. She sounded delighted. "You knew that, didn't you?"

Leonard uttered a gurgle like a year-old baby and tightened his grip. His little claw fingers were clamped around the beads like steel hooks.

"We have a walnut tree in our back yard," his mother told Cathy. "At this time of year, when the nuts are ripening, he'll spend hours out there, picking them up and looking at them. He even hunts for them under the leaves and where the grass is long, next to the fence. He knows them when he sees them."

There was pride in her voice, as if this were an accomplishment worth noting. Cathy heard a trace of invitation in it, too, asking for someone to agree that her interpretation wasn't wrong.

"If he has that much power of concentration, it ought to be a help in learning sounds," Cathy responded encouragingly, not at all sure she believed it.

Still, there was no denying his powers of concentration were more than she had given him credit for. As fast as she pried one set of fingers from the necklace, being careful not to press too hard on the fragile bones that felt as if they could be snapped like toothpicks, the second set twisted and pulled to gain a firmer hold.

"Now that's enough, Leonard. Let go," his mother said. She jingled her keys. "Look, sweetheart. Look what I've got. That's a good boy."

Leonard came slowly unglued from the necklace and turned to the new attraction. Cathy straightened, glad to have her necklace intact.

She really acts as if she cares about him, she thought, a trifle ashamed to be astonished by the discovery, but astonished none the less. It hadn't entered her head that, even to his mother, he could be more than an unlucky obligation that had been wished upon her, to be tolerated the best she could. But, in fact, he was a child, not a gnome; he was a flesh-and-blood little human whose mother wanted and loved him. It was a revelation that needed digesting.

"Here we are," called Roddy's mother, hurrying in from the hall. "Here's Roddy. We missed the elevator twice."

Cathy greeted them and reached once more for Leonard, being careful this time to keep the swing of her beads to a minimum. "Okay, fellows, let's be on our way. We're going to have company this morning. Dr. Paulus is coming to see how well you are doing, and we don't want our company to be there before we are."

"Lots of luck," Monica muttered, ushering her two patients past Cathy's group and into the hall.

The word had the shriveling effect of frost on the edges of Cathy's inner glow. Luck was precisely the commodity she needed during this next hour, but when Dr. Paulus was on the scene, it was a hard item to come by.

Roddy, on the other hand, was enchanted by the prospect of having an audience to perform for. "Shall we p'ay the marble game?" he suggested as soon as they were in the therapy room. He started for the cupboard where the marbles were kept.

"No," Cathy told him. "No marble game today."

It was too risky. The game consisted of a bottle into which Roddy dropped a marble each time he correctly identified the sound he was supposed to be listening for in the story Cathy read to him. Each time he missed, he had to pay a marble to her. There were twenty marbles altogether—which was twenty more than she cared to be groping for beneath the table and between Dr. Paulus' feet.

"Remember what happened to the marbles last week?" she reminded him, letting Leonard have a minute to rub his hands through Trudy's fur. Hopefully, he would have the desire out of his system by the time Dr. Paulus walked in. "Besides, we don't want to play the marble game every day."

Roddy wasn't fooled by that excuse. "I helped you pick them up. I'll pick 'em up today, too."

It was true. He did help, much to her surprise. He had sat watching at first, enjoying the spectacle of his teacher on her knees, sweeping her hands over the floor in search of the marbles Leonard had sent in every direction. Then he had offered, "There's one," pointing she had no idea where, and she had said, "Would you get it for me?" Maybe it was only that he had been ready to take part in the action, but thinking about it afterward, she was more inclined to believe he responded to the person-to-person appeal in her voice. At any rate, he had retrieved seven marbles in short order, some of them from such out-of-the-way spots as under the radiator and behind the wastebasket. Nevertheless, it wasn't an entertainment she wished to repeat for Dr. Paulus' benefit.

"I know another way you can help. Let's look at your notebook and see if you found any pictures with your new sounds in them that it would be fun to show Dr. Paulus when she comes in."

Roddy's return to the worktable had a tinge of reluctance in it, but he had his notebook open and was paging through it when Dr. Paulus did walk in two minutes later.

"I'm going to be visiting your class here every once in a while," she explained to the children as she seated herself in the chair at the end of the table. "But I'm just going to sit still and listen, so don't pay any attention to me. Go right on working with Miss Wheeler the way you always do."

Cathy squared Leonard on his chair and shoved him in close enough to the table so that it would take him a little time to squirm himself free. It was a foregone conclusion that he would squirm himself free eventually and start a restless wandering of the room, but, at least, he was periodically where he belonged. That, she reflected, is how we always do.

She turned to Roddy. "Can you tell Dr. Paulus what new sounds we're working on?"

"Chick-ken!" Roddy bellowed. He slapped a dramatic hand on the page in front of him. "See? Chick-ken."

"Good. Very good," Cathy applauded. He hadn't come near such clear ch and k sounds Friday. "You've been practicing. But what about your voice? How loud should it be when you talk to people?"

He replied in a mumble so low she couldn't tell if he were actually saying something or just making noise. Most of it was lost in the soft bump-bump of Leonard's heels against his chair legs. Roddy waited for a comment from her. When she merely stared at him, he dropped his head on his book and giggled.

Cathy scrapped her plan to do a tour of the room, Leonard leading and Roddy discussing, as they had done their first day together. Turning the two of them loose in the room when Roddy was bent on showing off by being silly would be to tempt fate beyond the bounds of reason. The tour was written into the lesson plan she had handed in to Dr. Paulus yesterday, of course, but it would be better to face the charge of poor advance planning than to be caught a second time floundering through a three-ring circus that was supposed to be a clinic session. I'd deserve anything she'd throw at me if I haven't learned that much. She silenced the qualm that fluttered in the wake of her decision.

"Try it again," she told Roddy. "If you can tell me about that picture so I know what you are saying, we can turn on the tape recorder and let you listen to yourself."

Roddy straightened up at once and pronounced in an almost normal voice, "A chicken and a lllll-lamb."

"Good! That's it." Cathy clapped her hands in a gesture more typical of Amy than herself. She knew Roddy liked to use the recorder, but it didn't always follow that giving Roddy what he liked produced full cooperation on his part.

The recorder stand was no more than three or four steps to her left, and, fortunately, not in a place where she would have to jockey it around Dr. Paulus to roll it close to the table. She did have to walk past Dr. Paulus to the cupboard where the tapes were stored, but that, too, she managed without stumbling into the chair or falling over her own feet. As a matter of fact, now that the period was underway, she was feeling far more poised and in command of the situation than she would have predicted.

Yes, and there was a tape, right where it should be —something she ought to have checked beforehand because supplies sometimes traveled to other therapy rooms and failed to return. But there, also, was a small hand—two small hands—grabbing for the workbooks piled on the lower shelf.

"No, Leonard," she said. "Leave those alone. You don't want those books."

Which was as great a falsehood as she was likely to utter today. For she and Leonard both knew that he did want them. He wanted to throw them on the floor. He wanted to taste them. He wanted to tip over a chair. He wanted to rock the mirror, to see if it could be dislodged from the wall. He wanted to trip on the cord to the tape recorder and disconnect the machine. He wanted to do anything and everything that would cause disruption. What he did not want was to sit quietly and not bother anyone. Unless . . .

"Come on. I'll show you something better."

She scooped him up and deposited him in his chair again. It was like lifting a bundle of rags. Then, not pausing to let herself dwell on the merit of her impulse, she pulled her necklace off over her head and put it into his hands.

"Here are the walnuts. Wal-nuts. Wal-nuts. You look at them for a while."

And don't, for heaven's sake, break them, she added mentally. Dr. Paulus, true to her pledge to be a silent observer, sat on without saying a word.

I wish I had a clue to what she's thinking, Cathy thought as she set the tape on the machine and threaded it. I wonder if her face ever gives anything away. What will it be like if maybe, one of these days, I'm able to glance up at her and know?

A fine-toothed thrill coursed to the tips of her fingers, and she put the microphone on the table quickly, for fear she might drop it. She hadn't meant to think of Dr. Rosenthal's promise right now. She mustn't think of it right now. She would be laughing as foolishly as Leonard in another minute if she did.

"Remember the story I read you last time?" she asked Roddy, and dug into her briefcase for the book. "About the little engine that could?"

By luck, the book was there among the other teaching props she kept in this briefcase. She had intended to bring today only the essentials she had written into her lesson plan but Greg's unexpected arrival had broken into her evening at just the wrong time last night for getting it done. Or just the right time. She was beginning to believe in the luck Monica had wished her.

"I know, I know," Roddy said. He took the book eagerly.

"Okay. Good. Now I'll switch on the tape recorder, and you tell me the story. The pictures will help you remember."

After that, the show belonged to Roddy. He flung himself into the telling of the story with a wealth of appropriate gestures and sound effects calculated to make it interesting. There were moments when he tottered on the thin edge of downright silliness, but a question or an added detail from Cathy served to steer him back into what was a valid speech experience each time.

Once or twice, she heard the necklace rattle on the table. She hoped Leonard wasn't making a project of demolishing it, but she couldn't let her attention stray long from Roddy. He was putting a serious effort into his l's and t's, ch's and k's, despite his dramatics, and he was the basket in which all her eggs were packed. Whatever remarks Dr. Paulus would have about Leonard, she would have to grant that Roddy had gained some ground in the past two weeks.

It was when Cathy rewound the tape and played it for Roddy to hear that she realized Leonard had been burbling and exclaiming to himself through most of the story. His contributions were recorded loud and distinct, but Roddy, bless his self-centered little heart, wasn't distracted by them for an instant. He listened in absorbed fascination to himself on the tape, and he had his answers ready whenever she stopped it to discuss a point.

"Hat hood. I said, 'Hat hood,' " he said as triumphantly as if he were scoring against an opponent. " 'The engine hat hood.' "

"Right," Cathy said. "Why do you suppose you said that? Were you maybe getting in too big a hurry? What should you say?"

"The engine that could. Could, could, co-hood!"

"Good! You're getting there. Let's hear how you said it the next time."

Cathy started the tape again, turning her head from Dr. Paulus to hide a grin. She had gambled that if anything could charm Roddy into attending to business, it would be the double importance of being both star performer and major critic, and the gamble was going to pay off. Her eggs couldn't be in a safer basket.

Another of Leonard's burbles punctuated the slightly nasal narration coming from the recorder. Its twin, exact as an echo, replied from Cathy's elbow.

Cathy did a startled twist. She hadn't known Leonard was on the prowl again. Here he was, squeezing himself in between her and the recorder stand. Could it be he was attracted by the sound of his own voice on the tape and was trying to imitate himself? She looped an arm around him, partly to restrain the hand he was about to tangle in the moving tape and partly to see what would happen the next time his private code chirped from the speaker.

What happened was that Leonard began a weaving action to escape. The necklace clattered to the floor in what was surely a dozen different pieces.

"I'll get it," Roddy yelled.

Cathy halted the tape. The click of the switch and the scrape of Roddy's chair as he dove were simultaneous.

Cathy dove, too. Her head met Roddy's with a sickening thwunk under the table.

"Ow!" Roddy howled, articulating perfectly. Disintegration of the remainder of the period trembled in the word.

"Ow! yourself." Cathy rubbed the spot on her forehead that was threatening to burst the skin, too jarred herself to be diplomatic. Talk about regaining enough vision to count fingers. Already she could see stars.

She started to laugh.

Roddy gulped and turned a sniffle into an uncertain snicker.

"Ow-wa! That's our sound," Cathy said.

Roddy's snicker became a full-fledged laugh. "Ow-wa! Ow-wa! We got to practice it."

Cathy was sweeping her hand across the floor without success.

"Here. I got them." Roddy leaned past her, and the necklace rattled, departing for the table top.

Cathy's grab to recapture it was too slow. She had to scramble up to join him in an inspection he was already making by himself.

A swift, fingertip survey assured her no links were broken, no beads missing, and none obviously chipped or damaged. It also revealed that Roddy was in no hurry to yield up the prize. He was handling the rough, nutshell surfaces with much of the same evident pleasure Leonard had displayed.

"These are acorns," he volunteered.

"Walnuts," Cathy said.

It was a harder word for him to pronounce, but he produced a fairly close imitation on his third attempt.

"What do you know about nuts?" she asked. "How do you get them out of the shells?"

Her ignorance delighted and astonished him. "You got to crack them."

He knew more than that. He knew you could use a

rock to crack them, and that they grew on trees, and that Santa Claus put them in his stockings at Christmas, and that his mommy cooked them in cakes and cookies and candy, and that he liked them because they tasted good. For the first time, Cathy was hearing him converse without her having to extract each sentence from him, like rusty nails from a board, and it was a conversation studded with the sounds he most needed to practice. She trusted that Dr. Paulus was taking careful note.

Leonard came to press against her and play with the walnuts, too, as she led the talk on from things to eat to ways of eating and how to tell if the meal were breakfast, lunch, or dinner. Roddy ended the period doing cheerfully for her the tongue exercises that on other days he tried to avoid or to dissolve into foolishness.

This new spirit of cooperation couldn't be just the result of Dr. Paulus' austere presence. The secret had to be in the necklace, Cathy told herself, in the realness of the walnuts, the novelty of something that could be touched by the fingers and weighed in the hand, instead of merely looked at in a book. The buzz of an idea began to vibrate in her mind.

The bell rang, and the power of speech was restored to Dr. Paulus. "Very well, Miss Wheeler," she said, rising. "Come into my office next period, and we'll compare our impressions."

That "very well" probably referred to nothing more than the bell, but Cathy heard congratulations in the rumble of the casters as she rolled the recorder stand back where it belonged. If she hadn't scored this morning, no one could. And this was only the start, if her idea worked.

"I'm proud of you," she told Roddy on the way to

the waiting room. "You did a fine job. And you were a good boy, too, Leonard," she added on a wave of generosity, although she had no reason to suppose her opinion affected him in the slightest.

Still, he had been good—for Leonard. She gave the limp little claw locked in her hand a gentle swing of approval. To her surprise, his fingers curled themselves around hers and tightened as if in genuine response.

Roddy ran ahead to meet his mother. "Know what, Mom? She likes us today." Turning, he demanded of Cathy, "Don't you?"

"I sure do like you," Cathy answered. "I like you a whole lot. You're my kind of guys."

A pin jab of guilt lent extra enthusiasm to her voice. Had she somehow failed to convince him before this that she liked him? To be honest, the question of like or dislike hadn't concerned her much, except as his behavior weakened or promised to reinforce Dr. Paulus' arguments. She had been looking on him and Leonard both more as problems to be solved than as real children who might be sensitive to whether the teacher's praise was heartfelt or mechanical.

"And we have a different kind of assignment for Friday," she went on as Leonard's mother joined them. "Roddy, you find three things that have your sounds in the names—things, not pictures this time. Maybe a crayon or a toy chicken or something like that. Something you can bring to class Friday without a truck to help you. Think you can do that?"

"That seems like a grand idea," Roddy's mother said. "I know we'll have fun hunting them up. I can think of a couple things already."

"Good! We want things we can pick up and handle." Cathy turned to Leonard's mother. "I'd like the same sort of thing for Leonard. Does he have any special things he's fond of—toys or walnuts or whatever?"

An image of Benjie in *The Sound and the Fury,* weeping over his sister's satin wedding slipper, flashed through her mind. She hoped Mrs. Perkins wouldn't think she was predicting a Benjie-type future of slobbering imbecility for Leonard. She hoped, too, that Mrs. Perkins would choose no objects that were likely to trigger a storm of tears.

"Walnuts— Yes, and he has a jar he likes to sniff. It used to have mentholated cream in it. Something like that, you mean?" Mrs. Perkins asked.

"The jar would be fine. Anything that he likes and finds familiar. I'm looking for objects that maybe he can relate to better than he does to flat pictures on a page. Something he likes to sniff as well as handle is that much more to work with."

Smell, touch . . . There must be objects that could appeal to even more senses at once. Her idea was lifting and widening like the wings of a new butterfly. Why hadn't she thought of it before?

The answer was that today—this week, from now on—everything was falling into place for her, everything was fitting together as it should. That was how it had been since she had walked out of Dr. Rosenthal's office—as if she were in possession of the magic bridle that bestowed on her the mastery of the wild, winged horse, Pegasus.

Or rather, she thought when she turned toward Dr. Paulus' office, it was as if she had a secret pocket into which she could slip her hand and touch a magic charm, a golden penny, whenever her luck was in need of renewing. She could feel that need collecting like steam on a chilled windowpane as soon as she was in the room and seated in the rocker at the corner of the desk.

"Before I express any opinions or make any suggestions, Miss Wheeler, I would like to hear your evaluation of this therapy session," Dr. Paulus said in a voice that was like a parfait glass, beautiful and frosty.

Cathy cleared her throat. What should she say? That of the five clinic sessions she had taught to date, today's was by far the most satisfactory? If the winter atmosphere in here was a clue to Dr. Paulus' opinion, that might amount to condemning herself out of her own mouth.

She cleared her throat again, and said cautiously, "On the whole, I believe I accomplished most of what I planned to cover today. I'm working on waking up Roddy's ears to the right sounds, so he's aware of it when he makes them and when he misses. I'm trying to get him in the habit of using them in normal conversation, too, not just when he's practicing."

"I see." Dr. Paulus shifted position, and her chair creaked like the protest of snow in January. "My impression was that you did a great deal of on-the-spot improvising today. The tape recorder, for example, doesn't appear on your lesson plan—an exercise, incidentally, which you did not complete. Your patient had criticized barely two-thirds of his recording when you abandoned the project for a new activity. Is it your general procedure to make spur-of-the-moment substitutions for the items in your lesson plans that you presumably have put some thought into drawing up beforehand?"

It was a question Cathy had known she couldn't hope to escape, but she hadn't known it could be phrased in such negative terms. Worse, there was some justice in it. Having to jump up in pursuit of Leonard every few minutes did call for frequent improvising to keep Roddy profitably involved in what was going on. Yet to confess herself unable to predict Leonard's next move, even when he was on the verge of making it, let alone prepare for it beforehand in a written lesson plan, would be to feed Dr. Paulus' mill exactly the kind of grist it wanted.

She closed her hand on the imaginary coin in her imaginary pocket, and the realization swept over her that here was a time when no answer could serve more to her advantage than the simple and direct truth.

"I've been trying to follow your advice that first day of clinic, when you told me a therapist has to get to where the trouble is before it starts. Roddy was set to be a clown today for your benefit, so, instead of letting him turn the tour of the room into a silly game, I substituted the recorder for the tour because he thinks using it is a special treat. The necklace was an accidental interruption when it dropped, but talking about it right away got him involved in spontaneous conversation we probably wouldn't have achieved if we'd finished with the recorder first."

"I see." The mercury rose not a single degree. "Your manner of improvising, however, eliminated what few activities your lesson plan contained for involving the non-talking patient. You devoted less than ten minutes of the session to him, including the time spent in reseating him and pronouncing walnut. In effect, you were working with only one patient."

Again there was justice in the charge, and again Cathy could afford an honest answer. "I have been working with Leonard. I've been looking for a way to hold his attention on something long enough to get some idea of language into his head. I've tried everything our text suggests, but there was something about this necklace today—" Her hand lifted to the strand of walnuts around her neck. "I'm wondering if I can reach him by using three-dimensional objects like this that he already recognizes and can examine and hold."

"It's possible." It was obvious that the idea didn't arouse the same measure of optimism in Dr. Paulus as it did in Cathy. "But it is also possible you missed an excellent opportunity for breaking through to him when you allowed yourself to be distracted from the tape recorder by that business with the necklace. He gave a strong indication that he might be attracted to the sound of his own jargon on the tape, but you failed to follow it up."

The beads under Cathy's fingers became hard knobs of dismay. She hadn't followed it up. She had meant to, and in the next second, she had forgotten all about it—forgotten what might have proved the most important incident of the entire semester. There was no defense she could invent for that and no way to repair the loss.

"I guess I did have my mind too much on Roddy," she admitted unhappily. "It's only in the last two sessions that he has started showing any real progress, and I was trying to encourage him in every way possible. Leonard's attention is so easily diverted by a different noise or a movement anywhere that I suppose I automatically assumed his interest in the recording was gone after the scramble to pick up the necklace. I didn't even think."

"Exactly," Dr. Paulus said. "It would be strange, however, if Roddy weren't showing progress, since he has already had two semesters of therapy."

Therefore, no matter what marvels of progress Roddy

might achieve this semester, Cathy should not expect more than a fraction of the credit for it to become part of her record. The credit for below standard achievement, of course, would be awarded to her in full. Dr. Paulus didn't plan on losing this game.

"But as you say," Dr. Paulus continued, "your retarded patient presents a greater problem than just lack of speech. The major part of your energies where he is concerned appear to be channeled into the purely physical job of keeping track of where he is and what he's doing at any given moment. The particular strain this represents for you under the circumstances could develop into an unhealthy situation for therapist and patient alike; certainly an unprofitable one. You're not obliged to retain a patient on your schedule that you find impossible to cope with."

Drop Leonard from her schedule? The rocker tilted slowly back as Cathy let herself be tempted. Imagine, instead of flittery, frustrating Leonard, she should be assigned a nice, normal little boy whose sole difficulty was a lisp—a nice, normal little boy who wouldn't go down on her record as a failure.

Except that it was dropping Leonard which would stamp Failure on her record. And there had been no mention of a nice, normal boy to replace him, probably because there wouldn't be one. The pot of winnings would have spilled itself neatly into Dr. Paulus' lap as soon as Leonard was gone and her delicately phrased "particular strain" and "under the circumstances" were translated into Cathy's file as "because of limitations imposed by her physical handicap."

Cathy's hand dug deep into the secret pocket to clutch her new gold coin—a coin whose full implications suddenly blared through her like a trumpet fanfare.

"I think I'd prefer to retain Leonard as long as I can, and maybe try a little harder," she said.

For somewhere in the nearing future, her physical handicap would be no more; she was on the threshold of freedom from those "limitations." The contest between her and Dr. Paulus was over. She didn't have to prove she could master speech therapy in spite of being blind. She could master it or fail or simply quit on the same footing as any other student. If she wanted to switch to another field, if she wanted to leave school and get a job, if she wanted to withdraw her savings from the bank and travel for a year, from now on, it would be as easy for her as walking through an open door.

"Very well. I will let the decision be yours," Dr. Paulus said. A pencil whispered on paper, noting perhaps the rejection of one more attempt to counsel surrender on reasonable terms.

Dr. Paulus had further comments on the clinic session, all of them concise, instructive, and antiseptically impersonal. . . . Cathy listened, jotted mental notations, and fought down a reckless impulse to rock to and fro and sing. She was singing, or at any rate humming to herself, when Amy caught up with her in the locker room after the interview.

"I was watching for you to go by the library," Amy said, a trifle breathless, "but as usual, you were traveling too fast for me."

"Or could it be you were busy dreaming about Larry when I went by?" Cathy asked.

"Isn't he great?" Amy bent to pat Trudy while Cathy stowed the morning's gear in her locker. "I told you, didn't I, that he's taking night courses in business at the university so he can be his own boss some day? Sure I did, because that's where he met Greg, and you know all about Greg."

"Do I?"

Amy laughed. "Well, if you don't, I have a feeling you will before long. He wouldn't go zooming off to show you his precious new car if that's all there's going to be to it, and you wouldn't be turning such a pretty pink, either."

Cathy plucked her lunch bag from the bottom of her locker and slowly stood up. Her grin was deliberately skeptical. "Tell me more."

Yet, wasn't there the faintest of jingles from that secret pocket, as if a second golden penny might have been added to the first?

6

"THREE GUESSES who that was," Mark said as Cathy hung up the phone and stood pondering a moment, her hand still on the receiver. "Wow! How soulful can you look?"

Cathy wasn't looking soulful, but it was hard not to grin at his mistake. He ought to have known she wouldn't have answered the phone here in the kitchen if she had been expecting a call. Most calls at this time of day, right around supper time, were usually for Mark, and she had answered the ring only because she was handiest to the phone, having just set down Trudy's supper for her.

"Okay, Sherlock," she challenged, taking the empty dog food can to the sink to rinse it, "see if you can guess."

"Swingin' Greg. Who else?"

"Wrong," she said, enjoying the implications in his sureness, as well as what was an ever rarer chance these days to contradict his guess.

"Olive Tyler," her mother said into the depths of the

refrigerator. "Mark, did you finish off my last quart of milk since you got home? Why didn't you tell me in time to send you to the store for more?"

Mark drained his mug with a gasp of satisfaction and thumped it onto the table. "Because I just finished it. Veterinary medicine demands a lot of nourishment, especially after you've spent the whole day in school first. Who's Olive Tyler?"

"Olive's the maid of honor in the wedding, Joan's cousin," Cathy told him, "and currently the rearranger of Joan's surprise shower."

"And that's who it was? How did you know that, Mom?"

The refrigerator door shut with a soft smack. "Because I heard her say, 'Hello, Olive,' and 'Good-by, Olive,' for one thing, and because I doubt that she'd be talking cake recipes to Greg, for another. Are you supposed to bring a cake now, too, besides the fruit salad and rolls?"

"No, instead of the fruit salad and rolls." Cathy dried her hands on the towel at the sink. "Nadine wanted to serve a lunch, but Mrs. Norton and Olive have decided the guests are likely to stay all afternoon at that rate, so it's going to be just cake and coffee. That's cheaper, quicker, and less bother, Olive says. It's such a complicated message that she was wondering if she shouldn't stop by and explain it all over again in person."

"Tonight?"

Cathy didn't miss the dubious note in her mother's question. "No," she said quickly. "I told her I have a pile of studying to get through tonight, and that I think I understand about the cake fairly well, anyway. And about the gift. This is the fifty-second time, I think, that she has reminded me I'm supposed to bring a gift."

Olive hadn't been too keen on stopping over, anyhow, which helped a lot in dissuading her. Cathy would have had a much tougher job persuading Greg to hold off if the call had really been from him and he had taken it into his head to drop by. The effort of convincing him that she was busy—or ought to be—was often as time-consuming as entering at once into whatever interruption he might be proposing.

Her studying had become somewhat of a rushed affair these last couple of weeks, occasionally receiving no more than a once-over-lightly treatment and a promise to herself to dig in deeper when she reviewed for midsemester exams. Lately, her parents were beginning to voice misgivings about the chunks her outside activities were biting from her normal study hours. Twice in past days her mother had released her from the chore of dishwashing on the grounds that "It will be a bigger help to me to know that you're getting your homework done." Yesterday, her father had said, "Hasn't this wedding crew—or your friend Greg—ever had school nights and study hours explained to them?" There were moments, fleeting ones, when Cathy wondered if she ought not to worry a bit on that score, too, but the problem wasn't really that serious yet. How could it ever be while she carried that wonderful promise in her pocket, reminding her that the future would soon be a treasure box she was free to choose from, not a solitary gem that must be bought with four years' worth of A's?

Saturday, the twenty-ninth of November: that was the date of her next eye examination. The Saturday after Thanksgiving; the last Saturday in November; the one day in this year she was living for. Even on a quiet evening like this, when no call or surprise visit from Greg pulled her away from her desk—Thursday nights Greg and Larry attended a business class at the university—her concentration on textbook material was broken at intervals by "Saturday, the twenty-ninth" wandering through her mind like a scrap of uninvited melody. The different ways of saying it combined themselves into a chant that often rocked her to sleep when she lay in bed at night, and, as often, woke her like the song of a meadowlark in the morning.

But what woke her on Friday morning of this week was the fizz of water running in the bathroom, the smell of coffee perking in the kitchen, and the superbass beat of Mark's radio vibrating the knowledge that she was in for one of her headaches this day. It was a hard, round pea lodged behind her left eye, waiting for her to move.

She groped for the bottle of eyedrops on the night stand. Slow and smooth, that was how to do it. These drops were not so effective as Dr. Rosenthal had intimated they might be, but they brought some relief, if she could get them in while the headache was still young.

"Cathy! Hey, Cathy!" Mark yelled from the foot of the stairs. He had a voice like a boat whistle when he wanted to be heard. "Are you getting up? Mom says breakfast is almost ready."

"Coming," she called automatically, and lay quiet, savoring the anesthetic coolness of the drops beneath her closed eyelids.

Either Mark was not deceived by her answer or he hadn't bothered to listen. His feet thumped the stairs in time to the beat from the radio, and his knuckles hit her door a cheery blow that swung it open. "You're not getting up," he observed, and, at once, was down on his knees, wrestling grunts of delight from Trudy. "Hi, there, old girl. How you doing this morning?"

Cathy turned her head slowly on the pillow, testing. Maybe, with an aspirin now and another later, she could just manage to survive.

"Hey, Cathy?" Mark said suddenly. His voice was a little muffled, as if it were being filtered through Trudy's fur. "They wouldn't take her back, would they? Like if you don't need her any more, I mean?"

Cathy missed a breath between heartbeats. Here was the question she'd been at pains to avoid asking herself. At the end of her training with Trudy, she, like the other students in the class, had signed her name to a promise never to mistreat her dog, sell it, or use it as a prop for begging. There was also a clause that pledged her to return her dog to the school, to be retrained with a new blind master, should death, illness, or restored vision make the services of a guide dog no longer necessary to her. The paper was just words when she signed it, a list of improbabilities too remote to warrant a second thought. Until now.

She sat up and swung her feet to the floor, forgetful of the wisdom of rising in easy, unjarring stages. "Trudy's too old for retraining. She's six, and she'll be even older by the time I've had the operations or treatments or whatever it is the doctor has in mind. They want younger dogs for retraining—two or three or four years old—that have a reasonable amount of working life left for their next owners."

She poked her toes toward Trudy, who lapped them with a wet, soft tongue, as if there could be no possible contradiction to such an argument. No one in his right mind could expect her to hand Trudy over to strangers as if she were a used car or a secondhand footstool.

"Maybe you could just keep on working her," Mark offered. "You could pretend you still *have* to have her. Like lots of kids wear dark glasses just for the heck of it because they like the looks, and you could, too. Who'd know the difference?"

"Maybe I will still need her without pretending." Cathy rubbed her left cheekbone and found the ache had penetrated there, too. "I'm not going to have twenty-twenty vision ever. That's for sure. The doctor said, 'vision enough to count fingers,' and that could mean anything."

She ought to remind herself of that more often. Glaucoma, the disease that had taken her sight, had done it in part by damaging the optic nerve, and she knew both from Dr. Kruger's attempts at explanation and from articles and books she had read on the subject that damage of that sort was irreversible. Whatever miracle Dr. Rosenthal foresaw, her gain was bound to be modest from most points of view. Common sense should hold her imagination back from the wild flights into the impossible that, every now and again, set her pulse to racing.

But what was a modest gain if the point of view was fixed at zero? She turned her face to the window, where the October sun was pouring through the panes in a blaze of heat she could trace with her hands but couldn't even guess at with her eyes. When you started at zero, each degree up the scale was a fantastic gain. Let common sense dictate what it pleased, the truly impossible would be not to believe that she could buy the world with that gold penny in her pocket—a world that included Trudy.

"Anyhow, you can say you've got to have her to get through school. That's no lie." Mark was writhing for the ball Trudy had lost under the dresser yesterday. "Teeth, tail, tongue, toes— She couldn't teach Loony Lenny his t's without you, old girl, could she?"

He gave the ball a toss that sent it, Trudy, and Cathy's head leaping simultaneously.

"Don't call him Loony Lenny," Cathy said, but Mark and Trudy were already out of the room and plunging downstairs in pursuit of the ball.

She began to dress, moving in slow motion for the sake of her head. It was too soon to worry about Trudy, she told herself. Perhaps she wouldn't have to worry at all. Who was to say that the question wouldn't work itself out happily, the same as everything else was doing for her these days?

That "everything" covered Leonard as well. For there were beginning to be flickers of response from Leonard.

She had been disappointed at first in his reaction to the trio of familiar objects she had asked his mother to bring. "I'm afraid these things are a little bulky," Mrs. Perkins had apologized, putting a bulging shopping bag into Cathy's hand. "But they are some of Leonard's real favorites. One is a piece of blue velvet from an old dress of mine, one is a balsam pillow his cousin made at camp a few years ago, and then there's that jar I told you of that used to have mentholated cream in it."

Roddy's contributions were a measuring cup, a toy car, and a stuffed, woolly animal he identified as a cat. He had them spread over the therapy room table before the door was shut, and he was full of the list of things his mother said he had to leave at home—a roll of carpeting, a catcher's mitt, and a real cat. When Cathy suggested they look at Leonard's things, his interest was no less keen, but Leonard had to be retrieved from the greater charms of slapping at his image in the mirror.

"Velvet," she said when she had him seated and the piece of material unfolded in front of him. "How soft and pretty, Leonard."

He let her stroke his hand over the worn nap, but his heels thunked an aimless rhythm against his chair legs, and his hand went to his chin to scratch when it was released.

Next, Cathy fished up the pillow from the shopping bag, if pillow were the correct term for a twelve-inch square of burlap, stuffed rock hard with nubby lumps of balsam. The balsam was real enough, though. She pinched a corner of the pillow and inhaled the spicy north woods fragrance.

"Mmmmm. Doesn't that smell good? Smell it, Leonard. Just like vacation."

Roddy had to smell it, too, and to deliver an approving "Mmmm." Leonard hugged the pillow against his chest and bent his face to the coarse texture of the burlap, then let the pillow drop to the floor and lie there, as if it held no significance whatsoever for him.

Cathy's hopes for anything better from the empty jar were feeble as she set it, still smelling faintly of menthol, on the table. Perhaps this whole idea was a mistake. It could be she was only confusing him by presenting here familiar objects whose meaning for him was tied to his surroundings at home. Perhaps he couldn't recognize them out of context.

Roddy swooped down on the jar for a noisy sniff and

pretended to gag. "Here, Leonard." He shoved it closer. "Ack!"

Leonard giggled, a different sound from his piercing laugh, and repeated Roddy's noisy sniff at the jar. "Mmmm."

Cathy's heart did a mid-beat flip. She had never heard him utter anything but his peculiar laugh and that parakeet burble she had caught on tape.

"Wonderful, Leonard!" She raised the jar to her nose. "Mmmm. Now you."

He bumped his face to the jar and laughed. Cathy went through the sniff and hum routine again for him, but this time he reached to finger her wrist watch, bypassing the jar completely.

Experience had taught her it was no use trying to call him back, once his attention had flitted elsewhere, so she turned her attention to Roddy for a while. At odd intervals during the period, however, she tested the powers of the jar and the pillow again, and twice more she won an "Mmmm" from Leonard. They weren't accidental sounds; they were intentional.

Since then, she had been trying other ways to hold his attention long enough to get him to imitate the sounds she was making. She had outlined her mouth in vivid red so he would watch her lips, had managed to record him so he would hear his own voice, and had searched through the house for more scents and smells that could be bottled and brought to the clinic. He was beginning to grasp the idea. She was almost sure of it. But every time, without fail, just as a triumph seemed about to materialize, he had been distracted by a shadow or the pattern in her skirt or some movement of Roddy's, and the moment was lost.

Today, though, she had one of her father's biggest

handkerchiefs tucked in her clinic briefcase. It was a wild idea that had presented itself out of nowhere while she was writing up her clinic notes last time, but it might just work. Her luck was growing. She could feel it.

And nothing's going to spoil it, she told herself firmly as she paused in the bathroom to swallow an aspirin before going on down to breakfast.

Whether it was the effect of the medication or her confidence, or a combination of the two, or whether she actually was enclosed in the aura of good luck these days, the pain around her eye had dulled to where it was livable by the time she reached the clinic. At least it was dulled enough so that, when she produced the handkerchief in the therapy room and showed it to the boys, she was able to tie it over her eyes without flinching.

"This is a blindfold," she said, in answer to Roddy's question. "I'm going to see how many of our sound things I can tell without looking. Then we'll see how many you can do. Watch me. Watch, Leonard."

She couldn't be sure he was watching, but she made a big display of opening and shutting the array of aromatic jars and cans she had collected for Leonard in past days: vinegar in one, mentholated cream in another, ground coffee in a third, after-shave lotion in a fourth.

"Now it's Leonard's turn," she said.

Leonard was halfway out of his seat, to go investigate something more interesting than what she was doing. She squared him on his chair and fitted the handkerchief across his eyes, knotting it at the back of his round head. His hands went up to touch the blindfold, but he didn't fuss or act dismayed by it, and he didn't try to push it off.

Cathy folded his fingers around the menthol-smelling jar. "Here, sniff. Mmmm."

She covered his hands lightly with hers, to follow his movements as well as to prevent him from dropping the jar. Leonard's style of disposing of an object when he was through examining it was simply to let go of it. He sat hanging on to the jar now, though, as if to shift it or relax his grip would involve risks he didn't dare to take.

She guided the jar to his nose. "Sniff."

He breathed in, then sniffed so hard that he reminded her of Trudy checking the shrubbery for a trace of rabbits. "Mmmm-mmm."

"Good, Leonard! That's good!" It was the most vigorous reaction she'd ever had from him.

She was surprised by a whimper of protest from him as she started to set the jar aside. "More?" she asked. "Do you want more?"

"More," Leonard said.

Cathy's hand froze on the round, squat jar. She couldn't have heard him right. "More" was the name she had been giving the jar ever since it had inspired his first "Mmm," her theory being that, somewhere along the way, he might make the association of sounds and ideas. But she wasn't ready for it to really happen. Perhaps, deep down, she hadn't ever seriously believed it could.

"More, Leonard?" She restored the jar to his hands.

"More," he said, as if he had been saying it all his life.

"Good for you, Leonard! That's good!" It was as much as she could do not to lift him up and whirl him around in a crazy victory dance. "Now let's try the lotion bottle."

The slender bottle of after-shave lotion brought no special response from him. Neither did the old perfume bottle full of the sharp smell of vinegar. But when she put the little muslin sack of ground coffee into his hands, saying, "Coffee," as she did it, he said, "Caff." There was no mistaking the sound, and no one but Dr. Paulus would have doubted its intention.

It was as if a light had gone on for him inside the blindfold. Or it was as if the bandage over his eyes had loosened invisible plugs in his ears, so that, at last, he could listen to the things he heard and begin to sort them out.

She couldn't keep him blindfolded the whole period, of course, although she was strongly tempted. Nothing else had ever kept him sitting this quiet for this long. Even after the blindfold was off, he stayed quiet for a short while, a little dazed perhaps by what had happened. Or perhaps, just perhaps, he was beginning to take notice of the tongue exercises she and Roddy started to do.

Mrs. Perkins was as thrilled as Cathy by the new breakthrough. "We were told not to put too much stock in the fact that he calls me Mama sometimes. They said it could be just gibberish syllables that don't mean anything, but this is different, isn't it? This proves his daddy and I are right, and he can talk some day—thanks to you."

She startled Cathy by planting a quick, dry kiss on her cheek. If Dr. Paulus were in the hall to witness it or were anywhere within earshot, she did nothing to make her presence known.

Cathy felt a pang of longing for Sister Bernard. It

would have been the cherry on the sundae if she could have burst into the office, certain that Sister Bernard was waiting there, willing and delighted to share her excitement to the full. The office welcomed no one any more.

"Dr. P. would say, 'How very nice, Miss Wheeler, but, of course, it's what you are expected to do,' and freeze you right out the door," Karen Bergen said as she and Cathy and Laura Riley headed for the library.

"Wrong," Laura said. "She'd never say 'How very nice' in a million years. Miracles should be standard performance, according to her. She wouldn't waste a pat on the back for anything that ordinary."

But in a way, Dr. Paulus would be right, Cathy realized at the center of the glow that warmed her. Teaching Leonard to talk was what was expected of her. Whether Dr. Paulus had expected that Catherine Wheeler could do it, or whether Catherine Wheeler herself had expected to do it was beside the point. Doing it was a speech therapist's job. But when the miracle happened, to her or to any therapist, it was a miracle, just the same. It couldn't be anything less. Was that perhaps what speech therapy was all about?

The glow was still with Cathy when she and Trudy cut across the campus that afternoon to the bus stop. Bands of sunlight like dusty and warm patches of left-over summer laced the walk, the chilled shadows of the trees slicing through them with the sharpness of a knife blade. Dry leaves capered ahead of her like kittens. Wind licked at her legs, tugged at her coat, and poured an exultant roar into her ears. Had the bus stop been on the far side of the boulevard, the wind would have been more problem than pleasure, drowning as it did the noise of oncoming traffic until the cars were almost upon her, but since she had no need to cross the street, she was free to lift her face to the wind and enjoy its rowdy insistence that, if she tried, she could fly.

She was alone at the bus stop. Probably, she surmised, she was early for the bus she wanted. In a lull between wind gusts, she thought she heard a car pull in to the curb a little beyond her, but she wasn't sure until there was a toot of its horn.

Trudy lunged for a door that snapped open. A voice, anonymous in the wind, called something from inside. Cathy, embarrassed, hauled Trudy back. The voice called again.

"I beg your pardon?" She went closer, bending to hear.

"I said, 'Climb in,' " the voice, still unidentifiable, shouted. When she continued to hesitate, he said, "It's me, Greg."

She and Trudy accepted at once. It took some doing to fold Trudy into the cramped space beneath the sports car's dashboard. "How did you know I'd be standing here at this moment at the bus stop?" Cathy couldn't remember ever detailing for him what her class hours were.

"ESP," Greg answered. "I was slaving over a hot typewriter an hour ago, wondering how I always rate the goody assignments like interviewing the lady with the albino squirrel in her back yard, when, suddenly I heard you calling to me: 'Greg, honey! Greg darling! I want you. I need you. Save me from this deadly grind.' " The car leaped forward like a prancing charger the instant Cathy shut the door, and he dropped his hand on her arm on the pretext of steadying her. "That was you calling, wasn't it?"

Cathy laughed and fastened her seat belt. "Whoever it was, I'd say she goes a bit overboard, wouldn't you?" She had yet to sort out how it was he organized his time—if he did have it organized. He was a part-time student at the university, she knew, and a part-time member of the staff of a small suburban paper, and his aim was to work in public relations one day, but he never seemed too busy at anything to yield to any whim that beckoned him.

"Do you mean you got up from your hot typewriter and walked away just like that?"

"Drove away," he corrected cheerfully. "Who could resist a message like that? I've only quoted you part of it, the mild part. I'll hold you to the rest of it later. But first we're going to fortify ourselves with supper at your house. Your mother's serving sloppy joes."

"Where did you gather that information? More ESP?" Her mother hadn't known herself what the supper menu would be when Cathy left this morning, and no one had been planning on a supper guest. He must have phoned her mother to learn what time Cathy's last class was over, and, in the course of the conversation, he had maneuvered her into inviting him to eat. The invitations her mother issued on her own initiative were generally the product of much forethought and for meals more elaborate than a ground beef concoction on buns. But Greg, Cathy was discovering, had a knack for maneuvering people into concessions that left them astonished at themselves when they paused to think afterward.

"ESP is only part of my talents. No secret is safe from me," he said. "I also have an uncanny ability to see into the future and make predictions. Such as we are about to stop at a bakery in another five minutes to pick up the rolls your mother needs."

"Incredible." Cathy pushed her wind-blown hair into place and grinned at him. "But if you were as good as you claim, you'd know today was no deadly grind. Today one of my patients said his first word for me."

And the best of her secrets, that brightest penny in her pocket, was yet totally unsuspected by his perceptive powers. She wanted him to share in that secret, but, so far, there hadn't been a right time to tell him, and the time for telling had to be right. Somehow it wasn't that easy for her to talk about it, even to her parents. Words would get themselves stuck in her throat and tears would well onto her lashes, no matter how calm and objective she thought she was going to be. It was ridiculous, but that was how things were.

"One word from one patient makes your day?" Greg asked. "Well, whatever turns you on." He touched his finger to her cheek as the car hummed at a stop light. "Me, I like action better than words."

Cathy's laugh was partly to cover the strange currents he knew too well how to wake in her. "Then I'll have to introduce you to Leonard."

"Forget it. Tonight I'm going to introduce you to Dudley Bruce Curtis III. His family owns a couple of hotels in Hawaii, more than a couple, maybe." The car broke away from the light with a surge of enthusiasm.

"And it's my golden opportunity to marry a millionaire?" Cathy asked, prompted by a faint sting at how quickly Leonard had been dismissed from the conversation.

"He's not your type. He's been at the university it must be three years now, and this is the first the guys have been able to talk him into throwing a party. It ought to be a good one, though."

So much for the movie they had talked about seeing tonight, Cathy thought. It was like Greg to want to go where the action was, if there was any. And there was no denying that, if Greg was there, there was usually some kind of action.

She smiled at him in spite of herself. If there were drawbacks to never knowing what they were about to do until he told her, there was also something exciting. Besides, remembering Leonard, she thought perhaps she was in the mood for a party tonight.

It was a party in the basement of a fraternity house, she learned, when she and Greg descended the steps into a roar of voices and tape-recorded music that evening. The noise bulged out to swallow them into itself the instant they came through the door, making her ears next to useless for gleaning any further information about her surroundings. Dudley Bruce Curtis III shouted what she took to be a welcome when Greg introduced him and she shouted a courteous reply, but she wouldn't know him again if she were to meet him on her own front doorstep. His voice, like that of everyone else, was anonymous in the general din. Her only real contact with the details around her was the brush of someone's sleeve against her hand, the dented table corner she clung to when Greg disappeared temporarily, the perfume of the girl who paused beside her to exchange a few shouted exclamations about the music, the sticky slosh-over of the paper cup of beer that was thrust into her hand from somewhere, and Greg's touch on her arm as he guided her to another part of the room, his hand leading her into the dancing, his arm keeping her close. There was nothing anonymous in Greg's way of touching her. Possibly that was why, even when reminders of her morning's headache began to vibrate through her head, she went on believing herself happy to be here.

I wonder if that's the effect Pete has on Joan, she thought afterward, kneeling on her bedroom floor to make peace with Trudy, who resented having been left home tonight and was saying so in whimpers and little reproachful yips. She rubbed her cheek against Trudy's head, murmuring, "Hush, hush," and wondering if Pete would put in an appearance at Joan's shower tomorrow, wondering how two people could be sure that what they felt was love.

She was still wondering as she sat on a straight-backed dining room chair in a corner of the Norton living room the next afternoon, listening to the chatter of a dozen women, most of whom she didn't know, and sipping from a cup of coffee that she didn't want. "Would you rather have coffee or tea?" Olive had asked her, and when Cathy said tea, had brought her coffee anyway.

Cathy was nominally one of the hostesses, but, as Olive had pointed out at the beginning, "All you have to do is chip in on the refreshments and bring a gift, of course." She had also mentioned once in passing, "We thought at first of having everyone at your house, but it will be so much more convenient at Aunt Lydia's. For one thing, there won't be all that carting of gifts back and forth. If they give them to Joan at home, they'll be there. And there'll be a carload of gifts, if everybody comes."

Cathy smiled vaguely and inclined her head toward a cluster of Joan's aunts and cousins, as if she were being included in their clucking inspection of a boxed assortment of towels and a kitchen canister set. The guest list was composed almost entirely of aunts and cousins, it seemed, none of whom troubled to pass to her any of the boxes that were being handed around to show off the gifts.

Cathy took another swallow of her coffee. It was lukewarm and bitter, but a furtive sweep of her arm to the right and left disclosed no table or stand on which she could set the cup. The choice was either to go on balancing a full cup or to drain it. Never mind. She could picture herself a year from now, charting the furniture in a strange room at a glance and strolling over to look at whatever she pleased without waiting for aid from anyone. Would it be, perhaps, at her own bridal shower?

"Here comes the bride, here comes the bride!" Joan's laugh hit high C as she did a twirl in the center of the room, her voice spiraling around her. "What I'd like to see is the groom," said one of the aunts. "Is Pete coming?"

"Not to a hen party like this. He wouldn't be caught dead," Joan told her. "I wanted him to be here at the start, to see me act surprised, but he wouldn't. He'll be here tonight to check the loot, but—" her voice took on a pout—"I don't know if I'll be speaking to him by then."

"That's the ticket, Joanie," applauded an aunt or cousin through a mouthful of cake. "You teach him that when you say 'Step,' you mean it."

Cathy downed the last of her coffee, oddly disappointed. She had been counting on seeing Pete and Joan together more than she realized. But why? She couldn't seriously be hoping for a revelation from them about how to judge whether love was real—real enough to pledge the rest of your life to it.

"Pete's mother got him taught already. That's my problem. Mrs. Sheridan hates me. She always has," Joan said, sounding not in the least disturbed. "Isn't that right, Cathy?"

"Mrs. Sheridan? Are you sure?" Cathy's memory searched back through back yard wiener roasts at the Sheridans, Halloween and Christmas parties in their recreation room, and impromptu gatherings around sheets of fresh cookies in their kitchen. "I thought Mr. and Mrs. Sheridan always treated any friends of Pete like members of the family. They seemed to like everybody. Or anyway, they did when they lived near us."

"That was before any of Pete's friends was going to be a member of the family," Olive said. She was crackling the tissue paper and gift wrap the gifts had come in, her intention being, Cathy gathered, to salvage the best for re-use at some future time.

"I'm not going to be a member of Pete's family," Joan declared. "He's going to be a member of mine. He has to forsake his father and mother and cleave unto me." She performed another twirl that staggered her into Cathy's chair and would have spilled Cathy's coffee on them both if any had been left. "Besides, Pete and I aren't friends. We're lovers."

There was a horrified gasp from one side of the room, a whinny of laughter from another, and an indignant "Joan!" from Mrs. Norton.

"Pay no attention to her," Olive said above the rustle of tissue paper. "She's been hysterical ever since she got that diamond on her finger."

Cathy sighed and slowly revolved the empty cup on her knee for want of something better to do. This wasn't the first time that she'd received the peculiar impression that Pete Sheridan as a person didn't exist; he was only a name tacked onto a featureless abstraction like "man."

"I may be hysterical," Joan said, "but I don't run up and offer guys free dry cleaning the same day I meet them. Look at her blush! Nadine, Mummie, Aunt Agnes, look at Olive turning red!"

"Ho, ho!" Olive's gift wrap had stopped its rustling. "All I did was tell the ushers they could have their suits for the wedding cleaned at our place. I thought I was doing you a favor."

"But you hoped you were doing *you* a favor," Nadine said, and Cathy was surprised at how easily that whispery voice carried above the buzz of other talk in the room. "You're angling to get Steve. All those devious questions to find out if he was married or engaged!"

"In case you're interested, Cathy," Joan said, leaning over the back of Cathy's chair but obviously speaking for Olive's benefit, "he is not. I asked him point-blank. That's the bride's privilege with other men. And he says he remembers you."

"That's nice of him," Cathy said. "Who?" Not that there were dozens of Steves who might be expected to remember her, but she wasn't about to offer herself as a target alongside Olive by leaping to conclusions.

"Who? Steve Hubert, that's who. I must have told you he's in town again, didn't I? His brother happens to be the assistant pastor at our church, and Steve's staying with him for the time being. Pete invited him to be an usher."

"But Olive thinks he's the best man," Nadine inserted.

This witticism provoked shrieks of mirth from every quarter. The shrills reminded Cathy of a flock of jays she had once heard heckling a sleepy owl. Only Olive did not remind her of a sleepy owl.

Cathy smiled benignly at her and directed her wish to Steve. "All I can say is, 'Lots of luck.' "

She hadn't ever met Steve's brother. He was away studying for the ministry during the time she and Steve had been dating—if dating were the proper term for a relationship that was more like the companionable chumming of two buddies than the heart-throbbing romance Joan had evidently been describing it to be. Cathy's memory of those days was a hazy mixture of rambling in spring woods together, hiking along the country roads, munching popcorn on a winter evening and discussing what might be the limits of outer space, tramping the lake shore in the summer and early fall and coaxing Trudy into the water to swim with them. As a matter of fact, Trudy had always received as much of Steve's attention as he gave to Cathy, which had seemed only right and natural at the time.

Poor Steve. The prospect of seeing him again did add a fillip of interest to the wedding, but what a boyish fellow he was compared to the sophistication of Greg. And if Olive had her mark on him, Steve and Cathy weren't likely to be allowed much opportunity for renewing old acquaintances.

Cathy let her mind slip back to Greg. What a contrast between this dreary afternoon and the vibrant world she had moved through last night!

"Why do you go to that stupid shower tomorrow?"

Greg had asked while they lingered over saying good night. "Come with me for the afternoon. I'll promise you a lot more fun than you're going to have there."

"I know, but I have to go to it." She had stirred in a halfhearted attempt to draw away from him and open the car door to get out. "I'm square, I guess." That was his stock accusation when he wanted to tease her.

"Square as a cement block," he had murmured against her hair, not letting her go. "That's what scares me. What happens when a guy that lives it a day at a time stubs his toe on something as permanent as a cement block—and likes it?"

That was a far piece from being a proposal of marriage, but it was the closest either of them had come to hinting that their relationship might be growing serious. What would she answer if he did propose? How would it feel to be standing in Joan's shoes and to know that, in three weeks, you would be committing yourself to another person for the rest of your life? How could you be sure you had chosen the right one? Plainly, no one was going to shed light on those questions for her at this engagement shower.

"Well, then, Olive," one of the aunts was saying, "you'd better start practicing to catch the bride's bouquet. There's not much time left."

Nadine chortled. "She's waiting for him to come get dry cleaned. And she's not too happy about the fact that he used to date Cathy."

Cathy rearranged herself within the confines of her chair's right angles and pretended not to hear. Surely this party must be drawing to an end. It would have been such a relief to pick up Trudy's harness, make some excuse about the time, and leave for home. It was seven blocks from the Nortons' house to home, a comfortable distance for her and Trudy to hike on a crisp afternoon. But Trudy wasn't here, thanks once more to Olive.

"There'll be so many people at the shower who aren't used to pets," Olive had informed Cathy on the phone, "and it will be so crowded, she might get stepped on. I'm picking you up and driving you home, so you won't want her, anyway."

Pets! As if Trudy were of no greater importance than a goldfish. And as if Cathy's right to move freely had been forfeited long ago. Olive might be due for a surprise one of these days, and part of it would be that Trudy would always be important, whatever the changes might be that lay beyond the next horizon.

"Look how quiet Cathy is," Joan directed everyone. "I'll bet you're going to have to move fast, Olive. I'll bet she's figuring how to get Steve back."

Cathy grinned reluctantly. There was no way to convince them, not even if she followed Joan and Pete right up to the altar with Greg. "No, I have no claims on Steve. And I'm not too good at catching thrown bouquets."

Not too good yet, a secret voice amended. But one of these days, one of these days—

"It's the bride who decides who catches the bouquet," Joan said, "and that's me. You girls all better treat me right. There's only three weeks left to go, and then—" she was off again on a staggering whirl around the room—"all my worries will be over."

Cathy set her coffee cup on the floor beneath her chair and joined in the spatter of applause for the performance—for suddenly she knew how it would feel to be counting off each day you had to live through until The Day arrived. It would feel the same as counting off the days to live through between now and Saturday, November twenty-ninth.

7

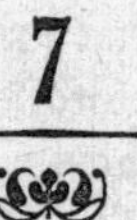

"THE DAYS DWINDLE down to a precious few: September, October, November . . ."

Cathy straightened with a guilty start in her corner of the pew, aware that she had been humming the song under her breath. A vocalist had been crooning it from the TV set when the Nortons arrived to take her along to the wedding rehearsal this evening, and the tune had been repeating itself in her head ever since. September, October, November . . .

She wedged herself more erect in the corner of the pew and planted her feet flat on the floor, to reduce the temptation to toe-tap the rhythm of the tune. If the choice had been hers, she would be sitting a few rows farther to the rear, but Mrs. Norton had marched her to the front pew and thrust her against it with the admonition, "Sit here, Cathy," and here she sat, trying not to hear more of the heated discussion in the aisle than was absolutely necessary. That meant she was obliged to hear most of it, for the Norton women, cousins included, possessed a penetrating quality of voice that even the hushing influence of being inside a church did little to diminish.

". . . Paying a pretty penny for this wedding," Mrs. Norton was declaring, "and we're not laying it out for a circus spectacle that will make everybody think we're too ignorant to know what's right."

"But we told you before," Joan protested. "We told you how we were planning the ceremony. Why is it such a shock now?"

"It's not unheard of for the bride to enter the church on the groom's arm instead of her father's," put in the minister. "We encourage innovations by the wedding couple if it makes the ceremony more personal and meaningful—"

"A sacred ceremony in a sacred place," Mrs. Norton interrupted him, "that's what's meaningful, isn't it? I never thought to hear you say you could change sacred things around to suit yourself, Dr. Schoenberg."

So the minister was Dr. Schoenberg. Cathy had been fairly sure he wasn't Steve's brother, Walter Hubert, but no one had bothered to perform introductions of any kind in any direction so far. Apparently, Steve wasn't here either, unless Olive had him off somewhere, offering him bargains in dry cleaning. But no, there was Olive in the center aisle, responding to a low reply from the minister, or possibly a mutter from Pete.

"What I want to know is, if this is the sort of wedding it's going to be, why did we have to go to the expense of buying special dresses and all? Why didn't you let us wear blue jeans and look really like hippies?"

The pew shuddered a little, and Nadine settled herself beside Cathy to whisper, "Olive's fit to spit tacks. She has to walk down the aisle with the best man if Joan comes in with Pete, and he's two inches shorter than she is. In those high heels tomorrow, she'll look like a giraffe with a pygmy."

Cathy couldn't muster much sympathy for Olive in regard to the spike-heeled sandals the bridesmaids would have to wear tomorrow. They were uncomfortable, as well as out of style, but Olive had insisted on their purchase because they were cheaper by twenty-nine cents than any others she had seen in visits to a total of five stores.

The best man was Chuck Sheridan, Pete's cousin from the northern part of the state. Mrs. Norton had consented to sharing that much information in the car. He was older than Pete, married, and the father of the toddler Cathy could hear banging her heels and occasionally conversing in one of the rear pews—three more counts on which Olive might be ready to spit tacks.

"What are the other groomsmen like? The ones we walk with?" Cathy whispered, more to keep conversation alive than because she was dying of curiosity. "Who are they?"

"One's Mac and one's Andy something. School friends of Pete, I guess, or from the army. They're okay. I picked Mac for mine." Nadine's giggle hinted that she foresaw more than just parading the length of the aisle for herself and Mac.

Cathy smiled at her from the security of not having to care whether Mac and Andy were okay or not. "Then don't you hand me any garbage about having to study on Sunday," Greg had said when she explained to him that tonight would have to be spent rehearsing and at the dinner that followed and that she would be tied up all day tomorrow with the wedding and reception. "We're not going to let this whole weekend be shot."

She could sustain herself through tonight and tomorrow by thinking ahead to Sunday.

"They must be army buddies," she murmured. "I don't remember any Andy or Mac from school."

When Nadine failed to answer, Cathy leaned toward her a little, supposing her murmur had been too low. "Are they here now?"

But Nadine was no longer beside her. She had risen from the pew much more lightly than she had dropped onto it, and Cathy was left talking earnestly to empty air. It was the type of blunder that mortified her more than any other, but there was no help for it now, except to dig into her purse as if she'd really been muttering to herself about some item inside she couldn't find, and to hope no one had been watching too closely. One of these days, she would be able to do her own watching, and such embarrassments would be a thing of the past. In twenty-nine days more, to be exact. Tomorrow was November first. *And the days dwindle down* . . .

"What's the use of being the bride if I can't do anything my way?" Joan demanded in a piercing quaver, halfway between wail and whimper.

"So let's quit arguing and do it." It was Pete, using a drill sergeant's voice that topped the others. "Okay, everybody. Come on. Let's get this thing moving."

"Now wait. Not so fast," Mrs. Norton began, but she was doused by an instant bumping of hips and knees against pews, a scuffle of feet on the marble floor, and a rumble of agreement that had a distinctly masculine cast to it.

Wire fingers bit into Cathy's elbow, identifying Olive before she spoke. "Stand up and turn to your right. We're going to rehearse. Andy, you take her."

She propelled Cathy, stumbling, into a pair of

sweaterclad arms that quickly became a rather sweaty hand circling her forearm, midway between elbow and wrist.

"Hello, Andy," Cathy said, catching her breath and her balance in the same gulp. "I'm Cathy."

"Right."

This was an acknowledgment, not a direction, she discovered, for he proceeded to steer her straight ahead along the aisle, like a shopping cart.

"It'll be easier walking if you let me take your arm," she suggested. "It will look nicer, more natural, too."

He shoved her onward without a sign of having heard. His fingers tightened automatically when she tried to slip her arm from their grip. She stifled a temptation to ask if he were an army M.P., accustomed to marching criminals off to justice. Very likely Olive's finesse in delegating responsibility had so unnerved him that it would be a while before anything could get through to his understanding again.

"Now, whichever way you decide on," Dr. Schoenberg was instructing everyone when she and Andy reached the group collected at the far end of the aisle, "this young lady—Nadine, is it?—and this gentleman will lead the way. Next, you, sir," he turned to Andy, "and this young lady. Like this."

He deftly released Cathy's arm from its shackles, and tucked her hand over the cuff of Andy's shoved-up sleeve. "There. That's fine."

Cathy and her partner paced up the aisle after Nadine and Mac without a stumble. At the front of the church, Andy delivered her to Nadine's side and silently retired to his place beside Mac. Then came Olive and Chuck, spaced half the aisle ahead of the bride and groom.

"And looking like you wouldn't believe!" Nadine tittered. "Her chin is right at the top of his ear, and she's scowling like maybe she'll bend down and take a bite. It's too funny."

"It looks horrible," was how Olive expressed it. "It's too much of the same thing. Just couple after couple after couple marching in. People are going to be watching for the bride to come in, even after you get right up in front, Joan, because it looks like nothing but bridesmaids."

"Can't they tell by the dress?" asked a tired voice from a nearby pew.

Cathy was puzzled for a moment to identify him. Then she realized he must be Mr. Norton, the father of the bride. He was such a quiet man that she had heard him speak barely half a dozen times in all the years she had known Joan. He hadn't offered a word this evening in the car. She wondered if he were voting to champion his daughter or to spare himself from having to be part of the spectacle.

"Anybody who doesn't know I'm the bride hasn't been listening," Joan said with disconcerting frankness. "I've certainly been telling everyone. I think it's beautiful, Pete and me coming in together. It says that we're sure of each other and what we're doing."

"It looks more like you're scared he'll duck out a side door and escape if you don't hang on to him every minute," Olive said. "It looks like you're having to drag him to the altar."

An amazingly loud "haw haw" of laughter burst from Nadine's whispery throat, accompanied by guffaws from at least two of the groomsmen, if not all three. "How about that, Pete?" one of them asked. Cathy didn't know which one, for she hadn't heard enough of them to sort out voices yet. "She's got the situation pegged, Sheridan," said another, and the laughter boomed.

"Stop it! Stop it this instant, I say." Mrs. Norton's hands slapped together with a crack like the snapping of a whip. "This is the Lord's house. If you can't behave like civilized Christians, you can all leave, every one of you. I'll wash my hands of this whole business."

"Promises, promises," came a corner-of-the-mouth mutter from someone. Cathy was almost certain it was Pete. And suppressed laughter gurgled here and there, like liquid in a corked bottle.

"Stop it!" It was Joan this time, hurling herself up from the front pew to stamp her foot. "You're spoiling everything. You're spoiling my wedding."

"Joan, for heaven's sake, act your age," Olive said coldly. "Don't go getting hysterical."

"And why don't you broom off to the place you usually haunt on Halloween? We'll call you when we need you," Pete said.

Cathy pressed her hands against a table behind her. Pete had always hated scenes. He would sulk rather than fight, if things didn't go his way when they were children, but that didn't mean he couldn't be provoked at last into action. And once that happened, he didn't care what got smashed.

"Well! Thank you!" exploded from Olive. "Peter!" Mrs. Norton cried. "Oh, Pete!" mourned Mrs. Sheridan from a spot somewhere to the left of the controversy.

Joan let out a scream that only when Cathy's heart faltered back to its normal rhythm did she recognize as laughter.

After that, there were too many voices saying too many things, and too many people milling in every direction at once for her to separate any of it into sense. She shrank tighter against the table, her hands mooring her there. The commotion surged around and by her without anyone troubling to explain what was happening —and she was just as glad not to have to know. This couldn't be typical of wedding rehearsals. It couldn't be.

"Take careful notes," Amy had teased her at lunch today. "The way things are shaping up between you and Greg, who can say when it will be handy to have a list of the do's and don'ts? I might like to borrow it myself, if Larry proposes just one more time."

"Weddings are for mothers," Monica had said. "Take my advice and save yourself a lot of grief: elope."

At the time, Cathy had thought Monica was referring to Amy's chances of marrying Larry if her mother got into the act. Amy's mother had only just tumbled to the fact that there was such a person as Larry, and she had yet to realize how important he was becoming in Amy's plans for the future, but, unless this romance were made of sterner stuff than any of Amy's previous ones, its days were numbered. Everyone hoped but no one—perhaps not even Amy herself, deep down—believed the pattern would be broken.

Now, though, Cathy wondered, shuddering, if Monica, who had two married brothers and a married sister, might not have been speaking from observations of weddings in general. Imagine Greg here as the groom, pressured into snarling at the bridesmaids, and herself, the bride, shouting reproaches at his friends. How could two people go off and live happily ever after together following a beginning like that? But it was impossible that they would have a beginning like this, she and Greg. For one thing, under no circumstances would her mother ever behave like Mrs. Norton. Surely, Greg's mother wouldn't, either—if Greg had a mother.

There was a startling thought. She slid her hands along the table edge behind her, easing herself farther from where Dr. Schoenberg was saying, "Joan, Peter, will you come with me for a minute?" She couldn't recall Greg's ever mentioning a mother to her. He had spoken once of his father, she remembered, saying gleefully it would drive his father up the wall, "If he knew I was driving a sports job like this on the salary I make." But that was the extent of background information on himself he had ever volunteered. He might be one of ten brothers and sisters and have uncles, aunts, and cousins that he reckoned up by dozens, or he might be a solitary motherless child, neglected by his father, for any clue she had. She didn't even know if he hailed from a farm, a city, or a suburb, or if this was his home state. Those were details that somehow had never entered their conversations or their thinking. It was curious how little you needed to know about a person in order to feel you knew him very well.

It was curious, too, how you could know everything about a person, as she used to about Pete, and find on meeting him again that you were strangers. "Oh, hi!" was all he had dredged up to say to her during the time he and Joan and the Nortons and Cathy had waited on the church steps this evening for the rest of the wedding party to arrive, and that scrap of communication was only at Joan's prompting, "Aren't you going to say hello to your old friend and neighbor Cathy?" "Hi, Pete, how are you?" had been Cathy's uninspired contribution. There was nothing more either of them had to say, then or since. The reason was partly, of course, that Pete was preoccupied and nervous in his role of groom, but a bigger part of it was that they didn't know each other any more, and that neither of them cared.

Someone tapped her lightly on the shoulder. "Would you like to take a seat for a while? It looks like things may be held up for a few minutes here."

It was a voice she thought she knew from somewhere, but she couldn't quite fit it to a name. Mac, perhaps? Or Andy? Or Chuck? No, not Chuck, for the arm he was offering her belonged to someone fairly tall. Not Andy, either, for this man was wearing a coat instead of a sweater, and his muscles weren't bunched taut with nervous strain as Andy's had been.

"Thanks," she said, deciding to postpone calling him Mac until the evidence was stronger, just the same. "That's a fine idea."

They skirted the knot of voices wrestling in semi-whispers and crossed to a side aisle. This was a narrower passage than the center aisle, but he brought her along it without any fuss and without grazing her knuckles against the wall. Whoever he was, he was the first person she had felt relaxed with since Mrs. Norton had marched up to the house to collect her.

"How will this do?" he asked, putting her hand on the back of a pew. "You're about four rows from the front."

"This is fine. Thanks." She smiled at him and moved in a little way, wondering if he meant to sit out the storm here, too, and rather hoping that he did. If he would say just a few words more, she was almost certain this vague sense of knowing him would crystallize into a name and identity.

"Cathy, there you are!" Olive's footsteps were clacking in rapid pursuit down the aisle. "I forgot there was nobody taking care of you. How nice of you, Steve, to step in and help her."

Steve . . . Cathy couldn't tell whether the chill that stiffened her smile was born of Olive's neat reduction of her to infant status or her own lack of perception in nearly calling an old friend by a stranger's name. But was the mistake altogether her fault or was there a subtle change in the voice she remembered, or thought she remembered? He *is* a stranger, she told herself, the same as Pete. And so am I.

"Well, go ahead, sit down, Cathy," Olive prompted. "We'll be back for you when Dr. Schoenberg is ready to rehearse again."

"It's a nice, roomy pew. Why don't we all sit down right here?" Steve suggested. "Unless maybe they need you up front for consultation."

"Me? No, thank you. I'm keeping my nose strictly out of that affair." Olive's laugh had a delicate shudder in it. "But I was glancing over the book rack a while ago, and there's one there I'd really like to have, only I don't know how to go about paying for it. I was hoping that, since you're the brother of the assistant pastor, you'd know what to do without bothering Dr. Schoenberg, and you'd come and show me."

Steve couldn't gracefully refuse. Cathy didn't know whether he would have wanted to if he could. She smoothed her skirt beneath her and sat listening to the departing footsteps, to the creaks and thumps of other people shifting in other pews, to the scattering of guarded voices, and thinking again: we're strangers. I'm a stranger here among strangers, a convenient body for evening out the wedding procession but not a real person to anyone. I don't belong here. I'm simply killing time, waiting . . .

Waiting . . . It was an odd sensation, like floating disembodied between two worlds, this alien one where she went through motions imposed on her by its local peculiarities, and the right one in which she would be set free as light when she reached it. It was a dreamlike feeling that wrapped her into itself at times—even once or twice when Greg was kissing her—with an insistence that only such a heat shield could have long resisted. Waiting . . . Waiting for the days to become a precious few . . . September . . . October . . . November . . .

How soon before November would be here? Cathy touched the dial of her watch. Six-thirty. In five and a half more hours it would be November first. Then November second, third, fourth, seventh . . . fourteenth . . . twenty-first . . . twenty-ninth . . .

"Cathy." It was Olive again, stooping above her like a kindergarten teacher directing a slow learner. "We're going to do a run-through of the traditional procession. Slide across the pew to the other end and I'll get Andy or somebody to pick you up."

For an instant longer, Cathy sat immobile. Not a muscle in her body would consent to move. But why waste energy resenting things and people who didn't really matter? I'm only marking time here, she reminded herself, and slowly she stood up.

"Or you could just step out into the aisle here and walk around like anybody else." Steve's hand cupped her elbow, drawing her out beside him. "I'll do the best I can to fill in for my old pal Trudy. How come you didn't bring her tonight?"

"A dog in a church?" Olive shrilled. She had somehow become wedged behind him and Cathy, and she was nearly treading on Cathy's heels.

"Why not?" Steve asked. "I understand Dr. Schoenberg's cat attends the eleven o'clock service every Sunday during the summer, when the doors are open and the sun hits that back pew. Trudy's no stranger to the inside of a church, either, if I remember correctly."

"That's true," Cathy nodded, "but she's not a member of the wedding party." She was beginning to think, however, that she might have cause to be glad Steve Hubert was.

"That's all we'd need," Olive said, inserting herself between them as they rounded the corner into the wider space leading behind the last pew to the center aisle. She unhooked Cathy from Steve's arm as if she were removing a coat from a hanger. "This wedding's going to be bizarre enough if Joan has her way, without adding a dog to it."

It became quickly evident, though, that Joan wasn't likely to have her way. Under the minister's brisk, concise directives, the procession formed as before, only, this time, Olive stalked in solitary splendor ahead of the bride and her father while Pete and Chuck waited up in front. They went through it twice more in that fashion, no one saying much until Joan suddenly burst into tears.

"It's my wedding and nobody will listen to me. Not even you. You won't listen. At least you ought to be on my side."

"Who knows any more what side is yours?" Pete asked. He was speaking low but the words had an angry impact that jarred the hush in the church. "First you want it your way, then it's okay the way your mother wants, and then you and she are both yakking at me about different things and everybody else is chiming in— Make up your mind right now: which way is it going to be? Because that's the way it is going to be. I'm leaving for the steak house in five minutes."

"I don't think you even care," Joan accused.

Her mother said, "This is my daughter's wedding, and it is going to be a nice wedding, Peter Sheridan, whether you like it or not."

Pete ignored them. "Come on, everybody. You might as well get your coats and start over to the steak house. We'll give you the decision at dinner."

Murmurs of "Good idea," "Sure, why don't we do that?" and "Maybe that would be best" swelled around and past Cathy in an immediate surge toward the doors. She wondered if she were about to be left stranded again, this time beside the choir seats, but Olive was there almost before the thought was formed, moving her along at a rate that demonstrated clearly there was no need for Steve to feel he must perform another rescue.

It was Olive's fault they were delayed at the coat rack. She had to search among all the hangers twice for a missing scarf, fuming the while at Nadine for having probably snatched it up as her own without looking. Nadine was already outside—as was almost everyone else—by the time Olive discovered that the rag she'd been kicking farther under the rack at every step was actually the scarf in question.

Car doors were slamming emphatically up and down the street when she and Cathy descended the half-dozen steps in front of the church. One car roared away from the curb like an ascending jet, and a second took off after it, a moment later.

Olive stopped dead still. "That was Aunt Lydia and Uncle Norman. You're supposed to ride with them, but they went off without waiting for you." She turned, scanning the array of cars that remained. "I guess I'll have to put you in with Joan and Pete."

Cathy stuffed her free hand into the depths of her coat pocket, wondering if Olive worked at constructing awkward situations for people or if it were a natural aptitude with her that operated like breathing. Surely among the four or five cars still here, all of them headed for the same destination for the rehearsal dinner, there must be room for an extra passenger elsewhere than in the one carrying the quarreling bride and groom.

"You can hunt up a ride for me, too, while you're at it," Joan said, cutting across in front of them on the sidewalk. She raised her voice. "Does anybody have room for me?"

"What are you talking about?" Olive demanded. "You're riding with Pete."

"I am not riding with Pete." Never had Joan enunciated more distinctly. "Steve, do you have room for me? I want to ride with someone I can trust."

A car door banged. Tires squealed. The car rocketed off up the street, leaving behind the angry smell of scorched rubber. Cathy would have known without a fresh burst of tears from Joan that it was Pete and that he had departed alone.

"My car's over here," Steve said.

Cathy jumped. She hadn't known he was standing on the steps just above her. He touched her sleeve as he came down to sidewalk level.

"Would you like to come, too, Cathy? You're looking for a ride, aren't you?"

It was Olive's turn to jump. Her grip tightened on Cathy's arm. "No, listen. I'll let her and Nadine go together in my car. I'll give Nadine my keys." Her tone became a solicitous coo. "Then you and I can look after Joanie."

Cathy was willing to agree. Under present conditions, Joan and Steve appealed to her as companions for a ride hardly more than Joan and Pete had. She was given no chance to voice her opinion, however.

Joan twisted a sob into a snort. "I couldn't think of asking you for such a sacrifice, Olive. You've done so much already." She thrust her arm through Cathy's on the other side and pulled. "Let's go."

Olive followed them to Steve's car, not quite releasing her hold on Cathy until Steve unlocked the doors. Even then, she suggested it might be better if Joan had the front seat and Cathy sat in the back, and offered again to go along. Joan's reply was to climb into the back seat and shut the door in her face.

So there were only the three of them in the car as it swung away from the church, and the interior was as uncomfortably crowded as Cathy had known it would be. Joan sniffled and swallowed and blew her nose and sniffled again.

"The Chisholm Steak House on Hawthorne Road—that's where we're supposed to be going, isn't it?" Steve asked when they had driven a few blocks.

"That's not where I'm going," Joan sniffed. "I want to go home."

Cathy turned to lean over the back of the seat. "Joan—" She couldn't think of anything else to say.

"Just leave me alone," Joan snapped, and returned to her handkerchief. "Just—leave me alone."

That pretty well established silence among them. Cathy readjusted her seat belt and turned her face to the window, wishing Greg were here. Greg's feelings about silence were the same as Nature's about a vacuum: he abhorred it. He would have the radio blaring by now and chatting to her and Joan as if nothing were the matter, not caring whether he always got an answer or not, so long as the emptiness was filled. In fact, if Greg were here, there probably wouldn't be anything the matter. He would have taken it as a personal challenge to befriend Pete, sweet-talk Joan, flatter Mrs. Norton, and manage Olive into some kind of compromise before everything fell apart. That is, if the fireworks hadn't spurred him to fan the flames instead, for the joy of keeping the action lively.

The car slowed for a corner. The turn signals clicked. Joan blew her nose. And the silence thickened.

Cathy considered asking Steve to switch on the radio, but it was very possible his car didn't boast one. Steve, she remembered, didn't mind interludes of quiet in his day. He was the type who grew restless near air conditioners, preferred sails and canoeing to motorboats, and would think of bringing a dining room table sooner than a portable record player to a picnic on the beach. How had they kept from being bored to insensibility when they used to go together, she wondered.

Without warning, Joan hurled herself forward against the front seat. "Don't stop. Go right on through. Hurry! Don't slow down."

"The light's red," Steve said calmly. "I'll have to stop."

"No you won't. It's about to change. Go through! Go through!" Joan leaned farther into the front, her elbow digging into Cathy's shoulder. "There, it's green. Go!"

"What's wrong?" Cathy asked. Common sense told her it couldn't be serious or Steve would be more worried, but the blast of a car horn beside them set her heart racing anyway.

"Don't look at him. Let him pass us," Joan commanded, every trace of sob and sniffle gone. "He thinks he's so smart. Turn at this next corner, if he goes straight ahead."

The horn-blowing car zoomed past them, its horn still blatting, but Cathy decided it was futile to ask more questions at this point. Joan's elbow continued to peg her shoulder to the back of the seat until Steve wheeled the car to the right, into a side street. That accomplished, Joan flung herself back where she belonged and gave her nose a quick, final blow.

Cathy slid her hand inside her coat to rub what was undoubtedly going to be too huge a bruise to be covered by pumpkin satin sleeves tomorrow. Provided, of course, there would be any occasion for wearing pumpkin satin tomorrow.

The car went on bearing right, its speed considerably reduced, she noted. "Where are we?"

"Crescent Park, I think it's called," Steve said. "It's shaped something like a watermelon slice. Keller Street, the street we were just on, is the straight side, and now we're on the drive that forms the crescent."

"Do you have to drive so slow?" Joan asked. "I meant for you to turn left back there. We could have got to the freeway. But if he saw us—" She interrupted herself with a shriek. "There he is! He must have come in from the other end. Don't let him stop us."

A car horn blared in front of them, sharp and peremptory. To Cathy, it sounded as if the oncoming car were rushing at them head on. A quick blast from Steve's horn shot her hands toward the dashboard to brace for a collision.

"Sorry," Steve said. His voice was terse, no pretense of casualness now.

He veered farther right and put on the brakes. The other car roared by, screeching to a halt behind them.

"Somebody's got to give in," he said to Joan's wail of protest, "and I'd rather do it this side of the morgue."

"Lock the doors. He's not getting in here," Joan cried, flinging herself from one side of the car to the other in a frantic race to press buttons.

The other car growled into reverse and halted again, beside them. Its engine went on chugging like a winded runner. A door snapped open.

Steve rolled down his window, and Pete's voice jabbed in at them. "Come on."

"No." But Joan's firmness was wobbly. "No."

"I said, 'Come on.' "

Cathy had never heard Pete use such a velvety tone. She could almost believe he was smiling, but if he was, it was a smile she wasn't sorry not to see.

"Leave me alone," Joan said.

Pete tried the door from outside. "Joan, open up. Get out."

Joan began to cry once more. Pete's sleeve rubbed the window frame as he reached in and unsnapped the rear lock. The door opened, and Joan climbed out.

"Thanks, Steve," Pete said, and closed the door. "We'll see you later."

Footsteps scuffed on the pavement. Then the door of the other car closed. The engine chug became a hum, and the car moved away down the parkway at a not unreasonable speed.

Cathy inhaled the frosty air spreading in through Steve's window. There was a cold dampness in it, as if rain might not be far off, but it smelled clean and uncluttered.

Steve switched off his engine. "What do you say we

give them a few minutes' head start? Or maybe it'll be too chilly just sitting here. Would you rather cruise around for a while?"

"To be perfectly frank, I think I'd rather walk the rest of the way." She tried to put a laugh into the words, but the result contained a flutter she hadn't intended.

"I can't say I blame you. That kid stuff isn't my favorite brand of fun and games, either. That's why I wanted to get onto some street quieter than Keller before I pulled over. Although, if it helps any, Pete wasn't shaving the margin as thin as it probably sounded."

Cathy frowned. She would have expected him to be tolerantly amused, if not fully sympathetic, toward Pete's desperate bid for reconciliation, but it was plain that he was definitely not amused. Had the safety margin perhaps been thinner than he wanted her to know? Or was this part of the difference between the old Steve and the new?

"Then it was no accident that you chose the park instead of the freeway. You meant to let Pete catch us," she said, trying to make the pieces fit. "Pete must have figured that out in a hurry, too. No wonder he said thanks."

"It wasn't so much a case of wanting to let him catch us as of not wanting to get mixed up in whatever stunts he'd be crazy enough to pull if he didn't. I'm not sure myself what the thanks were for." Steve paused, considering. "Except, I suppose, he probably thinks he has won this round."

"Well, he has, hasn't he?" She could smile, now that the scare was over. Pete's craziness did have a certain dash to it, a romantic masterfulness that was like something Greg might do.

"Has he?" Steve said. He rolled up his window and turned the ignition key. The car began to vibrate gently.

Cathy shifted within the confines of her seat belt to face him, but her impulse to object faded unspoken. Pete's dramatic pursuit had restored Joan to his car and his side, where she belonged. It was relatively safe to assume that the wedding was no longer in danger of being canceled—if such a danger had ever really existed. By walking away from Pete, then allowing herself to be reclaimed, Joan had demonstrated who was the important personage in this affair. And she had undeniably corrected the situation she was complaining of—that nobody was listening or paying attention to her.

"I guess I see what you mean," Cathy said reluctantly. "It's all been kind of a power struggle, hasn't it, to see who's going to be boss—if that's how you want to look at it? Joan may have to do it Mummie's way, but Pete's going to have to do things Joan's way, and Pete's not the sort of a guy who likes to give up doing it his own way. So nobody won this round."

"Well, you could say nobody lost it, either," Steve offered. His tone was growing lighter. "Maybe, from their viewpoint, they're both winners, and that will be the saving of them. My problem, I guess, is that I came in late this evening and walked right into the midst of the shouting, which did unpleasant things to my internal workings."

"And sort of shook your faith in the power of love to conquer all?" She stretched her legs to the warmth starting to flow from the heater as the car hummed into motion, following the curve of the drive.

"I'm afraid I got that pretty badly shaken for me a good while before tonight. To conquer or be conquered: that can make for a lot of scars that don't add up to my idea of love." He discounted a faintly reflective note with a short laugh. "End of this evening's lecture in Philosophy 101."

Not married, not engaged, Joan had said. Cathy wished she knew the whole story. Maybe that was the answer to the difference in him.

"Is that why you've come back here?" she asked cautiously.

"No, not exactly." He thought for a moment, and went on with greater conviction, "Not at all. That was over and done nearly a year ago. What brought me back here is the graduate program in geology at the university. For one thing, they have a new course in computer applications to geology that has my mouth watering every time I think of it."

"Computers and geology!" She shook her head. "I'm not even going to ask you how that works until I've been fortified by a good supper." But she wasn't surprised he could find geology mouth-watering. Steve and the natural sciences had always belonged together. She was glad that part of him wasn't changed. If any girl had been foolhardy enough to try pushing him into a different career, there would be no mystery as to why the romance had shriveled into scars.

"I couldn't give you a very lucid explanation of computers at this point, if you did ask. I'm only taking a couple evening courses this semester, and that's not one of them. For the most part, I'm a glorified stock boy at the A&P, but if I'm lucky, there'll be a teaching assistantship opening up next semester that will help a lot in financing and in study schedules and everything else."

"I hope you get it," she said, and meant it, but her

mind had already jumped to a new thought. "Have you ever met a fellow named Greg Breck there? He's taking an evening course at the university, too." The geology department, she realized, wasn't likely to be within elbow-bumping distance of Greg's class in public relations, but there was no harm in asking.

"Greg Breck," Steve repeated musingly. They were out of the park now, and he let the question dangle until they were past a loudly wheezing bus. "Greg Breck. Would he be a Viking-type guy: blond, blue-eyed, bearded, and of vital importance to you?"

"You do know him. I mean, that 'vital importance' bit sounds like something he'd say." She could feel herself reddening, and hoped the evening had grown too dark for Steve to notice.

Steve's chuckle banished that hope. "No, I don't know him, but he's been described to me. Rather accurately, it would seem."

"Joan?" she said, puzzled. "I remember she did meet Greg once, but I never mentioned to her that we were dating until the other day, when we all went for our final fittings. And then I didn't think she was listening."

"Maybe Joan wasn't, but her cousin was. What's her name—Olive? She told me."

"Oh," Cathy said. Olive, protecting her interests by establishing how little profit for him there could be in renewing old acquaintances, should he be so tempted.

"Right," Steve said on exactly the same note of comprehension.

There was an instant of hesitation. Then they broke into laughter together.

"Listen," Steve said, "would Greg be terribly upset—or would you, for that matter—if I gave it out that I've promised to drive you home after this dinner and that we have to leave about as early as politeness will allow? I have it on reliable authority—Olive's—that it may be possible to transfer her younger cousin to another relative's car for the ride home, which will leave Olive and me free to linger on at the steak house or elsewhere as late as we please."

Cathy grinned at him. "You've rescued me three times already this evening. It seems the least I can do for you is let you make it four times. We can say I've got a lot of studying to do. That's no lie."

"Good! It's a deal. I've heard about your passion for study. My informant also told me that you're on the brink of graduating from St. Chrysostom's speech therapy course with top honors, which means you have very little time to divert from your studies to other activities."

"I get the impression that your informant's major interest isn't accurate reporting. I'm not on the brink of honors or graduation or anything else. This is my junior year, so I've still got another year and a half to go." She curled her fingers around the padded arm rest on the door. "If I finish."

"If?" Steve said. "What does that mean?"

This was the first she had spoken that *if* aloud. Somehow, the sound of it in her ears lent the idea a substance it had lacked in her thoughts.

"It means I may not finish college. I'm not sure any more if a degree and a special career are worth the time and trouble of getting them. Worth it to me, that is. I'm not sure they're what I really want."

Steve whistled under his breath. "You *have* changed," he said, as if he were confirming an earlier observation.

Cathy hadn't thought that he, too, might be noting a

gap between the new and the old. He himself, or at least his voice, she was beginning to think, was not so much changed as matured, grown fuller, more deep, more firmly in possession of the qualities that had always been there. How did he see the changes in her, she wondered.

There was nothing in that voice to tell her the answer as he said, "This Greg Breck must be one 'vitally important' fellow."

Greg was part of it, of course, the most dazzling of the alternatives to college that could be hers. But she and Greg hadn't quite reached the place where he was The Alternative and not one of several. And Greg was not the reason why there could be alternatives.

"Suppose I told you that nobody's more important than a man I've just met once so far; that he's probably fifty and probably married, and I don't even know his first name but it doesn't matter; that I'm counting the days to our next date, which is November twenty-ninth."

Steve turned the windshield wipers on. "It's raining outside," he said mildly, "and I think it's snowing in here."

"No, it's true." She gripped the arm rest a degree harder to curb what wanted to become a jack-o'-lantern grin. "His name is Dr. Rosenthal. He's an ophthalmologist, and about six weeks ago he told me he believes there's a chance that I can see again."

Steve's right hand left the wheel to close around hers that lay on the seat. "Cathy, that's great! What's it going to involve? Surgery or medical treatments or what?"

"I don't know yet. I'm waiting to find out. I don't know how much vision I'll get back, either, but—" she had to squeeze the last few words past a fast-rising fog in her throat—"but I'm hoping."

"You bet you are!" His hand tightened its pressure before returning to the wheel. "November twenty-ninth?"

"The Saturday after Thanksgiving," Cathy said, and listened to the wipers repeat it and repeat it.

"But how does this bear on whether you finish college? I'm afraid I don't understand the connection."

She roused herself from the hypnotizing beat of the wipers. "It's mainly that college has always been something I *had* to do if I ever hope to be independent. The question of *want to* never entered in. But now, if Dr. Rosenthal is right, I won't have to keep doing things for the sake of proving to people that I can do them."

The rain patter on the roof was louder as the car slowed to a standstill at a traffic light. Cathy realized her explanation didn't rank high in coherence, but she didn't know how to say it better. It probably didn't matter, anyway, since he was asking only from polite curiosity.

His next question, put as the car started up again, took her by surprise. "Somebody's been giving you a rough time about proving you can handle speech therapy, have they?"

"Why, yes, as a matter of fact. Dr. Paulus, the chairman of the department. She's new this year."

Then, because she had said that much, she went on to sketch for him the basic details of Dr. Paulus' views. It was as brief a sketch as she could make it, for Greg's immediate reaction to any mention of the college or the clinic was always, "No shop talk."

Either the subject interested Steve, however, or he was a gifted pretender. He had another question when she stopped talking and a comment to spur her on after she had answered that, until she found herself telling him, not just about Dr. Paulus but of the clinic and Roddy and Leonard.

"There was a time when I was toying with the thought of going into speech, especially when I was in the announcers' club, back in high school," Steve confessed. "Maybe there's an affinity between geology and speech. Remember that ancient Greek who put pebbles in his mouth to cure his stutter? But that blindfold idea of yours sounds like a stroke of genius."

"Dr. Paulus has reservations. She admits that it works for Leonard, but she's afraid I'm training him to depend on a crutch that he won't be able to give up."

"What of it? Even if for the rest of his life he has to shut his eyes to talk, isn't that better than never talking?"

"I think so. And he is learning. He has about ten words he can say now, some of them plain enough for anybody to understand. I'm almost certain I can get him to putting sentences together by the end of the semester." Cathy flattened her shoulders against the back of the seat, savoring the triumph ahead. "That's going to be my Christmas surprise for Dr. Paulus."

"It must be kind of exciting."

"It is. I keep holding my breath for fear he'll forget everything between clinic sessions, but he doesn't lose much ground at all, and it doesn't take too long to revive what he does lose. I still can hardly believe it. It's like a brand-new miracle every session."

She paused, aware suddenly that this excitement was a thing totally apart from the thrill she was anticipating in the ultimate surprise she would have for Dr. Paulus. How odd that you could discover something unsuspected about yourself in the course of talking out your thinking with a friend. How odd, too, that she couldn't recall the last time she'd had a chance to try.

"Can you bear some more excitement?" Steve asked. The turn signals began their ticking, and the car swung left off the pavement and onto gravel. "The Chisholm Steak House is dead ahead, and you'll never guess what car we're following in."

"Not the bride and groom?" It was like stuffing her feet back into tight shoes after a spell of blessed respite.

"None other." Steve eased the car to an idling halt. "And here come the relatives, right on the heels of the parking attendant."

Cathy opened her window a crack. Mrs. Norton's voice knifed in. "Naturally, we've been worried. Going off in separate cars like that. Who knew what you were up to? If we can't have some consideration—"

Cathy shut the window.

"Too bad Pete didn't have a tape recorder along on that ride. It would be interesting to compare the facts with the version of tonight that they'll be telling on their golden anniversary," Steve said, and slid out of the car to come around to her door.

Fifty years. What would they be like, the lot of them, in fifty years? Let me live through the next twenty-nine days, she thought, and all my worries will be over. Then she remembered those were Joan's words on the day of the shower—and wished she hadn't remembered.

She stepped out onto dry pavement beneath a metal canopy. Overhead, the raindrops were clattering on the metal like a hail of fine stones but Joan's voice soared above the noise. "Yes, I can see. I see perfectly. So what?"

An eerie shiver pinched Cathy's skin. Halloween, she told herself, and cold rain. But she was glad to move closer to Steve and take his arm. It was good to have an ally here tonight.

"Oh, Steve! There you are!" Olive called. "At last!"

Steve's arm pressed Cathy's in a conspiratorial squeeze, and her shiver vanished in the warmth of struggling not to laugh. It was good to be an ally, too.

8

"WHICH KIND of wedding was it? Mama's or the bride's?" Monica asked Cathy at lunch the next Thursday. "You never did say."

Cathy gave her a one-sided smile. "We did it Mummie's way, of course. The wedding wasn't nearly as grim as the rehearsal, though. Everybody was on good behavior."

"Once the ceremony was over, the bride and groom probably didn't care that much about the details of it, anyway," Amy said, crackling open a bag of potato chips. "What mattered is that they did get married. All that fuss probably brought them closer together than they would have been otherwise."

"Maybe." Cathy cut through the skin of her orange with her thumbnail. She was remembering a snatch of conversation she had overheard at the reception. This had been when Mrs. Norton decided it was time to cut the wedding cake. Joan was ready and waiting, but Pete had been waylaid by first one group of relatives and then another, wanting to wish him well and offer jovial advice.

"Go get him and see to it that he comes," Mrs. Norton had counseled her daughter, in something less than a discreet undertone. "He's your husband now, and he'd better start getting used to it."

Joan had acted at once. Five minutes later, she was presiding over the cake with Pete at her side, and at her side he remained—as far as Cathy could determine—for the rest of the reception.

"I don't know about the bridal couple," Monica said, "but it looked to me this morning like Cathy did pretty well for herself. Or wasn't that tall-dark-and-handsome who delivered you this morning a bonus from the wedding? Greg hasn't dyed his hair and bought a razor, has he?"

"No, that was Steve, a friend from high school who was part of the wedding." Cathy worked loose a broad curve of peel. "St. Chrysostom isn't much off the route he takes to work, so when it was storming this morning, he called to see if I had an early class and if I'd like a ride to school. Really, he's Trudy's friend, and he knows how she hates rain."

"Trudy's friend!" Monica scoffed. "Is that what Greg believes he is? Or doesn't Greg know there is a Steve?"

"Greg knows about him," Cathy said. "He's not very worried. Steve's just an old friend."

Which was true on all counts. Greg had displayed a brief sharpening of interest when she told him of Steve, then had dismissed him and the wedding and the events of Cathy's weekend with a laugh. "Old friends hunting rocks, old maids hunting men—welcome back from the jungle," he said, "and let's see what civilization can do to make you forget."

And Steve *was* just an old friend. He had kissed her good night when he brought her home after the reception, but there had been none of the electric quality about it that she was used to with Greg. None, she suspected, had been intended. Steve was just an old friend.

"At least he's the kind of old friend that sticks by you," Amy said through a mouthful of potato chips. "Did Greg mention anything about Larry? Seeing him anywhere or talking to him or anything this week?"

Cathy shook her head. "Haven't you heard from him? What's wrong?"

"Nothing. Not a thing." Amy's laugh was as brittle as her potato chips. "Except that my mother got the brilliant idea Saturday of inviting us to New Concord for the weekend. Then, after she gave him the grand tour of the house and grounds, including the clothes in my closets and the souvenirs from our trips to Europe, and did a wide-eyed, 'how perfectly fascinating' probe into what a shoe salesman can hope to earn, she got sick so I had to stay with her and Larry had to drive back to town alone. He called me Monday night, but it was like neither of us could think of anything to say. I haven't heard from him since."

"How sick was your mother?" Monica asked.

Amy sighed. "Who knows? She does get these gall bladder attacks sometimes, and sometimes they do only last twenty-four hours, and she doesn't need the doctor—only somebody to stay with her. It's just that they happen at such convenient times—for her. I should have known better than to let her get anywhere near Larry. But I thought Larry was different."

Cathy bit into a segment of orange. She didn't really know Larry Tobin well enough to form a judgment, but for Amy's sake, she, too, would like to think his backbone was stronger and his love more durable than Mrs. Reinhardt's sabotage. Yet from what she had heard of the style in which Amy lived at home, she didn't wonder that even a sturdy young salesman who aspired to a store of his own one day might be staggered by the thought of having to match it.

"Maybe he just needs a couple days to get his bearings again," she suggested. "And maybe you weren't thinking too straight yourself when he called Monday, seeing as how you were out the next two days with the flu."

"That's a nice try, Cathy. Thanks. But I didn't have the flu." A potato chip crunched dolefully. "Tuesday was my day for Dr. Paulus to observe me in clinic, and I was feeling so dismal already, I didn't think I could take being ripped apart by her besides. So I called in sick Tuesday morning, and then I decided I might as well stay out yesterday, too, to make it look good. Not that I have to fake being sick on clinic days; I am sick."

"Why? What do you mean?" A ripple of dismay lifted Cathy's head. "I thought everything was going great with you."

"Maybe because everything's been going great with you," Monica said with a hint of superior knowledge that sent the ripples widening. "You've been living on Cloud Nine for weeks."

Cathy placed three orange seeds in the center of her paper napkin. It was something of a shock to learn she'd been concealing her private glow behind such transparent shutters. But Cloud Nine or not, she couldn't have been floating completely out of touch, could she?

"I know Dr. Paulus has tagged you a couple of times for getting up to clinic after the bell rang," she said, groping for a clue, "but I didn't know you were taking it that much to heart." Amy's tendency to be late was a failing nearly every professor in the speech department had protested at one time or another, without producing any marked results.

"Dr. Paulus doesn't tag. She vivisects you," Amy declared. "Twice last week she poked her head into my therapy room to complain that my patients were too noisy, then cornered me afterward to remind me of the importance of maintaining discipline. I'll admit the kids get pretty shrieky and wild when they're playing games, the same as any four-year-olds, but if I don't make a game out of the therapy, if I try to get tough and serious, Sally cries and Beth just shuts her mouth tight and stares at me. I've either got to fight them or Dr. P."

Monica tapped a paper cup on the table. "What it boils down to is that Paulus is the worst person in the world to have that job. She's not trying to teach us how to be professionals; she expects us to be professional already. Let her catch you having problems and does she help you solve them? No! You get a kick in the teeth from her and sixty days on bread and water."

"It's not just Dr. Paulus. It's everything," Amy said. "Speech therapy, the real thing, is nothing like I thought it was going to be. Sister Bernard was always so full of enthusiasm and pep, so dynamic and full of sparkle that you had to fall in love with her the first time she smiled at you—but I can't do it. I can't be like that. I don't think I believe enough any more."

Cathy raised puzzled eyebrows. "Believe what?" Amy made speech therapy sound as if it were founded on faith rather than practical science and as if Sister Bernard were its high priestess, who must be copied in every detail for one to receive its mystic powers.

"Now I don't believe that there's any worthwhile use to it, I guess. Last year when I listened to Sister Bernard talk, I used to be so inspired I could move mountains. I wanted to move them. But it's not the same without her. Nobody cares."

"And you don't think Paulus is at the bottom of that?" Monica asked. "She'll tear down everything Sister Bernard has built up here if somebody doesn't stop her." Her cup hit the table a sudden, hollow smack. "What we ought to do is walk out, the whole speech department. Walk out and refuse to come back until the administration fires her. I'll bet it would work."

"I'd hate to have to face her again if it didn't," Amy said with an audible shudder.

"That's assuming they let you back into school where you could face her," Cathy added. She couldn't do Dr. Paulus a bigger favor than to walk out before the end of the semester. Come what might, it was a favor she had no intention of granting.

"Okay, it would be a risk, but how much of a risk?" Monica pursued. "If the whole speech department walked out, that's a good third of the college. They'd have to honour our demands or close down."

"Do you suppose we could make them bring Sister Bernard back?" Amy asked wistfully.

Cathy rolled her paper napkin around the debris of her orange. "It might be a good idea to write Sister Bernard first and see if she's willing to come back," she suggested.

She didn't like the more than halfway serious tone

that was creeping into Monica's voice. Common sense told her that the lunch room roar had died away gradually. The lunch hour was nearly over. But she had the impression that everyone in the room had abruptly quit shouting.

"Why wouldn't she be willing?" Monica wanted to know. "We need her here more than that college in Oregon or wherever it is. If Paulus is so great, let them have her out there to start their clinic. We can send her a copy of the grievances we write up for the administration. Sister Bernard, I mean, and I'll bet she'll take the next plane heading east."

"Write her . . . That's a perfect idea, Cathy," Amy mused. "Or I could even phone her. If I could just hear her voice again . . ." She jumped up, gathering her milk carton, sandwich wrappers, and lunch bag together in a quick sweep. "I'm going to hunt up Sister Janice this minute and ask her for the address."

Cathy fished beneath the table for Trudy's leash and stood up, too. "That's better than fire-bombing the clinic. Trudy's afraid of thunder."

Monica remained seated. "Laugh if you like, but you haven't said a walkout wouldn't work. And neither of you said it may not be necessary, either." Her voice followed Cathy and Amy to the door. "Think about it."

Cathy didn't want to think about it. Or about Pete and Joan. Or about Amy and Larry, or Amy and Dr. Paulus. If a snap of the fingers could have disposed of Dr. Paulus to a remote corner of Mars and restored Sister Bernard to St. Chrysostom, her fingers would be the first to snap. But Thanksgiving was what she wanted to think about. Thanksgiving—only three weeks away now. Thanksgiving, and Saturday the twenty-ninth. She liked living on Cloud Nine, if that's what it was, and she wasn't eager to have holes shot in it from below.

Yet once made, the holes were difficult to plug. An unlooked-for wave of relief thrust up through Cathy the next morning when Amy trudged into the locker room, not only on time for clinic, but ten minutes early. "You must have gotten through to Sister Bernard last night," Cathy hazarded.

"No, but maybe today. Sister Janice didn't have the address handy yesterday, but she'll try to find it for me today. I guess she's not much of a letter writer." Amy paused to blow her nose. "Do you have any Kleenex I could borrow? I'm down to my last two, and my nose has started leaking like a faucet."

"Sure. Help yourself." Cathy reached into her locker for the box that was a standard part of her clinic supplies. "You're not about to get the flu for real, are you?"

"Wouldn't that be a joke?" Amy asked, digging in for a handful of tissues. "I might as well spend the weekend sick. I've got nothing better to do."

Which meant, Cathy understood, that Larry still hadn't called. "Maybe he's sick with the flu himself," she offered. "There's enough coughing and sneezing going on in the halls here to stock a hospital, and I shouldn't think where he works it would be much different."

"Thanks," Amy said, not sounding persuaded, and went on down the aisle to her own locker.

But it was quite possible, Cathy reasoned. Larry could have been temporarily laid low this week, and Amy herself might well be on the verge of a bad cold, if not the flu. That would account for Amy's low spirits and her talk of not believing in anything any more. Things couldn't actually be as grim as she and Monica had been painting them.

"Amy, listen," Cathy said, banging her locker shut to herald the birth of a new idea. "Why don't I have Greg suggest to Larry that the four of us go out together tomorrow night? The University Players are putting on *Blithe Spirit,* and Greg, as usual, knows somebody who can get him all the tickets he wants. Maybe all Larry needs is a little push."

Amy was enthusiastic but that evening Greg shrugged off the proposal before Cathy was finished explaining. "Right. We ought to set up something for the four of us again. Maybe next weekend."

He leaned his head out his window to greet the parking lot attendant, who was directing cars to various ramps and levels. "Hi, Lou! How's the world treating you?"

"I'm talking about tomorrow night," Cathy said as the car started up an incline. "It's important to Amy, and probably to Larry, too. Next weekend might as well be next year. Besides, it will be fun to have them along to share the play."

And that was true. She hadn't thought until this moment of how long it was since they had been with any real friends of hers. Greg's supply of acquaintances and friends was so unending that they seemed hardly ever to repeat anyone.

"Only we're not going to the play. We're going to the basketball game, and it's a sellout."

Cathy pressed herself into the curve of the bucket seat against the sharp swing left the car made at the top of the ramp. "A basketball game? Why? Tomorrow's the last performance of the play."

For the most part, she didn't mind Greg's habit of

choosing where they would go and what they would do without consulting her in advance. There were times like tonight when she still didn't know their destination when they were almost there, except that they were headed for some kind of a party somewhere and that, if Greg were involved, there was bound to be loud music and confusion. But the play was something they had talked over and agreed on together. He had known she was looking forward to it as a special treat, and he had told her himself, not forty-eight hours ago, that their tickets were waiting for them at the box office.

"A lot more people are going to the game than to the play," Greg said, as if this were reason enough in itself. He swerved the car hard left again and stopped the engine with no further parking maneuvers. "It's only luck that there were a couple of extra tickets for us."

"What's lucky about it if we don't want to go? You told me once yourself that you could think of better things to do than sit on the side lines and watch somebody else having all the fun."

Greg laughed and leaned to cup the back of her neck in a warm hand. "What difference does it make where we go, as long as we're there together? Anyway, there's a big bunch of us going, so it's got to be fun. Dud Curtis bought a block of tickets because one of the guys on the team is a buddy of his from Hawaii. You couldn't expect me to tell him we had other plans."

It was on Cathy's tongue to say that was exactly what she would have expected, but her attention was snared for an instant by the question of who Dud Curtis might be. Curtis . . . Hawaii . . . Dudley Bruce Curtis III, the hotel owner's son?

"Hey, there, Breck!" a male voice hailed them, echoing in the cavelike chamber of the parking structure. "I thought that was you following me in!"

He turned out to be a friend of Greg, headed for the same party as they were. He was also an effective end to the discussion. Who else he might be, Cathy didn't know, for if she had met him before, as both he and Greg appeared to assume she had, his identity had been swallowed up in the uproar and confusion of an earlier party.

Tonight's party proved to be of the same fabric, except that it was a gathering of friends in a discotheque rather than in someone's rec room or the basement of the fraternity house. When Cathy wasn't being jostled here and there in what passed for dancing on the crowded floor, she was sitting on a padded bench along the wall, sipping a lukewarm Coke and smiling brightly to her left or right, wherever a shout of unintelligible communication occasionally reached her through the crash of the music—just as she had been doing for she didn't know how many other evenings since she began dating Greg. Tonight, however, she couldn't persuade herself that she was enjoying every minute of the stale air and stifling noise. Tonight, everything was as flat as her Coke, which had somehow lost its carbonation while she was holding it. Worse, she couldn't even make herself believe that her disappointment over missing the play was the whole basis of the trouble, for a recognition was growing in her that this wasn't the first of these parties at which she had felt numbed to indifference within towering walls of sound.

And tomorrow night a basketball game, she thought, dampening her lips with the Coke, to give the appearance of being occupied in her isolation. Basketball—a game that had failed to thrill her in the days when she could see what was happening on the court and which had considerably less to offer, now that she couldn't. What fun could Greg possibly think she would have, sitting on a hard seat all evening, piecing together the action as best she could from the cheers and boos in the stands and the bits of information he and his friends might remember to toss her? Yet maybe she was being unfair. Maybe he did believe that where they were didn't matter as long as they were there together. But . . . She tilted her glass and downed the final, cloying swallow like medicine. But, once in a while, why couldn't the "where" be of her choosing?

"Are you sure the game is a complete sellout?" she tried again when, at last, she and Greg were in the relative quiet of the street, on their way to get his car. "Don't you suppose, if you suggested it to Larry, he could scrape up two more tickets somewhere and we could still go with him and Amy?" Whether Amy cared for basketball didn't matter under the circumstances, to Amy least of all, and if tomorrow night had to be a basketball game, inviting her and Larry along to dilute the monotony seemed a little enough concession to ask.

"No way," Greg said, swinging her hand to and fro in his. "Next week we'll minister to the lovelorn, maybe. This week is spoken for."

"By whom? Dud Curtis? What's so great about him?" She couldn't screen a grain of irritation from her voice. Amy and Larry were friends, the friends who had introduced her to Greg. Dudley Bruce Curtis III she wouldn't recognize if he stepped up beside her this moment and began talking, although he had been at one or two other parties she'd attended with Greg recently. He might even have been at this one tonight, lost somewhere in the din, but if that were so, he certainly hadn't put forth much effort to make his presence known.

Greg laughed. "How would you like to spend Thanksgiving in Los Angeles? Hollywood, Beverly Hills, Disneyland, movie studios—the works?"

"What?" She stubbed her toe against a corner of concrete projecting into her path—a step to a doorway or something—and did a hasty skip to catch her balance. Hand-in-hand was their favorite style of walking when Greg didn't have his arm around her waist, and she had the bruised shins and scuffed-up shoes to prove it.

"I'm serious," Greg said. "Dud's father will be in Los Angeles for Thanksgiving, and it's just possible he's in the market for a bright, ambitious, energetic PR man for his hotels. Namely me. Anyway, he's interested enough to pay my way out there to see him. And Dud knows a travel agent who'll fix us up as part of a tour, so your fare will be only peanuts."

Her lift of excitement for him broke into splinters of dismay. "My fare! It's you he wants to see. And I can't go. I can't."

"Now none of that square stuff. We'll be staying with Dud's married sister, all nice and proper and chaperoned and free of charge." He pulled open the door to the parking building and caught her close in the crook of his arm as the panels of steel and glass wheezed shut behind them. "Baby, we're going to live it up."

What an adventure it would be, if it could be. It couldn't be, of course. She knew that, even as reckless calculations began racing through her veins. Thursday, Thanksgiving, in Los Angeles . . . Saturday, the twenty-ninth, in Dr. Kruger's office . . . Not possible. Anyway, not practical. Yet—

"When would we be coming back?"

"It depends. If Dudley Bruce Curtis II likes me, we maybe won't come back at all. We may go straight on to Hawaii."

" 'We' meaning you and Mr. Curtis, I presume." Her laugh had a breathless wobble in it, perhaps because they were climbing the stairs to the level where the car was parked. "I have two weeks of classes and one of exams after Thanksgiving. So have you, for that matter, if you're planning to finish your night course."

"Why finish? I don't need it if I've got the job already. And you don't need it if you've got a guy who's got a job. Right? When I say, 'We,' I mean you in a little grass skirt in a little grass shack and me directing the whole, delicious luau."

Cathy stumbled on the top step, not altogether from the awkwardness of relying on the pressure of his arm around her rather than the hand rail for guidance. Was he hinting at marriage? Actually on the brink of proposing to her, at last, in so many words? Of all the places where she had imagined this moment might materialize, she had never thought it would be in an echoing cavern of concrete like this, smelling of gas fumes and oil. But one more word from her, one small, prodding question, and . . .

"What will we do about Trudy?" she heard herself saying instead. "You can't take a dog into Hawaii just like that. I read somewhere once that there's a quarantine of four months or more."

"So leave Trudy behind," he said gaily. "Give her to your brother. You won't be needing her in a little grass shack, anyway. Or in Los Angeles, either." His voice softened to a caress. "I promise you that."

Cathy flung a mental door shut on the shock waves

unleashed by the thought of disposing of Trudy as if she were a superfluous pair of jeans. Greg wasn't as callous as that sounded. He was too intent on persuading her to realize what it was that he was saying.

And here, at long last, was her chance to tell him of her own special hope for the days beyond Thanksgiving.

"I have to be here on Saturday, the twenty-ninth. That's the Saturday after Thanksgiving. I have an important appointment with the eye doctor in the morning, too important to break."

They were at the car now. Greg was jingling in his pocket for the keys. "What are you trying to do? Test my powers to dissolve problems? Get the appointment postponed. It can't be a matter of life and death, an eye doctor."

"It could be— Almost." She hesitated, willing him to grasp the connection between eye doctor and vital importance himself, willing him to help her by asking the right question. It had been so easy to tell Steve. But with Steve, she had been sure that he was listening.

Greg rasped the key in the lock and snapped the door open for her. "Then get the appointment moved up. They can squeeze you in earlier if they have to—if you tell them something ultraimportant has come up and you can't be there on the twenty-ninth."

Cathy ducked onto the seat and let him shut her in. She sat digesting his new solution in the moments it took him to walk around to the other side. He was right, of course. There was nothing magical about the twenty-ninth. Just as there was no immutable law requiring Christmas to be celebrated on December 25, or Thanksgiving on a Thursday. It was only in her mind that November 29 had assumed a peculiar cosmic importance—which could readily be superseded by a project of *ultraimportance.*

She knew that last thought wasn't quite fair. She hadn't told him yet what the appointment was for. But when she did tell him, would it alter in the least his ranking of priorities?

The question kept her silent as he slid in beside her. Music leaped from the radio with the flick of the ignition key. Then came the distraction of easing the car away from the one parked too close next to it, of paying the attendant at the bottom of the ramp, of exchanging horn blasts with other homeward-bound friends on the street . . . and the time for telling was gone.

Cathy lay awake that night through endless chimings of the downstairs clock, wondering why she had let the chance slip by her, wondering what had gone wrong with the whole evening. Nothing had gone wrong so far as Greg was concerned. He had taken for granted that the evening was a huge success; he always took that for granted. And Greg himself had been the same Greg as always.

There was the trouble. Greg's life contained only one real place, only one real happening at any given time: the place where he was and the thing he was doing. Events in another room, the heartbeat of another person had no genuine substance for him. He lived in the here and now, and he lived it to the hilt. That was a large part of his charm. But tonight she saw it also as a kind of barrier surrounding him, like the plastic bubble on an official car: so clear that he seemed to be mingling freely in the very center of the crowd, but so hard there was no way he could be touched from outside, and so small there was no room for anyone but him inside. She couldn't make him care about Amy's and Larry's unhappiness; she didn't trust him to care about her heart-held dream.

She rolled onto her stomach and dropped a hand down over the edge of the bed to where Trudy lay asleep. Trudy's nose pushed up, eager and cold, into her fingers. Cathy traced the velvety groove between Trudy's eyes and rubbed the stiff hairs at the base of the broad, curved ears, and, for a while, anger dulled the sharpness of her hurt. Greg would never understand, not even if Trudy were his own dog. He could fondle her, throw sticks for her, marvel at her beauty, then walk off and abandon her without a backward look because he couldn't hear her barking as he left. Greg had ears for music and laughter and new acquaintances' names, but he couldn't hear. If Cathy called him tomorrow to plead headache as an excuse for not going to the basketball game, he would hear what she said but not a word of what she was saying.

She did call him the next day. By then, the headache wasn't altogether fiction, and her throat had developed a sandpaper quality she could halfway believe might forecast a weekend bout with the flu. She more than halfway hoped it was flu, as she had hoped it for Amy, so that all this would end up being only the depressing effects of a virus, nothing worse—a virus that could be cured.

She called Amy, too, but Mrs. Greer, in whose home Amy boarded, said Amy had already gone out somewhere. Mrs. Greer didn't know where, nor did she know when to expect her back. Cathy pared her message down to the essentials: the date for the play had been called off and she herself was staying home with a touch of the flu. She didn't mention Larry. Mrs. Greer, who was a friend of Mrs. Reinhardt, had a Mrs.

Reinhardt sweetness in her voice that she didn't trust. Yet, as she hung up, Cathy acknowledged to herself she wasn't sorry not to have to talk to Amy. To discuss Larry would have led to a discussion of Greg, and it would be a while before she felt up to that.

It was a quiet weekend, the quietest Cathy had known since her first date with Greg. And the longest. The flu never quite materialized, but neither was she radiating vitality Monday morning when she met Amy outside Sister Janice's classroom.

"That's okay," Amy cut into her fumbled apology for Saturday night. "I decided to go home for the weekend, anyhow. I—I had some errands to do."

She pushed on by Cathy into the classroom without offering more. Except for lunch, at which the table was dominated by a dispute between Monica and Laura Riley on what constituted a truly liberated woman, Cathy didn't see Amy again to talk to that day.

Her intention of waiting to walk up to clinic with Amy Tuesday morning was changed by a shout from down the hall before she reached the locker room. "Cathy! Cathy Wheeler! Dr. Paulus was down here looking for you about ten minutes ago. She has a message for you."

"Thanks, Diane," Cathy yelled back, recognizing the voice as that of one of the seniors, and plunged into the locker room to rid herself of her coat and to gather up her supplies for clinic as fast as possible. She had no idea why Dr. Paulus should be hunting her out, but the mere thought of it caused her ribs to tighten up against her lungs.

The bustle of therapists and patients claiming each other in the waiting room, trading greetings and offering scraps of information, was an audible beacon as she and Trudy gained the third floor. She would have paused on the top step to smooth the ruffled edges of her poise, but Dr. Paulus apparently had been watching for her.

"There you are, Miss Wheeler," she said, crossing the hall to Cathy. "Mrs. Perkins phoned this morning to say Leonard is sick with the flu. She won't be bringing him to clinic today. It's unfortunate you couldn't have been notified in time to prepare for a clinic period with just one patient, but you won't have much difficulty, will you?"

"No," Cathy assured her automatically. "Thank you. Everything will be fine."

She hoped fervently that she was right as she went on into the waiting room. Leonard needed such a lot of repetition to fix in his mind what few crumbs of speech he had attained, neither he nor she could afford to have him miss a therapy session if they were to reach her goal of having him speak a full sentence or two by the end of the semester. There weren't all that many therapy sessions left in the semester.

Roddy presented himself at once. His hand closed next to hers on the handle of her briefcase. "Shall I carry this?"

"I'd be glad if you would," she told him, smiling. Roddy had become her right-hand man over the past weeks, carrying things for her, opening doors, selecting books from the cupboard, picking up the multitude of items Leonard contrived to drop. The briefcase was purposely packed with nonbreakables, so he could have the honor of transporting it to the therapy room. "You are a big help to me, Roddy."

"To my mama, too," he said.

His mother laughed. "He really is. We don't have a baby any more. We have a little boy who helps out everywhere and that we can depend on. I don't know how you've done it, Cathy, but it's a marvelous bonus."

Cathy wasn't sure how she had done it, either, or if she had. Roddy seemed to have responded naturally to the discovery that his help was truly useful to her at times. And it had been Leonard's presence that had forced her to have to be that honest with Roddy, so perhaps the thanks for the new Roddy should be Leonard's. Doubtless that was what Dr. Paulus would prefer to think.

In any event, Roddy himself was not interested. "Come on," he said, pulling her by the hand toward the door. Cathy yielded, and nearly bumped into Karen Bergen in the hall. Or rather, Karen nearly bumped into her.

"Cathy." Karen caught her by the arm. "Do you know where Amy is?"

Cathy shook her head. "Downstairs, probably. Her bus doesn't give her much margin, even when she's on time. Why?"

"I'm afraid she's in for a nasty surprise," Karen said in a guarded undertone. "Dr. P. is supposed to be observing in my room today, but she's changed the schedule so that Amy's it this morning. You know it was Amy's turn last Tuesday, but she wasn't here."

"I know," Cathy nodded. But how much did Karen know? Could it be that everyone was on the watch for tornadoes where she had been seeing only tranquil skies?

This was no time to ask. Roddy was trotting on ahead of her, and she had to keep moving. Her hand on the therapy room door, she heard Amy's chirp from the direction of the waiting room, "Yes, Dr. Paulus." The chirp had a mechanical ring to it, perhaps, but at least it was evidence that Dr. Paulus wouldn't be reading Amy out for tardiness this day.

"Can I sit in Leonard's chair?" Roddy asked, reminding Cathy that she had a more immediate problem than Amy's dilemmas to solve, namely, how to stretch a lesson plan designed to divide the period between two patients into one to fit just Roddy for the entire fifty minutes.

At first, Roddy was charmed to have the center stage to himself. "I got a poem," he announced as soon as the door was shut, and without prompting, recited:

"Lucy Locket lost her pocket.
Kitty Fisher found it.
Nothing in it, nothing in it
But the binding round it."

It was an array of sounds that would have utterly defeated him at the start of the year, and he was as proud of himself as Cathy was. At this rate of progress, he might, he just might be close to needing no further speech work by the finish of the semester, she thought. That was a long climb for a little boy to have made in the space of three semesters.

But without Leonard there to take a turn at tongue exercises, to share in the marble game, to be applauded for his efforts and to be eclipsed by Roddy, the novelty of being the solitary star began to thin as the period wore on. During the last quarter hour, Cathy was battling his old tendency to clown instead of work, a gremlin that hadn't put in an appearance in weeks.

She returned him to his mother unsatisfied by either his performance or her own, and spent the next hour in the library. On Friday, she would have two lesson plans ready, one tailored to the demands of two patients, the other trimmed exclusively to Roddy's measurements, in case—heaven forbid—Leonard should be absent a second time. Who could have dreamed in September that the day would come when she would be putting her whole heart into hoping for Leonard *not* to miss his clinic periods?

She worked until almost time for the bell, then decided to reward herself with an unharried few minutes in the washroom before the lunchtime crowd piled in. The halls were gratifyingly empty as she hurried downstairs to the lavatory opposite the locker room. She pulled open the door and stiffened to a halt under a torrent of voices that spilled out at her—spilled out and stopped short, as if someone had shut off a faucet. Trudy pushed on in beyond the door frame, and there was a spatter of laughter.

"It's Cathy Wheeler," Karen said. "Come on in, Cathy, and join the powwow."

Cathy entered far enough to let the door swing shut behind her. "Powwow about what?"

The torrent broke over her once more, in a half-dozen voices too jumbled together for her to identify any of them absolutely, aside from Karen's, and perhaps Laura Riley's and, rising above them all, Monica's.

"—quitting school, thanks to Paulus. I came down half an hour ago, and there she was, crying into her locker like it was the end of the world. She didn't take a single book with her when she left. Just shut up the locker and ran."

"Who?" Cathy's stomach knew the answer. It was like a swift drop in an elevator. "Not Amy?"

"Yes, Amy," Karen answered. "I told you Dr. P. was switching the schedule around so she could observe

Amy's clinic this morning without advance notice. Well, she did, and Amy's gone home. Probably for good."

"Because of Dr. Paulus?" It wasn't that Cathy doubted it. It was simply more than she could grasp in one breath. "I thought it was Larry she was worrying about."

"This has got nothing to do with Larry," Monica said. "I asked her. Paulus is at the bottom of it. What she did or what she said, I don't know. Amy said it was too terrible to talk about, and that's as much as I could get out of her, but she'd just come from Paulus' office. I know that for a fact."

"You know pretty well what Paulus did and said to her: the same as she says and does to all of us. There's no such thing as an accident or an honest mistake or circumstances beyond your control. There's only deliberate stupidity and carelessness and every other venial sin in the book. We're not students. We're inmates in a penal colony, and she's the warden." The deep voice belonged to Thelma Delaney, a sophomore who was in Cathy's tests and measurements class.

Cathy eased herself, with Trudy behind her, over to one of the sinks, as much to have something firm to hang on to as to get on with the business of washing her hands.

"But, my dears," Laura Riley mocked, "she's *professional.* She has *standards.* It's her duty to purge us of impurities."

The storm of voices burst loose again. Everyone, it seemed, had her own grievance to tell and was determined to tell it. Whatever Dr. Paulus had accomplished this semester, she had certainly made no friends.

"She's the one who ought to be purged," Monica said fiercely. "Right out of this school. We've had about as much as we can take. Hounding a student into dropping out is the last straw."

"Why don't we draw up a petition to have her removed?" rumbled Thelma Delaney. "We'd get enough signatures in a couple of days to shake up the administration so they'd either have to fire her or clamp down on her good and hard. I'll bet just about the whole school would sign, speech majors or not."

"We don't want her clamped on. We want her fired, period," said a girl Cathy didn't know.

Cathy jerked her hands from under the stream of hot water. Ordinarily, the water in this lav ran a scant degree above tepid, but today it was nearly scalding.

"Has Amy actually quit? Actually and absolutely?" she asked, turning to yank a paper towel from the dispenser. "Couldn't it be that she was too upset to really mean what she was saying?"

"It could be," Monica conceded. "All I know is that if she's not back in class tomorrow or Thursday, Paulus is in for big trouble."

Cathy dried her hands carefully. What fuel she could add to the blaze should she choose to tell of Dr. Paulus' attitude toward her. But she didn't choose to tell. That was a private war, *her* private war, and her heart was set on winning it independently, by herself. Besides, the blaze was already crackling at a rate that scared her a little. In the hubbub of voices around her, there was a unanimous theme: "Get Paulus." She could hear nobody saying, "Save Amy."

What could be done, however, to save Amy was a question with no clear-cut answer. Cathy's attempt to phone her that evening netted only the landlady, who sounded like a recording of their Saturday conversation: Amy was out at the moment, where she was Mrs. Greer couldn't say, but if Cathy would leave her number, Amy could call her when she returned. But Amy didn't call. Neither did she appear in school the next day, nor again on Thursday.

"She's gone home to New Concord," Monica said, stopping Cathy and Karen outside their first class of that afternoon. "I just spent two dimes worming the information out of her landlady. She's home and she has no immediate plans about coming back. So that settles it." She tapped Cathy on the shoulder. "Pass the word. Everybody who's got seventh hour free is to meet in the smoker. I've got the petition all drawn up."

To even the nonsmokers, this loungey, homey room —rarely, if ever invaded by the faculty—was the favorite hangout of the students for play or special work or meetings such as Monica was calling.

Cathy nodded grimly. She had seventh hour free. It was normally the time when she packed up to go home on Thursdays, but it wouldn't be today. Fifth and sixth hours might as well have been free for her, too, for any concentration she was able to give the lectures. Amy throwing away her most precious dream, that of becoming a speech therapist . . . Greg's splendor diminished . . . rebellion brewing within the walls of St. Chrysostom . . . The soft chup-chump of the notes she was brailling was like the sound of insect jaws chewing her Cloud Nine to shreds. She was afraid to wonder what would crumble next.

She knew before she reached the end of the hall after her sixth-hour class. "Miss Wheeler," Dr. Paulus hailed her from the door of her office. "Do you have time to step in here a moment?"

Cathy rejected in a single guilty breath the possibility that Dr. Paulus had wind of the meeting in the smoker and was out to sabotage it. This had to be about Leonard. Leonard was going to shave his chances and hers even thinner by missing another clinic period.

"Yes, sit down," Dr. Paulus said as Trudy led Cathy in to where Cathy's arm brushed the straight-backed chair that, midway into the semester, had replaced Sister Bernard's rocker. "I have some regrettable news for you. Mrs. Perkins phoned this afternoon to say that Leonard is more ill than they had supposed."

A quiver of smugness tickled Cathy's lips. Wait until she revealed she had foreseen this contingency well ahead of time and was prepared for another one-patient session.

"Their doctor," Dr. Paulus continued, "wants him kept home until after Thanksgiving."

Smugness fled in a rush of disbelief that sat Cathy forward on the chair edge. Absent for two sessions, yes, if that was how it had to be, but not through Thanksgiving. "Because of the flu?"

"Flu is no light matter for a child like the Perkins boy, who is frail at the best of times. As I understand it, he suffers from a defective heart, as well as his other disabilities."

Cathy was doing a frantic tally of the therapy sessions that remained: five that Leonard would have missed by Thanksgiving, four between Thanksgiving and exams in which to recover the lost ground. Her vision of Leonard, free of his blindfold, speaking an intelligible sentence or two on the final day, thinned away like smoke.

"He won't remember a thing when he gets back. We'll be starting over from zero."

"Perhaps not quite at zero," Dr. Paulus said. "If he does forget everything, you'll at least have the advantage of reteaching him what he once knew. It may be he will respond a great deal more quickly than the first time through."

Reteach him in four sessions what it had taken him how many laborious weeks to learn? At best, her record would credit her with nothing more spectacular on his behalf than a handful of half-articulated words, spoken only if his eyes were bandaged.

"What it will amount to is running to stand still," she said, her smile a wan gesture at veiling the bitterness pressing in on her. "Those last two weeks of clinic after Thanksgiving can't bring him up anywhere near where he might have been if we could have worked steadily." She swallowed a wild impulse to suggest she go to his home to tutor him.

"But he does have the capacity to communicate through language," Dr. Paulus said. "It may be a severely limited capacity, but its fact has been established. No matter how little he retains of this semester's work, he will at least have some foundation to build on next semester, if, hopefully, his health permits him to keep on at the clinic. He's losing a great deal by having to miss such a large chunk of time at this crucial stage of his clinic experience, but since there's no help for it, you can take comfort in the knowledge that your patient himself isn't lost. He'll have another chance, as many as he needs."

Cathy's lips were parted to ask how badly this halt to Leonard's progress was likely to injure the evaluation of her performance as a therapist, but her mouth closed without a sound as the import of what Dr. Paulus was saying struck her. I'm talking about me, she realized, but she's talking about Leonard. It's almost as if she cares what chances he may have, whether he gets lost in the shuffle or not. She! Dr. Paulus! The silver-plated iceberg showing concern for what became of another human being! Can it be that she does have a human heart and some warm blood buried somewhere in her, after all? And she's handing me an indirect compliment on my therapy work into the bargain!

That thought would have shaken Cathy enough without the sequel that came blistering at its heels: I'm the one who hasn't felt a twinge for anything or anyone but me and how my plan is affected. What's wrong with me?

"In the meantime," Dr. Paulus continued, "if you have any difficulties in adjusting your program to working with just one patient, I will be here to offer whatever assistance I can. Feel free to ask."

"I will. Thank you." Cathy wanted to ask if Leonard was seriously ill or merely being kept quiet while he recuperated, but she was ashamed to admit the question had occurred to her only now. "Thank you, Dr. Paulus," she said again.

Aftershocks of the interview were still rocking her when she and Trudy gained the lower hall and the locker room. In a daze, she shrugged into her coat, stuffed her human development notes into her briefcase, and drew her head scarf from her pocket.

Then she remembered the meeting in the smoker. She started to jam the scarf back into her pocket, but paused. What use would it be to sign that petition? Monica would be outraged if she didn't, of course, but aside from that, where was the point? What good would it do Amy to have Dr. Paulus removed?

Or me, either? she thought. Getting her fired won't make her admit I'm as capable a therapist as anybody else, which is what I wanted to make her do. And which isn't going to happen. My name on the petition would amount to nothing but spitefulness, like taking an ax to the barn door after the horse is stolen.

"Would Dr. Paulus be all that bad a chairman if Sister Bernard hadn't been so great?" Steve had asked this morning when he dropped by unannounced to offer her a ride to school.

Cathy stood thinking a while longer, then shook out the rumpled scarf and folded it over her head. Besides, she might not even choose to come back here next semester herself. In fact, she wouldn't lose much if she chose to leave right now and fly to Los Angeles with Greg. There was no way any more that the semester could end in the blaze of glory that she'd been planning. There still was Roddy, to be sure, but it was Leonard who was the real test of her resources, Leonard whose success would have been her crown of triumph. Why not yield to the persuasions Greg had crooned to her over the phone last light? Why not admit she may have judged him too harshly?

Lucy Locket lost her pocket.
Kitty Fisher found it.
Nothing in it, nothing in it
But the binding round it.

Cathy knotted the scarf firmly under her chin and picked up her briefcase. Her feelings about Greg were a muddle of yeas and nays. So were her feelings about quitting school. But there was one thing she did know. Her pocket was not empty. A single gold coin stamped November 29 remained tucked in its corner, round and solid and untarnished—and not to be tampered with. She couldn't change that date when it was only two more weeks away.

Trudy leaned into the harness, eager to be on their way, and Cathy pushed out into the misty cold of the November day, her mental fingers clinging tight to the magic coin.

9

"CATHY?" Her father's voice probed up the stairs. "I'm going to get the car out now. How close are you to being ready?"

"Right away," she called without moving from her dresser. "In a second."

She picked up her hairbrush for a last touch to her hair while her stomach did a slow roll and steadied itself. The hairbrush was steady in her hand, too, its strokes long and leisurely. They should have been light, quick strokes for this last bit of primping, but she couldn't seem to do anything lightly or quickly this morning.

It had been like that ever since she woke up this morning—a single, wild leap of her heart in recognition that this was the day, Saturday, the twenty-ninth of November—The Day; then a massive calm spreading through her, thickening and growing solid, like paraffin sealing in the sparkle and quiver of jelly. She had waited such an endless time for this morning to arrive that, now that it was here, she had to dig in her heels and hang on to each minute of it to double its length before she could make herself believe today was a reality. It was the way she felt during the first hours of Christmas sometimes, as if she must move with methodical care to savor every last drop of anticipation or the day's joyful promise would be fulfilled and over with too soon. Only this was different from Christmas because there had been Christmases before and there would be Christmases again, but today was a once-in-a-lifetime day.

"Cathy!" It was her mother this time. "What are you doing up there? Your father's waiting."

"Coming."

Cathy laid the brush down reluctantly. What she wanted to say was, I'm not ready. All of a sudden, it's happening too fast.

Or was the trouble that it wasn't happening fast enough? Perhaps this leaden feeling that gripped her was still part of the old game of filling in that stretch of empty time between now and then. She gave her hair a final pat, tugged at the jacket of the knit suit she was wearing, smoothed her hand down the front of the skirt, and walked unhurriedly down the stairs to put on her coat and harness Trudy. She couldn't hurry. She didn't dare, for fear that paraffin seal would crack open and the jelly beneath prove to be an explosive that would burst in every direction if it contacted the air.

"You certainly took long enough," her father grumbled as she and Trudy climbed into the car, but Cathy hardly heard him. An anonymous male voice on the radio was singing, "Today is the first day of the rest of our lives . . ."

Think sad thoughts, she commanded herself, reversing Peter Pan's formula for flying. Keep your feet firmly on the floor. She snapped her seat belt tight across her lap as an added precaution. Think of Greg.

The song was a favorite of Greg. For him, it confirmed his philosophy that there was nothing binding about yesterday, that it was unrelated to tomorrow or today.

She hadn't heard from Greg by mail or phone since his departure for Los Angeles on Sunday, nearly a week ago now. If he went on to Hawaii, as he hoped, or stayed in California, the alternative he'd been considering, it was doubtful she ever would hear from him again —unless at some future date, circumstances brought him back to town and her back to mind. Not that he had left here in a rage or brokenhearted at her refusal to go along. He had been so full of his own preparations and plans by the time she finally got it through his head that she wasn't going, he'd taken the disappointment in a noble stride that was almost unflattering. In spirit, he was already halfway to California and his focus on whatever wasn't to be a part of that was beginning to blur.

So it's over between us, she thought. Finished. And it hurts—a little. It would hurt a lot, if I'd think about it. If I could keep thinking about it . . . Suddenly a grin was urging up the corners of her mouth in complete disregard of everything.

She was still battling that silly grin on the ride up to the doctor's office in the elevator, and, for once, she was glad to be folded into the sobering hush of a waiting room. The chair her father directed her to received her into a nest too ample for conversation across either arm to be convenient, and too soft to encourage even the pretense of reading the Braille magazine she had brought along. There was nothing to do but breathe in the hush and relax into a paraffin sculpture of tranquility, and wait. And wait. And wait . . .

"Cathy." The nurse at the reception desk roused her centuries later—centuries too soon. "You can go in now."

Cathy scrambled to her feet as if she had been startled from sleep. Her clutch on Trudy's harness was as much for balance as guidance, but, in an instant, that odd sense of tranquility swirled back to insulate her. She walked through the inner door and found the examining room as calmly as she ever had, although she was strangely short of breath when she arrived.

Dr. Kruger's calm was a match for hers. He adjusted the height of the examining chair for her and proceeded with the routine tests she knew so well, as if this were as ordinary a visit as any other.

"I understand you've been having headaches," he said, just when she was beginning to think he would never say anything to the point at all. He rolled aside the metal tray of instruments. "How are the eyedrops? Any help?"

"Yes, some," she nodded. "If I get them in early enough. The eyedrops Dr. Rosenthal gave me, you mean?"

There wasn't a reason on earth to suppose he might not mean the drops Dr. Rosenthal gave her, but she wanted to establish Dr. Rosenthal as a fact by speaking his name aloud.

Dr. Kruger grunted, a sound she took for confirmation. "These headaches," he asked after a moment's heavy silence, "are they predictable in any way? For instance, do they come more frequently at one end of the week than the other? Or when there's a shift in the weather? A storm in the offing?"

"I don't know. I haven't thought of connecting them to anything like that." She frowned in an effort to think back, but her mind skittered away from concentration. She didn't care about the headaches' causes. She wanted to talk about their cure. "I used to think they came when I was most under pressure and everything else is going wrong, but sometimes they come out of nowhere, when everything else is going right."

That day when Leonard said his first word, for instance. Hadn't she had one of those headaches that day? Right now, she couldn't quite remember.

Dr. Kruger had more questions to ask. Where did the headaches start? How severe were they? How long were they likely to last?

Then he was stooping over her again, telling her to look up, please, to look right, look left, look down, while he examined her left eye once more. Nothing touched her, but she could trace the movements of the lights she guessed he was using by the rustle of his sleeves and the warmth his hands cast on her cheeks. Nothing was said, either, but his very silence whispered to her that he must be rediscovering the hope that Dr. Rosenthal had found.

She shifted her hands on the chair arms and was surprised to have them skid on a thin film of moisture that had somehow collected under her palms. Yet she was as calm, as in control, as ever.

Dr. Kruger straightened up. His light rattled onto the metal tray. "It's difficult to see much in there, but there's evidence of scar tissue drawing inside that left eye. That could account for some whopping headaches and no doubt about it. Let's try a stronger version of those eyedrops and see if they don't do a better job of keeping you comfortable."

Scar tissue. Was that the key? Scarred material blocking her vision? She waited for him to go further in his explanation, but he had crossed to his desk and was scribbling out the new prescription.

"Is it—" She had to run her tongue over her lips, which, unlike her hands, were too dry. "Do you think it should—could be removed?"

"Removal is a possibility. Maybe a probability eventually. But let's give these drops a chance first. We don't have to worry about anything as drastic as surgery to get you through the school year in fairly good shape, I'm sure."

Cathy mimicked his dead-pan tone. " 'Drastic' depends on your priorities, doesn't it? I think I could manage not to worry about taking some time off from school if it were in a good cause." She coughed on a swallowed laugh. "About how much time would I have to be out?"

"Well, there'd be about three days in the hospital." Dr. Kruger tore a sheet of paper from his pad. "Then, generally, we figure on six to eight weeks after that before the swelling is down enough for the prosthesis to be fitted."

"Prosthesis." She knew that word from her therapy studies. It meant a man-made substitute for a missing part of the body. The word was a generic term for things like dentures and artificial limbs and devices worn by some cleft palate patients to help in articulation. And . . .

"Yes," Dr. Kruger said. "A plastic eye."

The chair arms pressed into Cathy's palms. He wasn't talking about removing scars that obstructed her vision. He was talking about removing entire eyes, every last hope of vision.

Then she recognized where the misunderstanding lay. "Remove the left eye, you mean. But what about the right one? Dr. Rosenthal thought there's a chance of restoring some sight in that." She was proud of how evenly she said it.

Dr. Kruger squealed his chair away from the desk. "Dr. Rosenthal told you that? Not in so many words, did he?"

She refused to hear his incredulity. "It was practically a promise. First he asked me—" how well she remembered every detail of that conversation—"if my schoolwork wouldn't be easier if I could see. He said that twenty-twenty vision would be like wishing for the moon, but that it didn't do any harm to hope. He asked if I would settle for vision enough to count fingers, and told me to come again in a couple months so you could keep track of what was happening. He said I could be certain you'd do everything that was medically possible and that I—" Her throat rebelled suddenly and she had to gulp. "That I should never give up hope—hoping," she finished in a whisper.

For there was no actual promise in anything Dr. Rosenthal had said. Repeated here in the sterile practicality of this office, the promise evaporated from his remarks like perfume too delicate for the antiseptic air. Those remarks were only scraps of idle sociability, loosely strung together on a thread that didn't necessarily lead anywhere.

Dr. Kruger cleared his throat. "Well—" He stood up and cleared his throat again. "I suppose it is true there's no harm in hoping—"

Cathy waited for him to continue until the pause became unbearable. "But in my case hoping won't do any good?" Her voice remained a husky whisper, but she couldn't risk the stress of clearing her own throat. Something might break.

"I'm afraid—yes." Dr. Kruger exhaled softly. "There's always room for hope, I suppose, in a general sense. But research hasn't come up yet with anything that even remotely points to a replacement for the optic nerve, which is what you would need. The nerves are gone in both eyes."

Cathy nodded carefully. More than ever, a sudden move could be her undoing. She believed his diagnosis with a root-deep certainty of its truth that her faith in Dr. Rosenthal never had achieved. But she had believed—wanted to believe—Dr. Rosenthal, too.

"Why would he talk as if—tell me to keep hoping?"

"He didn't mean to mislead you intentionally, I'm sure. It may be he was indulging in some wishful thinking, to brighten up his findings for you, and wasn't aware of the interpretation that could be put on his comments." In a faintly tightened voice, he added, "Dr. Rosenthal always acts from the best of motives."

Cathy understood. Out of the goodness of his heart, Dr. Rosenthal had sought to inject a ray of sunshine into what to him seemed an impossibly bleak existence. Well, he'd injected it, and now she was more blind than she had ever been before.

She stepped down from the chair and clamped her hand hard around Trudy's harness, which, along with Trudy, rose to meet her. With her other hand she reached toward Dr. Kruger for the prescription.

"These new drops, I use them the same?" The same as what, she had to leave unsaid.

"No, these I want you to put in three times a day, headache or not. If we're lucky, there may not be any more headaches. Provided, of course, you don't get hit on the head with a baseball." His dry chuckle was barely distinguishable from a cough.

Cathy made a smile, and the danger of tears somehow receded. "When do you want me back?" she asked in a voice that was very close to normal.

"Not until spring. We can wait until school is out. June, probably, unless some problem comes up, of course."

He walked with her to the receptionist's desk and stood by while Cathy was booked for a return visit in June.

"Okay, then," the nurse said cheerily. "That will be the first Saturday. In the meantime, have a merry Christmas."

Christmas. Cathy could have laughed, but she responded instead like a talking doll whose string had been pulled. "Thank you. Merry Christmas to you."

"Right. Merry Christmas," Dr. Kruger said, sounding no less mechanical than she.

He waited until Cathy was crossing the room to her father but not quite until she was out of earshot before addressing his nurse in a terse undertone. "Get me Dr. Rosenthal on the phone."

Cathy hurried her arms into the coat her father held for her. "Let's go, Daddy," she murmured, afraid this might be one of the times he would suggest speaking a few words to Dr. Kruger himself.

To her relief, he didn't argue or ask questions, and they left, Trudy tugging at the harness as if she, too, sensed that they must escape that office or suffocate.

A sidewalk Santa Claus was ding-dinging a monotonous bell on the street corner. Cathy wondered why those bells, supposed to remind people of the Christmas spirit of joyful giving, invariably had such a dreary clang to them. It was more like a call to grim duty than to gladness. She wasn't sorry to pass by quickly in the wide arc that was Trudy's means of expressing her distrust of people dressed up in peculiar costumes and making peculiar noises.

Our tastes don't run to make-believe, Cathy thought. Even in the name of charity. Especially in the name of charity.

"Woop! 'Scuse me." Somebody barreling along the sidewalk barged into her. The blasé soprano skidded up a startled notch. "My God! A dog!" Then stupidly, backing away in mumbling confusion, "Oh, a blind dog. Sorry."

Cathy's body became a robot shell encasing her, a creation of welded steel and bloodless plastic, programmed to walk on at a steady pace without a glance to left or right. Were Mark here, he would be cutting capers of concern about the "poor blind dog" the length of the street. Cathy had been known to cut a few such capers herself on past occasions. But not today. She couldn't even spit out the bitterness that rose to her tongue: "You can see where you're going. Why don't you look?" She could only walk stonily on—and on and on and on the endless miles to the parking lot around the corner and the shelter of the car.

"Well?" her father prompted when they were in the car and underway at last. "What's the story on counting fingers?"

"It was a false alarm." She spread her hands in her lap and bent her head, as if the explanation were printed in the creases of her palms for her to read. "Dr. Kruger says both my optic nerves are dead. Apparently, Dr. Rosenthal didn't have all the facts."

If that was not precisely what Dr. Kruger had said

of Dr. Rosenthal, it was true, nonetheless. He did not have all the facts. Not about her. Not about Catherine Elizabeth Wheeler, who did not need or want or knowingly accept charity from any source born of any motive.

Her father received the news quietly. "It's just possible Dr. Kruger doesn't have all the facts together, either," he said, slowing for a turn. "There are other doctors we can consult. We don't have to take his word alone."

"No, I don't want to. He's right. I know he is. Too many doctors add up to too much—too much confusion."

Her hands clenched on themselves at the thought of having to live again in the dream world she had inhabited for these past two and a half months. She saw it now not as a dream but as a distorted nightmare. Even deeper than her shock, keener than her disappointment, was the humiliation burning in her. To think that to Dr. Rosenthal she had been so pitiable an object that he fed her false hopes in the belief that this was all that could possibly make such a wretched existence bearable to her. A phrase bit into her mind from a poem by Marianne Moore she had memorized once for an English class in high school: *Charity riding an elephant.*

Her father didn't press the argument. She suspected he would probably call Dr. Kruger and clarify the facts for himself, but she didn't care. He was good at knowing when enough had been said for the moment, and that was what counted. The next hurdle would be to tell her mother and Mark without provoking outbursts of sympathy or indignation, neither of which she could stand up to just now. She tensed as the car did the short, familiar turn into the alley and pulled to a stop at the garage.

But when she left her father tinkering with the sluggish pulley for the overhead door and let herself into the house, there was no one around. It was early for Mark to be home from his morning chores at the veterinary hospital, and, judging by the thuds and thumps from upstairs, her mother was cleaning in the bedrooms. Trudy dashed upstairs to investigate while Cathy hung the harness and leash and her coat in the front hall closet.

"Cathy?" Mrs. Wheeler called from the top of the stairs. She came into the living room as Cathy was closing the closet door. "You're home earlier than I expected."

"There wasn't much to stay for, I guess." Cathy released the door knob slowly and gave the door a final push as if all that was important was whether the sometimes uncooperative latch caught or not. "There's no change except that Dr. Kruger gave me a stronger prescription for my headaches. Dr. Rosenthal was wrong. What he said was more hoping than possibility, and it appears I took him too seriously. There's no way, Dr. Kruger says."

"None at all? Oh, Cathy."

Her mother made a quick step toward her, but to Cathy's relief, it was only one. Consoling arms around her now and a shoulder to cry on might put a crack in the dam that could never be mended.

Instead, Mrs. Wheeler asked, "What have you done with your father?"

"The garage door doesn't want to go up the way it should. He's still down there arguing with it." Cathy offered her a one-sided smile. "Let's face it. This is going to be one of those days."

"It's beginning to look that way," her mother agreed. "You missed some phone calls this morning that I'm afraid you'll be sorry about, too. The phone has been ringing steadily for you ever since you left."

"Who's been calling?" Cathy's immediate thought was Greg. She was surprised by how little interest the idea aroused in her. Had their feeling for each other been real or only another part of her delirium?

"Well, the first call was from Amy Reinhardt. I should say the first two because she called twice within a half hour."

"Amy! Where was she calling from? Can I call her back? What did she want?"

No one had heard from Amy or of her since that day she had vanished from St. Chrysostom in tears. Monica claimed to have put in a long-distance call to Amy's home in New Concord, but the phone had rung and rung without anyone answering. Amy had no notion of the hornet's nest that had been stirred up in the college on her behalf. The Monday following the delivery of Monica's petition to the president's office, a notice had appeared on the speech department bulletin board:

> To the members of the junior class: Your communication of Wednesday, November 12, has been received and is being given the careful study proper to its contents.
>
> *Sister M. Regina, Pres.*

Nobody was quite certain about what was meant by "careful study proper to its contents," but there were those who predicted an explosion in the offing—and also those who were troubled by second thoughts about the petition, now that it was too late. There were also uneasy mutterings that Monica and Karen had padded the list of signatures with names of girls who had failed to attend the meeting or had been reluctant to sign for themselves, and louder mutterings from those who did sign about people who were braver at making promises than keeping them. Ugly words like "forgery," "turncoats," "radicals," and "cowards" had hung in the air like hot smoke the last week before Thanksgiving vacation. Cathy herself was undecided yet whether the instinct that had prompted her not to sign had been valid or just a self-centered betrayal of her friends, but it was evident already that the price was to be a definite cooling of Monica's friendship and perhaps that of others, too. Amy was the one person who could tell her why it had to be so.

"I gather she was in town with her mother to pack up the things she had left behind and do a little shopping. She said she wouldn't be anywhere you could reach her. She was so sorry to have missed you that I think she wanted to say more than the reason she gave for calling, but—" Mrs. Wheeler paused to pick up a newspaper lying on top of the television set. "Well, I've got it right here, an item she saw in last night's paper. It's about Leonard Perkins. An obituary."

Cathy set her purse down gently on her father's overstuffed footstool. "Say that again."

"You'd better sit down," her mother advised. "I'll read it:

> PERKINS, LEONARD; 4321 N. 67th; Friday, November 28; aged five years. Beloved son of Leon A. and Edith née Walsh; grandson of

Leonard and Thelma Perkins and Harold and Virginia Walsh; great-grandson of Oliver B. Walsh. Survived by aunts, uncles, and other relatives. In state at the Compton Funeral Home, 1616 W. Spring, 8 P.M. to 9 P.M. Saturday, November 29.

Cathy did sit down, lowering herself onto the edge of the footstool as though it or she might break. "That is Leonard," she said foolishly. "Those are his parents' names and that's his address. But I never guessed he was that sick—"

Her mother smoothed the newspaper page. "He must have been their only child."

"Yes," Cathy said. It sounded like a stranger's voice, commenting on a stranger's business. She couldn't seem to pull her thoughts together into anything coherent.

"Steve—he was another of your phone calls—offered to take you to the funeral parlor this afternoon, if you want to go. But he'll be calling back around noon. You can make your arrangements with him then."

Death and funeral parlors on this day that was to have been champagne and celebration. Cathy swayed with a giddy desire to laugh. The ring of the telephone saved her.

"That will be Mark," her mother said. "He called about ten minutes ago, to see if you were home yet and what Dr. Kruger said."

"I'll get it." Cathy pushed herself up off the footstool. What she said to Mark, and later to Steve, she afterward didn't remember, except that Mark's reaction, following a groan of regret, was, "Well, at least nobody's going to be able to grab Trudy away." She repeated this to Steve, when he phoned again, before he could utter anything sympathetic, and his understanding chuckle had reassured her that she could leave the subject without lingering until it grew painful.

The difficulty was that everything forbade lingering for the same reason. It wasn't until the receiver was back in its cradle that she thought to wonder why Steve should volunteer a part of his Saturday afternoon to escort her to visit a funeral parlor on behalf of someone he hadn't ever seen. She couldn't even remember if she had thanked him.

"I don't remember either, so it can't be too important," he said, breaking into the apology she began as soon as she was seated beside him in his car. "If I were making some kind of sacrifice, giving up something I'd rather be doing, then I suppose you could thank me. But not until then."

"Okay." She found that smiling was easier than she had expected. "You get no thanks from me unless I discover there is something you enjoy more than Saturdays at a funeral home. Under those conditions, maybe I'm the one to be thanked." The smile went lopsided and was gone. "I can think of lots of things I'd rather— I don't know what to say to them, to his parents. What is there that isn't trite or stupid?"

"Don't worry about it. They're not looking for words of wisdom. It's that you care enough to come that counts. Anyhow, that's how I felt when my dad died. I was fourteen then, and I don't remember a thing anybody said to me, but I can still name off just about everybody who was there." Steve touched her shoulder lightly. "Be yourself and everything will be fine."

She let herself believe that up to the second the car eased in to the curb and he turned off the motor. She stopped believing it when her feet crossed the mat-covered threshold of the silent building and noiseless doors shut her into a hush that absorbed every natural, commonplace sound from the whisper of clothing down to the tiny jingle of the ID tag on Trudy's collar. The pepper scent of chrysanthemums and the weighted odor of roses kept too warm too long thickened the air into bands of panic tightening against her throat. She didn't belong here. She had no right. She was an intruder, a fraud.

"Perkins?" a man's voice inquired. Not a stir of air, a shush of carpet had forewarned of his approach. "Would you like to sign the book before you go in?"

Steve declined on the grounds the family didn't know him, but he lent his pocket comb as a guide to indicate the line along which Cathy painstakingly drew the loops and curls of her name.

"We're not the first ones here," he murmured, leaning over her shoulder to read. "This page is more than half-filled, and it's only three-thirty."

Cathy could hear people talking in the room beyond. Leonard must be in there. Leonard lying quiet and undistracted by his surroundings, for once. Leonard lying quiet now and forever. How could she walk in there and offer his mother a shallow "I'm sorry"? What meaning was there in that? What use could it be now, when being sorry came too late?

Yet that was what she did say, with her hand clasped tight in both of Mrs. Perkins'. "I'm so very sorry."

"Thank you. You're so good to come." Mrs. Perkins pressed Cathy's hand harder. "Only don't be sorry. We've always known we were keeping him on borrowed time. The doctors gave him less than a year when he was born, but he would have been six his next birthday. And this year, when he was starting to learn—" She faltered, still holding Cathy's hand. "We can't ever thank you enough for what you've done for him and us. The work you did with him, the words he was beginning to speak—we'll never forget it."

Leonard's father joined them. His handshake was moist and calloused and, like his wife's, reluctant to let go. "We sure do thank you. You and that St. Chrysostom's school over there. Me and my wife aren't Catholic, but we can't ever say enough good about that bunch of people there. No other place we went to would even give Lenny a chance, but that Dr. Paulus, she said the only way to know was to try."

"She's such a lovely person," Mrs. Perkins said on a note that was almost awe. "She cares so much. Who would have thought she would trouble to come down here today? And you, too. But that's so like you people."

"Do you mean Dr. Paulus has been here?" Cathy couldn't wholly hide her astonishment.

"She left just a few minutes ago. I guess Lenny kind of got to her like he did to anybody that knew him—like he must have got to you for you to work so hard to help him. There was a lot of love in that little guy, whatever else you say. A lot of love." Mr. Perkins turned aside and blew his nose.

Cathy wasn't sure what expression her face was wearing, but she felt as if it were one wired on. She was aware of Steve nearby, hovering in the background, hearing, registering all this. But perceptive as Steve sometimes was, he couldn't know—how she hoped he couldn't know, he or anyone—the wretchedness that was twisting inside her.

"Is that the same Dr. Paulus you've been telling me about?" he asked when they were in the car again.

Cathy shook her head in wonder. "It doesn't sound like the same person, does it?"

But then, the Cathy Wheeler the Perkins had described sounded like no one she knew, either.

"I saw the name Jacqueline Paulus up near the top of the page you signed," Steve said, "if you want to count that as physical evidence. She didn't put 'Dr.' with it."

"Jacqueline." Cathy tested the texture of it on her tongue. "Jacqueline Paulus. Funny, I never pictured her as having any first name besides Dr. I never pictured her as having enough heart to feel sympathy for anyone, either, but, now that I know she went out of her way to show the Perkins she cared, I'm not really surprised. And that's about as much sense as anything seems to be making today."

Steve's hand left the wheel to give hers a quick pressure. "You've had a rough day."

Rough? That was a mild term for what she had endured this past quarter hour, trapped between Leonard's coffin and banks of flowers, receiving outpourings of thanks she didn't deserve. For she had not done a thing for Leonard. Everything she had accomplished with him had been done strictly for herself. When she first heard that he was gravely ill, hadn't her only thought been how will this damage *me?* And since then, had she given more than a passing thought to how he might be faring? Each repetition of the Perkins' gratitude for her selfless dedication to their son had been like another strip of adhesive tape being ripped away to reveal something festering underneath.

Cathy rolled her window halfway down and tipped her face to the jet of November cold that streamed in. "I feel as if I haven't had fresh air to breathe in ages."

"What would you say to a walk in the woods at this

hour?" Steve asked. "We aren't far from the north end of Ridge Park and our old tramping trail where we used to let Trudy run, and there's still a fair amount of daylight. I'd like to stop off and take a look around for a glove I lost in there Monday."

"I'd say let's, yes," she agreed. It was the least she could do in return for the favor he had done her this afternoon. "I haven't been in those woods since I can't remember when."

The car swung off the paved street and jounced onto a dirt road, jarring fragments of recollection from the dusty corners of her memory. Unexpectedly, she knew there was no place she would rather be heading for than the living quiet of the woods.

Trudy's memory was in operation, too. She was on her feet, uttering little yelps and whines of recognition before Steve put on the brakes. Cathy unbuckled the harness and tossed it onto the back seat. At Steve's "All clear," she opened the door, holding onto the leash, and let herself be tugged up a path to the top of the slope where the woods began. There, well beyond danger of Trudy's dashing into the road, she unsnapped the leash and set her free. Trudy hurtled into the underbrush like a cork popped from a bottle. The crack of dead twigs and crash of dry leaves marked her progress as plainly as a line on a chart.

Steve laughed, linking Cathy's arm through his to walk on along the trail. "I catch sight of a fox in here every once in a while, but we won't do it today. Not unless he's deaf. Any creature that has ears to hear and legs to run or wings to fly is long gone already."

Trudy burst out onto the trail ahead of them and came prancing and panting to nuzzle Cathy's fingers. Then she was off on another pell-mell flight that would circle back in a few minutes to touch home base again. She wasn't about to risk getting lost or left behind. Her joy in the rare freedom of being able to range as she pleased foamed away some of the gloom from Cathy's somber spirits.

"Right about here is where my glove came up missing," Steve said when the trail led them down into a hollow. "It's quite a way in, though, and no path. I didn't think about your nylons—"

Cathy slid her hand from his arm. "Say no more. I'll wait here."

Steve guided her a few steps off the trail to a knee-high log. "At least you can wait in rustic comfort, compliments of the forestry department. I won't be long. I've got a pretty good idea of where I must have dropped the thing."

She had no sense of being deserted as his departing footsteps crunched through the drifts of fallen leaves. Neither was she worried about how long he might have to search. The threat to her stockings of burrs and raspberry brambles had been only a small part of her reason for choosing to stay here and wait. What she wanted more than anything else was to be alone for a while.

Trudy crackled up to her to investigate the log. After snuffing beneath it, she climbed up beside Cathy, stood there for a wobbly instant, and launched herself forward to splash through the windrow of leaves behind it.

Cathy smiled in spite of herself. "Show off! You elephant."

The other elephant she had encountered today raised its unwelcome head: *Charity, riding an elephant . . .*

Before she could block it, another image from the poem presented itself: *envy, on a dog.* Like a zigzag flash in a kaleidoscope, the whole reference tumbled itself together:

> envy, on a dog, is worn down by obsession,
> his greed, (since of things owned by others he
> can only take *some*).

Envy, obsession, greed: the words dug into her with determined barbs, like the sticktights she had just discovered clustered on the hem of her coat. Could it be called anything less than an obsession, the way she had slept and eaten and breathed nothing but the dream of seeing again these last months? Wasn't that why that —she might as well admit it—mingled with the bitterness and disappointment, there was a kind of relief, as if she had been released from some form of captivity? It was her fault as much as Dr. Rosenthal's that she had fallen such a willing victim into his trap; hadn't she come to him brimful of envy of the sight other people possessed? As for greed, she had been scrambling to claim as her own, not some of *anything* but *all* of *everything*: her dog, her sight, the right to remain in the speech therapy program as a blind student, the triumph of walking out on the program as a sighted person, the glamor of a serious romance, the security of being tied to no final commitment. Why hadn't she recognized that "all of everything" was an equation that canceled itself out? The end result was nothing.

Cathy hunched deeper into her coat. Once again, she had the sensation of being newly awakened from a delirium. It was as if she had been far away for a long time. A lot of her values had fallen into sad need of repair during her absence.

She pulled the last of the sticktights from her coat

and stood up. It was too chilly to sit here, just thinking. Steve wouldn't be disturbed if she walked on a way by herself.

She scuffed a step or two through the brittle weeds and found the hard-packed groove that was the trail. A squirrel was dancing on a limb over her head, mewing and rasping his protest against the intrusion of outsiders into his woods. A short distance to the left, Trudy emitted a series of violent sneezes, apparently the price of inhaling too much dirt from the excavation she was enlarging. Farther on, the pert buzz of a chickadee was notifyng the world of his presence.

Nevertheless, the woods were quiet, peacefully quiet. Cathy moved slowly, pushing aside the drooping wands of branches that tickled her face. The clean, crisp air cut through the cobwebs the day had cast around her. A tang of damp wood and ripeness rose from the earth, speaking of a steadfast continuity she could almost lean against.

It's all here, she thought, tilting her head to listen and inhale. There were acorns on the path; she could feel them roll under her feet. There were crows gathering at the remoter edge of the woods; she could hear them talking. None of the world had been erased for her. It was as much within her grasp today as it had been yesterday. It's all here, she repeated to herself, and I'm here, alive to it, being.

She thought of Leonard. It was Leonard for whom the world had stopped. Her loss today had been only a fantasy woven from the flimsiest of threads, at best. Leonard's loss was the day itself, and yesterday, and whatever tomorrows there might have been. For her, they were still all intact.

She kicked a stick that lay across the path, then bent

to pick it up. Trudy was there at once, begging for her to throw it. Cathy tested its balance on her hand. The grosgrain texture of the bark was intriguing, the solid weight of the wood a satisfaction. When she sent it whistling as straight and far as she could launch it, she was alive to the smooth flow of motion from her shoulder and arm down to her heels.

Today is the first day of the rest of my life, she remembered, and turned with a smile toward the crunch of Steve's approaching steps. Somehow, his presence in no way disrupted the tranquility that was soaking into her, like healing oil into chapped skin.

"Not frozen yet?" he asked.

"Not a bit. I love it here. I'd almost forgotten."

"So had I. Until one day I happened to be driving by and here it was." He fell into step beside her as they began to walk on. "I've remembered a lot of forgotten things since I've been back. And some things I'm not sure I even knew I knew."

Cathy stumbled on a root in the trail, and Steve's arm dropped across her shoulders to steady her. It felt good there, and she was glad he let it stay.

The trail led them upward to the crest of the ridge. There the wind sliced into them with a stinging forecast of winter, urging them closer together and driving them back down the hill. They retraced the trail without talking, partly, Cathy surmised, because Steve's face was chilled as stiff as hers, but more because there was more to communication than just spoken words, for another surmise was flickering awake in her—that the effect of the woods on her would not be quite the same if Steve weren't here, too.

"You didn't say if you found your glove," she said

when they reached the comparative warmth within the protection of the hollow.

"I did. Right where I left it."

"You make it sound as if you'd left it there on purpose."

He lifted a branch out of their way with his free hand and let it swish into place behind them. "I'm ashamed to say I didn't think quite that far ahead." The arm on her shoulders became a pressure that drew her to a standstill. "But I do admit to being an unblushing opportunist."

Cathy laughed to cover a sudden flutter of comprehension that couldn't be true. She bobbed her head in a mock curtsy. "Why, Steve, I didn't know you cared."

"Try me," he said.

His kiss was quiet and undramatic, a nice kiss of the sort she had learned to expect from Steve. Then he linked her hands behind his neck and kissed her again. This time, it was like nothing she had expected, and for a space the November woods were at the height of summer.

It was one more twist to this tangled day that was going to demand some earnest thinking over to unwind.

10

CATHY'S FINGERS idled on the typewriter keys, groping for inspiration that wasn't there, then typed a final sentence. She rolled the exam paper out of the machine and slipped it into sequence beneath two other single-spaced sheets. The set of questions she had brailled for herself at Sister Janice's dictation lay on top. This wasn't the best exam she had ever written, but it was better than it would have been if she hadn't spent the past two weeks cramming to catch up on the fine points she'd let slide during the semester.

She tapped the papers together on the typing table and stood up to cross the little cubbyhole of an office and lay them on Sister Janice's desk. The rest of the girls in the human development class were taking this exam in 349, the big classroom down the hall, but since there was no typewriter in that room, Sister Janice had volunteered the use of the one in her office. "I'll be popping in and out most of the period," she had said, "but I'll try not to disturb you. If I'm not here when you're through, you can just leave the papers on my blotter."

She wasn't here. If Cathy were to trust the evidence of her ears, no one was anywhere. Not a voice or a footfall was audible through the open door. The length and breadth of the building was charged with that tautly subdued atmosphere of exams in progress. Typing an exam was always faster than writing it by hand, no matter how much brain racking preceded each answer, so it wasn't unlikely that she was the first to be done.

She borrowed a paper clip from a tray at the upper corner of the desk blotter and laid her papers in a neat pile in the center of the desk. A check of her watch told her it was twenty minutes past two. Her appointment with Dr. Paulus wasn't until three. The next question was how to fill the time between.

She walked back to the windows beside the typing table to warm her cold hands in the sunshine pouring through the panes in a flood that denied Christmas could be only a week away. Probably she should be rehearsing what she intended to say to Dr. Paulus, but she had been ready to say it almost from the day classes had resumed after Thanksgiving vacation. If the choice were hers, the distasteful interview ahead of her could have been over and done with that very week. It had been Dr. Paulus' decision that, "We might better postpone discussing next semester until after you're through with your exams."

Cathy was obliged to admit that there had been other, more pressing, demands on Dr. Paulus recently. Girls who had signed Monica's petition began being called to the president's office in ones and twos right after Thanksgiving. For a while, disquieting rumors had circulated that girls who had merely lent moral support to the petition by complaining about Dr. Paulus among themselves would be called in, too, but that didn't happen. What did happen was that Sister Regina summoned the petitioners to her office as a group last week, there to deliver their charges to Dr. Paulus in person and to hear her reply to each. The encounter had ended with several girls in tears, Laura Riley among them. Others, like Karen Bergen, were reduced to sheepish mumblings, and those of Monica's ilk remained ominously silent. No one seemed disposed to go into much further detail for the benefit of those who weren't at the meeting, but it came as a surprise to hardly anyone when Sister Regina's office issued a statement the next day to the effect that the administration had found nothing in Dr. Paulus' actions that was unjustified or irregular and that the college considered itself and its students fortunate to have a person of her professional caliber in the speech department.

"Why should it be a surprise?" Cathy had overheard Monica declaiming to a cluster of girls in the lavatory. "Nuns aren't above being jealous the same as anyone else, and a department head as popular as Sister Bernard—well, let's just say our beloved college president gets to look like a lot bigger wheel without the competition. Regina's not going to bring her back if she can help it. She's got a lot more to gain by sticking by Paulus, so long as they figure we'll swallow that garbage about professionalism and 'a matter of faulty communication' every time Paulus cuts somebody else to bits in her tricky barbed wire." She had snapped a paper towel from the dispenser and crumpled it viciously. "It's been Dr. P.'s ball game this semester, but next semester she may find out that the honeymoon is over."

Nobody had ventured to laugh at this mixture of

metaphors. Nobody had asked precisely what Monica meant by them either. At last not while Cathy was still within hearing. Perhaps, like her, they hadn't really wanted to know.

Cathy turned from the window at the sound of footsteps in the corridor, but they went on by. The pace was so brisk that she felt it must be someone bent on a definite errand. Trudy, alerted for the moment, laid her head back down on her paws with a clink of her collar and a sigh.

Cathy echoed the sigh and sat down again at the typing table, for want of anything better to do. The honeymoon was over for her, that was sure, in more ways than one—or it would be when she walked out of the speech department this afternoon. All those bright, golden dreams— Nothing but fool's gold, most of them.

"Honeymoons don't last forever, I can tell you," was how Joan Norton—Joan Sheridan—had put it the other day when she phoned to invite Cathy to a fondue party she and Pete were giving during the holidays. "You wouldn't believe how it can get on your nerves, trying to think of what to talk about to the same person morning after morning and night after night. Mummie says I ought to get a bottle of tranquilizers and take them, but everything around here is so tranquil already, compared to the wedding and all that fuss and things, that I could scream."

And there, Cathy thought with a faint shudder, but for the grace of God go I. She retrieved the typewriter cover from where it had fallen under the table and smoothed it over the machine. Three nights ago, the doorbell and a yell from Mark had pulled her from her studying and down the stairs into a pair of arms that lifted her off her feet in a hug that assumed nothing ever changed unless Greg Breck wanted it to.

"I came back to get my car," he explained. "And to tie up a few loose ends I left dangling. But California's the place! The hotel deal didn't pan out like I expected, but there's a bunch of other leads I'm going to follow up as soon as I get out there again." Then, as if the weeks of total silence between his departure and this moment were less than yesterday, he had clapped her on the shoulder and turned her toward the stairs. "Go hop into your jeans and a warm jacket. We're invited to a December beach party this guy I know is throwing at his lake cottage tonight. It's going to be wild."

Cathy had felt her backbone lengthen and lock taut. "Just like that? I've got exams to study for. Tomorrow at eight o'clock is my first."

"Forget exams," Greg ordered in a tone of command that would have been suicidal if her father weren't too busy in his basement workshop to be aware of what was happening upstairs. "If you don't know it now, you won't know it tomorrow, and what's the difference, anyway? You don't have to graduate *summa cum laude* to suit me."

"I'm not doing it to suit you," she had said before she could stop herself. Her attempt to undo its bluntness was no improvement. "I'm doing it for myself."

She doubted that he grasped the full import of what she was saying, but when she continued to refuse, something of it began to register. "You may be sending me off to the arms of another woman," he warned, only half-jokingly.

That should have cost her a pang of some kind. She hesitated, waiting, but there was none. "I guess I'm not the jealous type."

Greg hesitated, too. Perhaps he was wishing Mark wasn't sprawled on the floor in front of the TV set across the room and that her mother would find an errand to take her upstairs to the linen closet or down to the basement. Cathy herself wasn't sure but what a little more privacy would have made everything easier, but there wasn't much else that required saying under any circumstances.

"Well, okay," Greg had yielded finally. "I'll be seeing you around."

And that was the end of that. It was possible that he might call or even drop by again, but she calculated that the chances were pretty slim. The most painful part was that she felt no pain whatever. Yet it was barely over a month since the idea of honeymooning with him, of submerging the rest of her life in his, could set her heart to beating like pigeons' wings.

That was why she wanted to go cautiously where she and Steve were concerned. The fact that Steve understood her misgivings was itself a pledge that he and Greg were not the same, but he agreed that there were good reasons for them not to let themselves grow too serious too fast. Among them was the distance both she and Steve still had to travel to gain their degrees. Steve's undernourished finances might mean he would have to drop out of school entirely for a year and get a full-time job somewhere, if the teaching assistantship he was hoping for went to someone else. As for where graduation lay in Cathy's future now—

She gulped down a lungful of air and held it to the count of ten to quiet a nervous flinching in her stomach. Her finger sought the button on her watch that let the crystal fly up so she could touch the minute hand beneath, even though she knew it hadn't moved more than five minutes beyond its last position. What wouldn't she give to have this afternoon and its business irrevocably settled and behind her?

Light footsteps approached the office door, paused, and came in.

Cathy twisted on the narrow typing chair. "Sister?"

"Oh!" It was a squeak of surprise near the desk. "I didn't see— I thought this room was empty."

"Amy!" Cathy said, and almost overturned her chair in her eagerness to reach the desk before the newcomer could vanish. "What are you doing here? Where have you been?"

"Don't ask. It's such a dreary story." The plaintive little chirp was definitely Amy's. "Anyway, what are you doing here? I thought nobody'd be around today and I could scoot in and scoot out without any fuss."

"You'll have to scoot fast," Cathy said, easing herself between Amy and the door, for fear Amy might just try it. "Everybody's around today. They're up to their ears in exams."

"You're kidding! This isn't exam week. Last week was."

Cathy pointed to the desk. "There's my development exam, hot from the typewriter. And half the junior class is down the hall, working on the same thing."

"I could have sworn exams were over last week and I could just duck in today to pick up my leftover stuff and duck out again. In fact, I did swear, on my word of honor." Amy's laugh was very like a gasp of dismay. "Maybe if I lie low in here between bells, I can still make it. How was the development exam?"

"Thorough." Cathy's shrug was wry. "You might say a prayer for me, if ever you have an idle moment."

"Why not?" Amy's laugh this time was light and brittle. "A prayer, the alphabet, three blind mice— They all come at the same price."

Cathy's mouth gaped, but without a syllable to reply. Amy gone cynical? It was as if a snapdragon were suddenly to breathe flame.

"Oh, Cathy, I'm sorry!" The flames were out as swiftly as they had ignited, and the old Amy was beside her, a repentent hand on her arm. "I meant nursery rhymes in general, not that one. I wasn't being personal or—"

Cathy covered the hand with her own before it could escape. She hoped the impression wasn't that she was hanging on to Amy to make her stay, but that was exactly what she was doing.

"Listen, Amy Reinhardt, the only way you can hurt my feelings is to disappear again without telling me what's wrong. What happened to you? Where have you been all this time?"

"Different places. Home, mostly." Amy made a feeble attempt to regain her hand, then let it stay where it was. "I—I had the flu. Can you imagine that? After all the faking I did, the real thing hit me like a truck. So I went home and gave it to my mother and we've been taking turns having relapses ever since."

"How are you feeling now?"

"Fine. I mean—" Amy turned her head away to rasp out a small, dry cough. "Getting over getting better is the worst part, if you know what I mean."

Cathy shook her head. She didn't know what Amy meant, but more disturbing, she wasn't sure that Amy knew either. Amy was tossing words at her at such a rate that it was rather like listening to a record playing at the wrong speed. The sense was getting lost in the sound.

"You knew that my patient, Leonard, died," Cathy said, remembering that Amy had cared enough to phone about it.

"Yes. At least somebody got lucky."

"Amy!"

"Well?" Amy challenged. "What do you expect me to say? That the world's all sunshine and miracles and love? Don't you for one minute believe it." She snatched her hand from Cathy's and retreated to the window. "Don't look so shocked. You can't believe that life's a glorious party for everybody, just because everything's always so easy for you."

Easy? The charge stung like a slap, and Cathy's mind jumped ahead to the pending interview with Dr. Paulus. Amy should know how easy that was going to be.

"I can't believe anything if you don't let me know what you're talking about," she countered with a degree of warmth. "What is it that's gone wrong?" Then, on a spurt of inspiration, "Is it Larry?"

"Larry? I'd forgotten there was such a person. He's never phoned me or answered a single one of my letters since I went home, so obviously there isn't." Amy was rearranging Sister Janice's African violets on the windowsill. The saucers grated as though they were being slid across gravel. "Besides, my mother and I are leaving on a six-week cruise after the holidays. As long as we're together we don't need anybody else."

"Does that mean you won't be in school next semester?" Cathy couldn't bring herself to say, "won't be allowed back," but that was what she was thinking. A wintery finger touched her heart. Had Monica been right all along?

Flower pots clinked in abrupt collision. "I won't be

in school again ever. Two and a half years is enough time thrown away on nothing."

Cathy picked her way around Trudy, lying watchfully between the desk and the typewriter, and stepped to the window. There were beginning to be voices in the hall now, and she was no more eager than Amy to call attention to Amy's presence here, especially not just yet.

"Amy," she said in a low voice, "is it because of Dr. Paulus? Is it something she did that drove you out?"

The pots stopped their grinding to and fro on the sill. "I told you I got the flu. I had time to think while I was sick, and I realized I could be having a lot more fun doing other things than studying and making lesson plans. I couldn't take it another day, so I've quit."

"I can't believe that," Cathy said, and it was the truth. Amy's enthusiasm had never waned, even when they had slogged through March snowstorms together last spring to perform hearing tests in downtown grade schools as part of their audiometry course. "What about Sister Bernard? Did you ever write that letter to her?"

"Sister Bernard!" The name splintered into jagged laughter that was totally unlike Amy's.

"What about Sister Bernard?" Cathy asked, already half-discounting the answer. Could it be that the flu story was the whole truth after all, and that Amy was still under some sort of medication that was temporarily changing her personality?

"Do you really want to know? Shall I tell you about Sister Bernard and what she's been doing since August? Do you really want to know where she is right now?"

"She's in Oregon some place," Cathy answered reasonably. "At some school helping to put together a—"

"She's ten miles outside of New Concord, at the nuns'

nursing home at Oakwood," Amy said. "She had a stroke this summer, and she's been a vegetable ever since."

"You're not serious!" The quiver in Cathy's voice was both anger and alarm. Amy had to be suffering some kind of delirium to say anything so outrageous. For Amy even more than for anyone else, Sister Bernard had always been the embodiment of competence and wisdom.

"She's a vegetable at Oakwood, and she's never coming back," Amy said as if she were biting off a thread with each word. "I found out that day I decided to write to her. I stopped in at the mail room to buy a stamp, and I asked Sister Hilda, that vagueish little nun that helps sort mail sometimes, if she could give me Sister Bernard's address. She told me she thought that just Convent Hospital, Oakwood, would do it, and started to look up the zip code for me. Then she got all flustered and said she was wrong and to forget Oakwood and that students shouldn't bother Sister Bernard, and that I'd better ask Sister Superior or Sister Regina or somebody like that if I wanted more information. That was Friday, so I went home for the weekend to go check up at Oakwood myself."

"And Sister Bernard was there?" Cathy's mind was reaching back in spite of herself, back to that day they had discussed writing to Sister Bernard. Wasn't that the day Amy had been so worried about the effects of her mother's hospitality on Larry? Yes, and Amy did go home unexpectedly that weekend, for that was the Friday they had planned to ask Greg to set up a double date with Larry for *Blithe Spirit*—a plan Greg couldn't be troubled to carry out. But none of this was proof that anything in Amy's wild tale was so.

"They wouldn't let me in, naturally. Not past the front desk, anyway. They weren't giving out any information about their patients, either. But my mother got busy and made a few phone calls here and there, and we found out. My mother always knows someone somewhere where it counts." It was difficult to know if the rasp in Amy's throat was meant to be a rasp or a bitter chuckle. "I didn't want to believe it any more than you do, but when I got back here and screwed up the nerve to tell Dr. Paulus what I'd heard, she admitted that it's true. Sister Bernard has been there all this time, hidden away from snoopy visitors and everyone else who might spill the big, dark secret."

The cold steel edge of the typing table behind her was carving its contours into Cathy's hands. "Why?" She was questioning no one detail of the revelation but the enormity of it as a whole.

"Why not? They've been stuffing us full of hot air and baloney here from the first second we hit the campus. What's one lie more, or a dozen? You know, it's really funny when you think of it." Amy flung around from the window, expelling a burst of laughter so harsh it sounded as if her throat must be scraped raw. "Here we've been knocking ourselves out for the noble cause of communication and conquering disabilities and earning the rewards that come from service to others, and all the while there is Sister Bernard, our glorious ideal, lying there without a voice or a mind or even the power to turn over in bed."

"Hush! Not so loud." Cathy side-stepped along the table, intending to close the door, but the thought of being shut in here with this strange, explosive Amy caused her to hesitate.

"Why? What's the matter?" Amy demanded, her volume rising. "Don't you see the humor in it? Me, I thought she was so beautiful and indestructable and strong that I even considered entering the convent when I was a freshman so I could be more like her. And do you know what my mother said? That my head was full of mashed potatoes. Isn't that a laugh?"

"Girls, please," Sister Janice said from the doorway, and the door clicked shut. "Lower your voices. I could hear you halfway down the corridor."

"Oh, Sister," Amy said, sounding dismayed rather than contrite. "I didn't expect to see you. I was going to leave you a note."

"I'd have been sorry to miss you, Amy," Sister Janice said, "but you might have expected the entire school in here if you kept up that shouting."

"We were talking about—about . . . That is, Amy was telling me—" Cathy discovered that, far from being capable of a shout, her voice was unequal to much better than a squeak.

"I gathered fairly well what Amy was telling you. I also know that Dr. Paulus trusted her not to repeat the story among the students."

"Because it isn't true?" Cathy didn't know which answer she wanted less: that Sister Bernard was indeed ill or that Amy was hysterically lying.

"Last summer, at a convention, Sister Bernard suffered the first of three cerebral hemorrhages," Sister Janice said more gently. "The other two occurred while she was in the hospital. Her speech was affected and her left side paralyzed, but she's at our Oakwood convent now and making good progress toward recovery. We're hoping that, eventually, she may be well enough to be part of St. Chrysostom in an active way again."

Cathy wished she could sit down. She tried to focus

on the positive parts of the information, such as they were, blocking out the shadowy remoteness of "may be" and "eventually." The result was a welling up of resentment so swift and hot it took her by surprise.

"There's nothing wrong about having a stroke, nothing shameful in it. Why has it been hushed up like a wicked secret?"

"You are quite right. There is nothing wrong or wicked or shameful in any of this," Sister Janice said firmly. "Perhaps a policy of frankness would have been the wiser course, but it was Sister Bernard's own wish, expressed in the hospital while she could still speak, that her condition be kept from her students as long as possible. She wanted her absence to cause as little upset as possible among you. Also, if Sister Bernard has any failing, it is her hatred of being fussed over and worried about and given special treatment and attentions beyond what may be absolutely necessary."

Cathy wasn't ready to accept everything quite yet. "What about the story that she was in Oregon, starting a clinic?" she challenged. "Who made that up?"

"I don't know how that story got started," Sister Janice admitted. "Or rather, I don't know how Oregon and Sister Bernard came to be connected in it. It was Dr. Paulus who was invited to help organize that speech clinic. She gave up that opportunity to come here on short notice for Sister Bernard's sake—and the college's."

"But nobody ever tried to put the rumor straight." Cathy was beginning to understand Amy's sense of betrayal, for her own was nearly as great. "All those times the teachers had us say an extra prayer before class for Sister Bernard's intentions and we always thought it was that clinic—Dr. Paulus could come here for Sister Bernard's sake, but she couldn't trust Sister's students to be mature enough to handle the truth like adults."

Sister Janice let a book thump onto her desk, and her tone hardened. "I don't deny that we who love Sister Bernard may all be guilty of having taken the easy way out. But as for maturity, can you honestly say that Dr. Paulus has been overwhelmed by evidences of student maturity this year?"

Cathy had no answer for that. Certainly, Dr. Paulus' highhanded methods were not calculated to win her many friends among the students, but the student reaction to her from the start—hostile, sullen, resistant, intoxicated by the image of themselves as victims—didn't lend itself too well to an unqualified defense, either. As for many of her own attitudes this semester, Cathy had evaluated them enough since Thanksgiving to know when she had lost her argument.

It was Amy who spat out, "Maturity! What's that besides a word? That's what Sister Bernard always said we should be: mature, responsible, reliable. And then what does she do? Falls apart at the seams and makes a mockery of the whole idea."

"Amy!" Cathy was shocked into a laugh. "You're talking as if her illness were deliberate."

"No, I know better than that," Amy said. "Or maybe I don't. All I do know is that she's not what I thought she was. Nothing's what I thought it was. Everything's gone wrong."

She was crying. Cathy moved to put an arm around her, but Amy lurched aside and crumpled into the chair at the desk. The muffled sound of her sobs told that she had buried her head in her arms like a little girl.

It was at this moment that the bell chose to ring.

Trudy heaved herself to her feet, recognizing the signal for what it was, and poked her nose into Cathy's damp hand, ready to leave. Cathy looped the leash over her wrist automatically, but stood where she was, undecided.

"You have an appointment at this hour, don't you?" Sister Janice asked in an undertone. "Go on. Don't be late."

Cathy picked up her purse and her folder of typing paper from beside the typewriter, but still indecision held her. She wanted to help Amy, to comfort her. More than that, she wanted to be reassured by Sister Janice that Amy wasn't beyond whatever help anyone could offer.

"Shall I come back here afterward? Amy?"

There was no break in Amy's sobs, no sign to indicate that she had heard.

Sister Janice gave Cathy's shoulder a pat that combined understanding with a gentle push toward the door. "Don't press her. She needs a little time."

Cathy eased the door shut behind her as carefully as if she were leaving a sick room. There was a second small snick after the click of the latch catching, and she knew that Sister Janice had turned the lock.

She stood outside, her hand reluctant to quit the knob. The hall was throbbing with footsteps and voices released from the exam hush by the bell, but the desire for sociability had left her. Her mouth felt lined with paper toweling. There was a drinking fountain about ten steps to the right of the door. She located it and took a long, cold drink that left the toweling intact and settled into her stomach like thickening plaster of Paris.

Sister Janice had neglected to ask her to keep Sister Bernard's illness a secret. Was that an oversight or had she lost faith in the value of trying to preserve the myth that all was well? Either way, it didn't matter. Cathy had no urge to peddle her new knowledge to anyone.

Yet if the fact had been known to everyone, Monica's forces would have been demoralized before they could unite. Even afterward, a statement from Dr. Paulus, a corroborating explanation from Sister Regina, could have drained the blood lust from the rebellion in a single gesture. Whose decision was it that the truth should not be told? Surely no one in the administration would have required of Dr. Paulus that she place Sister Bernard's privacy above the risk of damage to her own career. But to imagine Dr. Paulus willing to make such a sacrifice on behalf of another person, Dr. Paulus capable of caring that much about another person? That thought trailed Cathy down the hall to the chairman's office, lending a sliver of support to her morale, which was going to need all the strengthening it could get.

There was no response when she knocked on the open door and waited for permission to enter. Cathy knocked a second time, to satisfy herself no one was there, then nudged Trudy on in to the chair by the desk. Dr. Paulus might be occupied elsewhere temporarily, but she would be here by the time the second bell rang, the time that was the official start of the appointment. She would be here because she believed in being punctual. Dr. Paulus did live according to the rules she imposed on others. There ought to have been a particle of solace in that observation, but as Cathy folded her skirt under her and squared her purse and folder on her lap, she couldn't help reflecting that a little less perfection to face would be a lot more comforting.

"Good, you're here already," Dr. Paulus said, coming in just as the bell burst through the echoes in the hall.

Cathy bit the inside of her lip to conquer a wry smile. Her powers of prediction were in good form. She could probably predict just as accurately that this was one meeting that would go off without serious conflict. So why did she feel as if she were waiting for a dentist's drill?

Dr. Paulus opened a drawer in the desk. "I have a gift for you."

"For me?" A corner of Cathy's folder bent under her hand, although she was positive she hadn't jumped.

"You weren't expecting one?" Was there the faintest shimmer of amusement in Dr. Paulus' serene voice? "It was delivered in this morning's mail, along with a similar package for me. It's from Mr. and Mrs. Perkins."

She put a small, square box into Cathy's hands. A crisscross of narrow ribbon held it closed, but there was no gift wrap, no bow, no ornamentation of any kind that spoke of Christmas. A folded card without an envelope was tucked under the ribbon. Cathy slipped it free, but the blank page offered no clue to the quick sweep of her fingers.

"Would you like to have me read it for you?" Dr. Paulus asked.

Cathy would rather have postponed the reading for the privacy of home, especially when it was a communication as personal as a note from Leonard's parents was likely to be, but there seemed no graceful way to refuse. She handed the card over.

"It says THANK YOU on the front. Inside, there is a quotation from Proverbs: 'A word fitly spoken is like apples of gold in pictures of silver.' Then there's a note: 'Dear Cathy, We would like you to have this to remember Leonard by and to remind you of our thanks for what you did for him and for us. Very truly yours, Leon and Edith Perkins.' "

The clock on the desk was ticking rapidly in a barely audible whisper that filled the room.

"Thank you," Cathy said, receiving the card again. The words were a whisper, too.

There could be no question now whether to open the box immediately or to save it until she was alone. She fumbled the ribbon off at the corners and lifted the lid. A ball of heavy metal met her fingers. No, not a ball. An apple, complete with stem and a saw-edged leaf, and a dimple at the blossom end.

"It's gold. Gold-colored metal, anyway," Dr. Paulus said. "An apple of gold. It's the same as the one they gave to me. It looks like something freshly picked by King Midas."

Cathy revolved the little paperweight—for a paperweight it apparently was—in the cup of her palm, visualizing its golden sheen. *A word fitly spoken . . . our thanks for what you did for him and for us. . . .*

"I can't keep this." She restored the apple to the box and folded in the lid. "I don't deserve it. I didn't earn it."

"That's obviously not what Mr. and Mrs. Perkins think," Dr. Paulus said. "You taught their child to talk, didn't you?"

"I didn't do it for them. I didn't do it for him, either." The ribbon was resisting Cathy's attempt to fit its unbroken loop onto the box as it was before. "I did everything so wrong this semester."

The ribbon snapped in two where its ends were taped together, and, for a dreadful instant, she was blinking against the threat of tears.

"Doing things wrong seems to have been a common malady this semester," Dr. Paulus said into the brief silence. "None of us appears to have been immune." She seated herself behind her desk. "The best anyone can do is to profit by her mistakes. It's what's meant by 'Learning the hard way,' I suppose."

Cathy let the papery ribbon slither into a heap in her lap. She had never dreamed that Dr. Paulus would admit to being to blame in some degree for the upheavals this year had brought, much less that she could sound genuinely rueful doing it.

For the first time, Cathy experienced a riffle of sympathy for the woman across the desk from her. What must it be like to be thrown into a new job where you were urgently needed, only to have your efforts balked at every turn by frictions, failures, and mutiny?

This new insight by no means altered the basic differences between herself and Dr. Paulus, but it gave Cathy the courage to say what she had come to say.

"Dr. Paulus, I've decided to drop speech therapy. I'd like to switch over into special education. It's what you suggested at the beginning of the semester."

"Yes," Dr. Paulus said, without a trace in her voice of surprise or satisfaction or any of the other condescensions Cathy had been steeling herself to accept. "May I ask what has prompted this decision?"

"I want to go into teaching mentally retarded children. I've checked in the registrar's office and with Dr. Ellis in special ed. The way is fairly clear, as soon as I have permission from you."

"Let me rephrase the question," Dr. Paulus said. "What I'm asking is why you've decided to drop speech therapy."

"Because—" Cathy rubbed her thumb to and fro

along the edge of the box, as if a suitable answer might present itself in Braille there. She had dozens of reasons why she should learn to help the mentally retarded, why she practically owed it to Mr. and Mrs. Perkins to become more receptive and knowledgeable where other children like Leonard were concerned, why it was a type of work she could enter with the smallest taint of self-interest. Trust Dr. Paulus to ask the question the wrong way around, so that none of these forward-looking answers fit.

"Because of the clinic work mainly, I suppose," she said warily. She had prepared herself to be eating humble pie but that didn't improve its flavor. "I'm not happy about how I handled most of it. I don't think I'm right for that sort of thing. It wasn't what I expected."

"What is it that you expected from the clinic or from yourself? You demonstrated the imagination and resourcefulness necessary to teach one patient the first words he ever spoke, and you achieved a rapport with your other patient that helped him mature enough to accept the discipline he needed. You are aware, of course, that your cleft palate patient has been discharged from the clinic, that his speech is satisfactory?"

"Yes, I know." Cathy tasted again the peppermint sweetness of the huge candy cane Roddy had thrust upon her during their last therapy session and her rejoicing as he said, without a flaw in his enunciation, "Take it. It's for you. A Christmas present from me." She was warmed again by the pressure of his mother's farewell handclasp and her delighted, "He's grown up such a lot this fall, I can't believe it. We're so glad he had you for his therapist." That hour was a memory to be cherished always, yet it had only underscored the decision to withdraw.

Cathy swallowed and faced the waiting stillness behind the desk. "I'm glad that you think I did a good job—" at any rate she would have been glad under different circumstances—"but that's the whole point: I did it just to prove that I could, to make an impression. The patients were nothing to me but a means to an end. It was all mechanical. I never got involved enough to really care about them."

"Indeed?" A pencil tapped a light tattoo on the desk. "It appears to me that the situation is quite the reverse. If you are intending to throw away five semesters of speech therapy as an atonement for what you consider your sins of omission, I should say you are far too much involved emotionally. You cannot live your patients' lives for them, Miss Wheeler. Or die their deaths, if that is truly the reason for your quitting the program."

"No, it's not. I'm not. That isn't what I'm trying to say." Cathy grabbed for her purse and the box as they lunged toward the edge of her lap. Her recent sympathy for Dr. Paulus was ebbing fast. What pleasure did this woman derive from twisting an act dictated by a sense of ethics and stark logic into something foolish and melodramatic? "Anyway, what do my reasons matter? You never did think I belonged in the speech therapy program."

"That is true. And I would still have strong reservations had you chosen to remain. Nevertheless—" The pencil tapped twice more, then clattered abruptly among other pencils, as if it had been tossed into a tray. "Frankly, Miss Wheeler, I'm disappointed in you. I had judged you to be made of sterner stuff."

"Disappointed! How?" The preposterous suggestion brought Cathy forward in her chair.

"For one thing, I noted that your name was missing among the signatures on Monica Vohl's petition. Since you might be presumed to feel you had at least as much provocation as the others, I wondered at your self-restraint. Apparently, I misread its significance. I didn't realize you had already given up the battle and were in full retreat."

What stung most was the filament of truth at the core of the lash. "I'm not retreating from anything," Cathy said. She had to clench her fist to resist shouting it at her. "Signing that petition would have been giving up. It would have amounted to saying I needed half the college to help me fight my private battles. Which I don't."

"Fortunately, the signatures numbered somewhat less than half the college," Dr. Paulus said dryly. "On the other hand, perhaps one should applaud your discretion in choosing this auspicious moment to pull out. I don't foresee that the climate in the speech department is likely to become noticeably more congenial in the near future than it has been this past semester. Probably, you will be more comfortable in special education, all things considered."

A coward! crackled through Cathy's brain. She's calling me a coward! She thinks she's been too tough for me.

Her retort crackled, too. "There's nothing in this past semester I wouldn't do again or couldn't do again if I had to, and nothing more that speech therapy has to offer that I'd be afraid to try. If I were just worried about being comfortable, I might as well marry the first man who asks me, like him or not, and forget the whole thing."

"I see." The silver voice was infuriating in its cool

detachment. "You don't consider, then, that dropping your therapy major is equivalent to forgetting the whole thing?"

"Speech therapy and special ed aren't that far apart. A lot of what I've learned already will apply. After working with Leonard Perkins, I'd say it's almost a natural combination." Even as Cathy fired them, the words transformed themselves from angry, defensive flack to a sunburst of new meaning.

"If I really could combine them," she said carefully, trying for control of the excitement igniting her, "if I could take courses in teaching retarded children and keep on in speech therapy both, that would be perfect. Would that work?"

"It's a thought to explore," Dr. Paulus said, and began riffling through papers. "A more promising one, at any rate, than being reduced to marrying the first man who asks you, like him or not."

Cathy emerged from the office a quarter hour later unsure whether to congratulate herself on having accomplished a miracle or to suspect that she had been expertly manipulated into doing exactly what Dr. Paulus wanted. For a compromise between two fields of study, her schedule for next semester was heavily weighted on the side of required courses in speech therapy. Even the single special ed course it boasted, Introduction to Teaching the Exceptional Child, was acceptable as a substitute for a more generalized special ed course required of speech therapy majors. "This way, if your enthusiasm fades on closer acquaintance, you'll have lost nothing," Dr. Paulus had said pointedly, "and if it doesn't, you'll have enough of a foundation to judge just where you want to go from there."

By rights, Cathy should have been seething with futile indignation, but as she swung around the corner beside Trudy, it was as if she were moving for the first time in weeks without the drag of restricting chains. If I've been manipulated, she marveled, it was into doing what I really wanted most to do, too. How could I have got so mixed up trying so hard to think straight?

By some trick of association, that brought Amy back to mind. She slowed her pace and gave Trudy a "Right and in" as they neared Sister Janice's office. Trudy swerved and came to a halt, her muzzle raised to touch the knob of the closed door.

Cathy patted her by way of praise, then gently tested the knob. It was locked. That must mean Amy was still inside. The door of this office was rarely if ever shut during class hours under normal conditions. Cathy could knock, of course, to learn if she would be interrupting, but should she?

It was the memory of Amy's accusation, "Everything's easy for you," that turned her from the door and started her on down the hall. It would be callous, if not actually cruel, to burst in there now, flags flying and trumpets blaring as they were within her, and offer sympathy to a friend whose world had gone to ashes. Everything was easy for her, and she wasn't actress enough to hide every trace of its radiance—not quite yet, anyway.

I'll put my folder and things in the locker, she decided, and come back up here after I've settled down a little. She couldn't simply go on home, abandoning Amy, but she didn't want Amy to end up hating her, either.

Christmas music was drifting through the ground floor corridor. The carol was "We Three Kings of Orient Are" when Cathy drew close enough to identify it, and the source was either a radio or a phonograph in the alumnae office—a radio evidently, for, as she passed the door, the music was replaced by a mellow male voice:

> 'Tis not the weight of jewel
> Or plate.
> Or the fondle of silken fur;
> 'Tis the spirit in which the gift is rich,
> As the gifts of the wise ones were;
> And we are not told whose gift
> Was gold
> Or whose was the gift of myrrh.

The voice faded beneath the rise of chimes and violins that became "Joy to the World." Cathy hugged her folder tighter to her, lodging the Perkins' box riding on it more securely against her chest. In her case, she knew whose was the gift of gold and what was the spirit behind it.

And what of the gift of myrrh, that "bitter perfume," as the carol described it? Wasn't that what she had received from Dr. Paulus, not just today but beginning with their very first interview? She could be grateful now to Dr. Paulus for having jarred her out of her complacency about her choice of a profession; she was grateful to her—or should be—for jolting her into a recognition that her work in speech therapy was not something she wanted to throw away.

But I can't say truthfully that I like her, even so, she reflected. I doubt I ever will. Which—comprehension leaped into focus—was precisely how Dr. Paulus preferred it.

Cathy nearly missed Trudy's signal that they were at

the door to the locker room. Of course! Dr. Paulus wants me out of the program or else so mad I'll work my head off to stay in. Which I did, and which, one way or another, she'll see to it I keep on doing. It's top quality performance she's after, not personal popularity. She doesn't need to be liked, anyway not by students. She's sufficient unto herself. And every word she said to me upstairs was calculated to produce the effect she got.

A fleeting indignation thinned Cathy's lips as she juggled her armload to open the door, but the next thought brought a grin. Dr. Paulus was by no means the stupid automaton Monica painted her. If she planned to profit from her mistakes of this semester, it well might be that the honeymoon was over, but not on the terms Monica was looking to dictate. That promised to be a bout worth watching.

"Cathy! Cathy Wheeler! Wait a second, will you?" A young man was walking swiftly, now sprinting, toward her from the far end of the hall.

"Yes?" Cathy let the half-open door glide shut. She had an idea she ought to know him, that the voice was familiar, but his identity eluded her. "What is it?"

"I'm looking for Amy," he said before he had quite closed the distance between them. "You wouldn't know if she's been here this afternoon, would you? Or is she going to be here? I had a note from her a couple of weeks ago, saying she thought she'd be paying this place a final visit on the seventeenth." He added, as if Cathy might otherwise dispute it, "That's today."

And he was Larry Tobin. "She's in Sister Janice's office, on the third floor, right now. Anyhow, I'm pretty sure that's where she was a few minutes ago." Cathy's welcoming smile was tempered by the recollection of

Greg's airy assumption that a girl was a form of robot to be switched off and switched on again whenever it suited his convenience. "But what do you want of her? She said she hasn't heard from you since she left school and went home."

"It figures. Every time I phoned her she was either sleeping and her mother wouldn't disturb her or she was out and her mother didn't know when she'd be in. I tried writing, but Mama probably hands out the mail the same way she delivers phone messages. I wouldn't put it past her."

Cathy nodded. "It does figure. It's hard to believe, but that's the sort of thing Amy's mother would do. Amy really has been sick, though. I suppose that helped."

"Look, I've got to talk to her. Third floor, you say?" Larry moved a step or two beyond her before swinging around. "Mama's not up there, too, is she?"

"No, but that's no guarantee she's not lurking somewhere near. Better hurry. Do you know how to find Sister Janice's office?"

She would have gone along to show him, but the sketchy directions she offered him first were barely out of her mouth before he was dashing for the stairs at a run. The "Thanks, Cathy" he tossed back at her from the region of the landing struck her as fair evidence that he—and undoubtedly Amy, too—would not count it a breach of friendship if she failed to follow. Maybe there was hope for Amy's future yet.

So we can go on home with a clear conscience, she told herself, nudging the door wide open enough to let her armload and Trudy pass into the locker room together. Only I'm glad it's Amy's solution and not mine.

The thought surprised her, for she liked Larry and certainly she had nothing against love.

Except that there was such a gallery of teeth and claws and twisted shapes that masqueraded under the name of love. There was Amy's love for Sister Bernard, for example, like a vine taking its strength and height from the tree it clings to and doomed to collapse utterly when the tree fell. Or there was Mrs. Reinhardt's love for Amy that was actually a prison with ever-thickening walls. And there was Greg's kind of love that absorbed the other person into himself, like a spoonful of sugar stirred into his lemonade. And Joan's kind of love, designed for display, all satin ribbons and eye-catching wrappings around an empty package. And Dr. Rosenthal's version of love that had inflicted the cruelest hoax of her life on Cathy because his feelings were too tender to perform one quick pinprick inoculation of the truth.

She lifted the little golden apple from its box for another look before setting it on her locker shelf, out of harm's way, while she put on her coat. There was also the kind of love Mr. and Mrs. Perkins had for their son, a kind that could have been excused for being as thin or ragged as the worst but that was, in reality, a mixture of gentleness, patience, and faith that somehow balanced the ugliness of the others. And there was Dr. Paulus, too; her kind of love was like a cold, bright flame, guarding her profession and her sick friend's right to privacy.

I don't like her, Cathy repeated to herself, snuggling into the fleecy lining of her coat, but I think I do rather admire her. Maybe it's because I have an inkling now of which way she'll jump and why the next time we cross swords, I won't be running scared any more.

"Noel, Noel," the alumnae office radio was chorusing when she and Trudy entered the corridor again. She leaned into the pushbar of the heavy outer door and was released into the thin, clean, chill outside.

The sense of restricting walls fell away as she turned her cheek to the chisel-edged wind. Leaves rustled along the walk, a crow cawed from a lofty tree, traffic rumbled on the boulevard, unrolling the broad landscape of campus around her.

"We're free," she said to Trudy, whose ears were perked toward the complaining crow.

Cathy snatched a sharp, tearing breath from the wind. Yes, free! Free to be herself again, to belong to herself, to own the mastery of herself.

Dr. Paulus had said you can't live another person's life for him. It was a worse mistake to surrender parts of your life to someone else to live for you. That was what she had done this fall, yielded up her rights to her identity: to Greg for the excitement of a new experience; to Dr. Rosenthal in exchange for a pipe-smoke mirage; to Dr. Paulus from a lack of genuine conviction; to Leonard, almost, from a muddled sense of guilt.

But she was whole once more. Whether her eyes could see or not, she was whole. That was the real gift of gold that had been given her, and as the poem had said, it came with no specific giver's name attached. Yet the treasure was hers, and she would let no part of it—of herself, of Catherine Elizabeth Wheeler—be lured from her keeping soon again. She had her own road to travel.

"Forward, Trudy," she said, and together they sprang down the steps to the walk.

Someone gunned a car engine in the parking lot. The car's horn tut-tutted, and she was sure, even before the car eased up beside her in the driveway, who the driver was. It was turning into that sort of a day.

"This is what I call fine timing," Steve said, swinging the door open for her. "I pulled in just five minutes ago, and I was afraid I'd be too late. I knew you had that appointment, but I didn't know how long or short it might be."

Cathy laughed at a vision of Dr. Paulus glancing from her window to discover her accepting a ride from a young man already. "You may be too late at that."

"Too late for what?" Steve asked as she and Trudy climbed in. "On a cold day like this, don't tell me you're not in the market for a nice, warm ride."

The warmth in the car was pleasant after even so brief a time as she had been standing in the wind. It was always pleasantly warm where Steve was, but she smiled at him from the bright citadel of her new-found self. "Only if it's going my way."

"Oh?" She could feel the intentness of the look he gave her before he reached across to punch down the stubborn lock button of the door. "Well, I've got a pretty good idea where I'm going. That's why I knocked off work early this afternoon. They called from the university today to say the assistantship is mine, if I want it."

"Steve! How wonderful!"

Her lunge to hug him was hampered by the bulk of Trudy, crowded in the space between the dashboard and her knees, but Steve met her halfway. Being met halfway, she realized, and meeting halfway imposed no forfeit of rights on either side. There were such things as roads that ran parallel, and ways of giving that could build rather than destroy.

"Now what's this business about being too late?" he asked. "Who's too late? And for what?"

"It's a long story." She laughed, loosening her scarf and settling into the seat. "But I think maybe I was wrong. It's not too late—for anything."

ABOUT THE AUTHOR

BEVERLY BUTLER lost her sight at the age of fourteen. She learned to read and write Braille and under the guidance of her dog, Sister, she finished high school and graduated *cum laude* from Mount Mary College. Miss Butler was granted a Woodrow Wilson Fellowship for advanced study, and in 1961 she received her M.A. degree from Marquette University. Miss Butler now lives in Milwaukee, where she teaches writing courses at Mount Mary College and writes novels and poetry. She has received the Johnson Foundation Prize of the Council for Wisconsin Writers. Her popular novel, *Light a Single Candle*, was awarded the Clara Ingram Judson Award for outstanding literary merit. Based on the author's own experience, it tells the story of how Cathy Wheeler lost her sight at the age of fourteen, and with her guide dog, Trudy, accepted the challenge of going back to public high school. This title is also available in an Archway Paperback edition.